HARDCORE

AN ASHLEY HALE THRILLER

LARRY A. WINTERS

Everything in the world is about sex except sex. Sex is about power.

— OSCAR WILDE

1

THE MAN WATCHED her with a flat, unpleasant stare.

He had hollow cheeks, a receding hairline, and thin lips. Ashley tried to ignore him, but it was impossible to look across her table at Sean and not see the gaunt face over Sean's shoulder. The man with the hollow cheeks was talking to another man at his table, but every few minutes, his gaze shifted and his stare settled on her.

His attention was probably harmless. She had dressed up tonight. Her neckline was low—nothing like the tops she used to wear, but low enough that she felt a chill from the air-conditioner. She had taken extra time with her lipstick and eye-shadow. Wasn't it natural for a man to notice an attractive woman in a restaurant?

Maybe. But she was relieved when the lights dimmed.

Darkness swallowed the waiters, the busboys, and the man with the hollow cheeks. The candle on the table flickered, but its glow revealed little beyond the tablecloth and the silverware. Sean watched her with a bemused and slightly drunken grin.

"You look anxious," he said. He lifted his wineglass and drank.

She was, but not because of the man with the hollow cheeks. Sinatra's baritone crooned *Strangers in the Night*. It seemed like the same series of old standards played every time she and Sean came here. Probably one greatest-hits CD, looped endlessly. *It must drive the staff nuts.*

Ashley tried to smile. She sipped from her glass and swallowed the crisp, ice-cold water slowly. What could she say? *Well, honey, I just happened to rifle through your underwear drawer this morning, innocently of course, and I noticed this box, and I opened it, so I know why you suggested going to Silvestri's tonight, and I'm ready to say yes, hell yes, but that doesn't mean I'm not nervous, okay?*

Two waiters delivered a platter to the table to their right. The smell of mussels in marinara sauce wafted over. She looked down at her salad. She had barely touched it.

"Not anxious," she said. "Just happy."

Sean leaned back, and she thought he was going to reach into his pocket right then, but he didn't. He exhaled and rearranged the napkin on his lap.

"I'm happy, too." The skin around his eyes crinkled when he smiled, making him look older than his thirty-five years. "You remember the first time we came here? Our first date?"

"I remember," she said. "You ordered spaghetti carbonara and ruined your shirt."

"Yeah, but the rest of the evening was pretty great."

"It was."

Tonight, he had not splashed any sauce on his shirt, and she was glad. He had worn her favorite, a blue and green striped Hugo Boss dress shirt. She had bought it for him for his birthday. The tapered cut emphasized the smooth lines of his torso and drew her gaze from his square, broad shoulders to his slim waist.

She watched the material tighten against his left biceps muscle as his hand slid into his pants pocket. Her stomach fluttered.

Then he stopped.

The man with the hollow cheeks approached their table. His mouth hitched upward in an awkward smile. Candlelight flickered off his teeth. His stare moved from her cleavage to her throat to her face.

"I thought it was you," he said.

Ashley breathed in. She forced herself to sit up straighter instead of curling in on herself. Her first thought—of course—was that the man recognized her from *before*, but she pushed that thought away. Two years had passed. Most of her titles were out of circulation. It was just as likely that she'd met this guy at the bank, that he was stopping to say howdy and tell her how much he appreciated TD Bank's favorable interest rates.

Jesus, not now.

A waiter brushed past on her other side, carrying a pitcher. He paused at their table and leaned the pitcher over her goblet. Ice cubes and water tumbled into the glass.

"Ashley Hale," the man said. "This is amazing."

The name made her stiffen. Sean's hand came out of his pocket and settled on the table. Empty.

"Do you mind?" Sean said. "We're trying to eat."

The man offered a half-smile and then returned his attention to her. "I don't mean to bother you. I just have to tell you how great you are. The energy you bring to your scenes. And you have the most amazing body. I mean, beautiful. Your legs, and your ass."

Even in the muted light, she could see Sean's face turn red.

"That's flattering," she said. "Thanks for the kind words."

She looked at Sean. It was going to be tough to get the mood back, but she could do it. This wasn't the first time her past had intruded at an inopportune moment. It happened. The man would leave. There would be more wine. Dessert.

"So what are you doing in New Jersey?" the man said. "Feature dancing somewhere? I'd love to come see you."

"No, I—" The man leaned closer. He reeked of cologne and garlic. "I stopped performing a couple years ago, actually. Listen, we … we'd rather not be disturbed." Her hands fumbled with the napkin on her lap, and she made a fist, squeezing the starchy material.

The man glanced at Sean. "Would you mind taking a picture with my phone?"

Sean's face darkened.

"Please?" the man said. "I've been a fan for years."

Ashley was deciding how best to intervene when Sean's face broke into a grin. He said, "Sure, man, no problem."

He grabbed the man's phone and took a picture of himself.

"No," the man said, "I wanted—"

"Dude, Ashley's retired from the business. But me? I'm an up-and-comer. My cock is like twelve inches long. You want a picture of it? You can pose with it if you want."

"Uh, no—"

Ashley chewed her lip to stop from laughing. She'd seen Sean goof around in private, with her, but never in front of people. His surfer drawl was so convincing, she could almost forget he worked at an accounting firm, crunching numbers all day in a small office with no windows.

"How about my nuts, man? They're kind of my trademark. I'm calling myself Balls Deluxe. You know, because my sack is so huge."

Ashley lifted her napkin to her face and covered her smile. A stray piece of romaine, wet with Caesar dressing, dropped onto her skirt.

"I ... I just wanted a photo of Ashley. I'm a big fan."

"I know, you mentioned that. But if you think she has a great ass, you should see mine."

The man plucked his phone from Sean's hand. "I need to get going. My friend is waiting in the car. Ashley, it was amazing to finally meet you."

Ashley managed to say, "Thanks," without kicking off a fit of laughter.

"It was amazing to meet you, too," Sean said. "Balls Deluxe. Spread the word."

The man hurried to the door, bumping a few chairs on his way. People stared after him. He disappeared out of the restaurant.

Ashley burst out laughing. "Oh my God."

Sean smiled and blushed. "I had to get rid of him somehow."

"That's one way to do it."

He raised his hand and signaled for the check. "Let's get out of here."

She had to fight to keep her smile in place. Apparently, there had been a change of plans.

"I'll brew some decaf at my place," he said. "After that pathetic pervert, I need a change of scenery. Sound good?"

"Yeah. Sure. Sounds good."

———

THE DASHBOARD CLOCK read 8:50 PM. Traffic was light on 287, but Sean weaved between cars anyway. His smile was gone, replaced with a frown and a distant gaze. He was pushing eighty in a sixty-five-mile-an-hour zone. Ashley did not ask him to slow down.

Sometimes she missed LA, the sun and the freeways and the flashy cars. Even in summer, New Jersey wasn't the same.

He's dealing with it, she thought. *That's what he's doing right now. By the time we get home, he'll be fine. Leave him alone. Sit quietly. Let him brood.*

"Crazy night," she said.

"Yeah."

"You were funny."

He shot her a sideways glance. "Thanks."

"But—" She cringed. Commanded herself to shut up.

She listened to the throb of the BMW's engine, adjusted the air-conditioner vent so the icy air stopped blowing against her neck.

"But what, Ashley?"

"Nothing."

He turned in his seat. Stared at her instead of the road. "I hate when you do this. Just tell me what you were going to say." She smelled wine on his breath.

"It's nothing. Just, you know, when you called the guy a pathetic pervert."

Sean rolled his eyes.

"I'm just saying," she said. "It doesn't make him pathetic. Or a pervert."

"No. He's just a guy who beats off to porn. Nothing pathetic or perverted about that."

He glared at her. She turned to stare out the window. Why had she said anything? Five minutes ago, there had still been a chance to salvage the night.

"So now you're going to ignore me?" he said. "That's real mature."

"I don't want to fight, Sean."

"And I do?"

He stabbed the power button on the stereo and filled the car with noise.

———

AT HIS APARTMENT, Sean kicked off his shoes and tossed the Hugo Boss shirt over the back of a kitchen chair before disappearing into the bathroom. Not a good sign. It was difficult to imagine him proposing in his Fruit of the Loom tank-top. She lifted the shirt from the chair and carried it into the bedroom. She hung it in the closet. Touched her palm to the blue and green stripes before sliding the door closed.

Wetness gathered in her eyes. She blinked it away.

While he was still in the bathroom, she moved to the dresser and opened the top drawer—the one he'd given her. Anticipating post-proposal celebrations, she had worn a g-string under her skirt. Now it seemed like a badge of her past. She balled it up and shoved it deep in the drawer and pulled on a comfortable pair of panties. She heard the toilet flush.

"Hey." He stood in the doorway, one hand braced against the doorframe, a dark patch of hair visible in the shadow under his arm. "Let's not fight," he said.

"Okay."

"I'll put on a pot of decaf. We'll watch some TV." He turned and headed toward the kitchen.

Watch some TV? She sat on the edge of the bed. The man at the restaurant had derailed her evening. Did she have to allow him to ruin her life? Screw that. Sean was still wearing his pants. Presumably, the ring was still in his pocket. If he wasn't going to initiate things, she would.

She heard the sound of the coffee maker percolating. An aroma of hazelnut and cinnamon drifted in from the kitchen. At least he was making the good stuff.

She found him sitting on the couch. He had the remote in his hand and was scrolling through the list of recorded shows on the DVR. Ashley swiped the remote and turned off the TV.

"I want to talk," she said.

"About tonight?" He turned to her with a concerned-boyfriend expression. "That guy was an asshole. It happens."

He patted the cushion beside him, but she remained on her feet.

She took a deep breath. "Do you ever think about getting married?"

He laughed, but his concerned expression looked a little more genuine. "What?"

"Marrying me. Do you think about it?"

"I guess I have. Once or twice."

"I think we should get married."

His mouth gaped. No words came out. Finally, he said, "Ashley, this is kind of coming out of left field, you know? I don't think I'm ready yet. For that kind of ... step." He seemed to read something in her eyes and stood up. The couch squeaked. "Are you okay?"

"You were planning to propose to me tonight. What changed? The guy at Silvestri's?"

He laughed, but it sounded forced. "I wasn't planning to— I don't know why you thought that, Ashley. It's not true." He spread his hands. "Having a nice dinner, that was the extent of my master plan for the night. Honest."

"Honest?"

She lunged for his pocket. He caught her wrist. His fingers tightened painfully around it. She smacked his stomach with her free hand. He let go and tried to back away from her, but his legs hit the couch. She drove her hand into his pants pocket. He tried to push her away. She braced herself, dug her heels into the carpet. Her fingers explored the soft lining of his pocket. She touched metal. A hard, circular object. She tucked it between two fingers and yanked it out of his pants.

A diamond solitaire.

"What's this, Honest Abe?"

"Jesus Christ." He was panting.

"You carry this around for good luck, like a rabbit's foot?"

"Ashley—"

"Do you want to marry me or not?" She heard her voice break.

He turned away from her. Rotated his neck. She heard the joints pop. "I thought I did, okay? I thought I was ready. But I'm not."

"Because of the guy in the restaurant?"

"Because of ... everything."

"What the fuck does that mean, Sean?"

"I'm just not ready."

"Because I used to work in porn?"

"I didn't say that."

"But that's what you're not ready for, right? Marrying a slut? A whore?"

"I never said anything like that!"

She grabbed her bag from the kitchen counter, opened the door of his apartment, and stepped into the hallway. The warm air smelled like curry—a neighbor cooking.

"Wait!"

She heard his footsteps behind her. She did not turn around. The stairwell took her to the ground floor. Her Altima was in the parking lot.

"Ashley, hold on!"

She slid behind the wheel, locked the doors, and started the engine. The headlights popped on automatically. Sean charged into their glare. Eyes wide and arms flapping. She pulled out of the space and drove past him.

Her phone emitted a piercing trill. When it did not stop, she pulled it from her bag and looked at its screen, expecting to see Sean's name. She didn't. She saw Gail's. It had been so long since Gail had tried to call her, she had forgotten that the woman's number was in her contacts.

Christ, how bad can one night get?

She let it ring.

Instead of driving home, she found the nearest highway and ground the pedal into the floorboard. The Altima leapt forward, pushing her back against the cloth seat. She focused on the road, on the rhythm of tires on asphalt. A habit nurtured in Los Angeles, she supposed. *Car therapy.*

Her phone beeped. A voice mail message.

She held the phone in her hand as if weighing it. Why listen to Gail's message now, when she was already upset? What good could come of it?

With a sigh, she listened.

The voice was strained, urgent: "It's Gail. I mean, Mom. Tara's had an accident. She's dead." And then, after a pause: "Please come home."

2

THE SAN FERNANDO VALLEY lay no more than ten miles from the ocean, but you wouldn't know it. The surrounding mountains trapped the heat and smog. Palm trees creaked. Heat mirages glittered above the pavement. Ashley woke in a strange bed drenched in sweat. It took her a moment to remember the small Travel Inn room. When she had arrived the night before, she had opened the window. Now the odor of hot asphalt rolled into the room, along with the hum of freeway traffic.

Tara's had an accident.

She looked at the rolling suitcase on the floor. She did not remember packing. Her memory of the time between her argument with Sean and her arrival here was fuzzy. She remembered a phone call with a United Airlines customer sales rep. She remembered a middle seat in coach. She must have rented a car at the airport. A Hertz keychain lay on the motel room desk. She wondered what kind of car they had given her.

Was this what grief was like—temporary brain damage?

She tasted salt. Her forehead was dripping. She rolled off of the bed and closed the window. It stuck. She had to push hard to grind the pane along its track.

She hefted the suitcase onto the bed and unzipped it. She had been lucid enough to pack underwear. That was good. She plunged her hands past bras and panties and found some blouses, tank-tops, a couple skirts, a pair of jeans. Toiletries and makeup. And her phone charger.

She closed her eyes and breathed.

Her phone was in her purse, still in airplane mode. She knew that she should get it now, turn off airplane mode, and call Gail, but knowing the right thing to do and doing it were different things.

According to her watch, it was 1:23 PM. Jesus. She'd slept half the day. Gail was probably wondering why she had not heard from her.

There was no sense putting the moment off. Ashley would keep the encounter brief, limit the discussion to Tara's death. And then she would fly home. There was a reason she had not packed her black suit. There was no way she was going to Tara's funeral.

———

THE RENTAL TURNED out to be a little yellow Ford Fiesta. A cardboard evergreen dangled from the rearview mirror and infused the small car with an overpowering scent of pine. She yanked it free and stuffed it in the glove compartment, then pulled out of the motel parking lot. Driving sparked her energy. As she navigated the crisscrossing boulevards of the Valley, her spirits lifted. She had avoided LA for two years, but now that she was here, she could not help feeling a sense of comfortable familiarity.

Gail had suggested meeting at the house in Tarzana where Ashley and Tara had grown up, but Ashley had refused and suggested Tara's apartment instead. The prospect of meeting in the home of her dead sister seemed less emotionally painful. Ashley wondered what a therapist would say about that.

Tara had been renting an apartment on the second floor of a two-story building in Northridge. Ashley climbed out of the Fiesta. It was Sunday afternoon. The parking lot was full. Judging by the number of luxury automobiles, rent was not cheap here. Sunlight gleamed off of the windshields of Audis and BMWs.

So Tara had been doing well. The thought brought a bittersweet smile to her face.

She jogged into the shade at the edge of the building and found a cement stairwell leading to the second level. There was a metal railing, but it was too hot to touch. She climbed the flight of stairs. At the top, an outdoor walkway extended along the side of the building. She walked along it until she reached the door labeled 2F. It opened before she could knock.

The woman who stood in the doorway had a few more gray streaks in her hair than Ashley remembered, and she seemed to have shrunk an inch or two. She had given up contact lenses for thick, plastic glasses. But her face was familiar enough.

"Hi, Gail."

Gail seemed to deflate. "I thought that today of all days, you might find it in your heart to call me Mom." She stepped backward and invited Ashley into the apartment of her dead sister.

————

"TARA AND I RECONCILED, YOU KNOW," Gail said. Ashley could feel the woman following her through the apartment, although her shoes made no noise on the carpeted floor. Gail had always had a light step. "For the last year, we've been very close."

"Really? I figured you just showed up for the reading of the will."

Ashley did not dare turn around or stop walking. She did not want to see her mother's face.

"Why bother?" Gail said. "She left everything to Rob."

Ashley toured the two-bedroom apartment. Tara had lived well. Ashley recognized some of her sister's old furniture—the couch, the kitchen table—but most of it was brand new. The headboard in the bedroom looked like cherry wood and smelled of furniture polish. Ashley ran her fingers over the smooth surface. She listened to the quiet hum of the air-conditioner and imagined Tara sleeping in the bed, or dressing in front of the matching wardrobe.

"What are you looking for?" Gail said.

"I'm just looking."

Tara had set up the second bedroom as a home office and gym. There was a desk with a monitor on it. A slide-out tray held a keyboard and mouse. There was a docking station for a laptop, but it was empty, its connectors exposed.

"Where's the computer?"

"The police took it," Gail said.

Now Ashley turned to look at her. "The police?"

"After the accident."

Two bookshelves stood against a wall. One held rows of books, the other displayed framed photographs. The photos showed Tara smiling with various men and women. Most of the photos appeared to have been taken at industry events.

A gleam drew her eye to a glass display case set against the wall opposite the window. Reflected sunlight made the glass opaque. She had to open the door to see inside. Four shelves. The first held an AVN award with the name Tara Rose engraved on it. It was an award Tara had won during her second year in the industry. Best Group Sex Scene—Video. She was nineteen. Tara had never managed to win another AVN award—*take one of mine,* Ashley used to tell her, after she'd amassed a crate full of them—but she had apparently picked up a XRCO award a year ago. It stood on the second shelf, next to a faded photograph in a silver frame. Ashley wondered if Tara had tried to tell her about it. There had been so many calls she had not answered. So many voice mails she had deleted without listening to.

She crouched to get a closer look at the photo in the silver frame. At first she thought it was an old picture of herself, but then she realized that she was looking at her mother as an eighteen or nineteen-year-old. One of Gail's beauty pageant victories.

There were no photos of Gail in Ashley's New Jersey apartment. She had never known Tara to display any, either. *I guess they really did reconcile.*

The third and fourth shelves held souvenir coffee mugs. Ashley did not need to lift them out of the case. She already knew what each looked like. She owned the same ones. Tara and she used to buy them together back when Ashley was still working in the industry. She and Tara did strip club tours together, feature dancing in cities across the country, and they always came home with a matched pair of gaudy mugs. It was a sister thing.

There was one from New Jersey, with the words *The Garden State* arching above a perfunctory illustration of an eastern goldfinch, the state bird. Ashley remembered carrying two goldfinch mugs to the counter at a Turnpike rest stop. At the time, she never would have believed she would one day wind up living in the state, working at a bank.

Ashley closed the display case's door and walked across the room to the exercise machine that stood in a corner near the windows. It was a tall Bowflex resistance system. Ashley was surprised to see it here. Tara had always enjoyed leaving her apartment and going to the gym. She had liked the classes and the social aspect.

"I don't think you should touch that," Gail said. She lingered in the doorway, looking uncomfortable.

"Why not?"

"There's a couch in the other room," Gail said. "Let's talk in there."

"Why would the police take Tara's laptop? What happened?"

"Please. I need to sit down."

Ashley felt a knot in her stomach. She followed Gail to the living room and sat on the couch. A cloud of Tara's perfume rose from the cushions. Trish McEvoy. Ashley had not smelled it in years.

The room was quiet. The only sound was the barely audible air-conditioner. In Tara's last place, you could hear dogs barking and the chop of circling helicopters.

Ashley gestured to an empty space in front of them. Where a TV stand should be, the carpet was indented with a pale square. "Did the police take the TV, too?"

"Rob did. When he moved out a few months ago. I guess it was his. Tara never got around to replacing it."

"Moved out?"

Gail smiled ruefully. "He dumped her."

Ashley looked at her, surprised. "And she still left him everything in her will?"

Gail looked at her hands. She shrugged her bony shoulders.

"What kind of accident was it?" Ashley said.

Gail twisted her fingers together. "Ashley, there wasn't an accident. I didn't want to tell you the truth over the phone."

"What do you mean, *the truth*?"

"Tara killed herself."

Ashley sprang from the couch and stared down at her mother. "What?"

"The police—"

"No. I know Tara. There is no way. No way. She would never—"

Gail met her stare. "I told the police the same thing. But, you know how it is."

"What does that mean?"

"It means, a dead porn star? Come on. I doubt the investigation was exhaustive."

"What are you saying?"

"I'm the one who found her. Thursday afternoon. She had been dead for ... I don't know. Since the night before. It was awful."

Found her? Ashley felt lightheaded. The room was beginning to close in. She sat down, using the armrest for stability. "You found her?"

"God." Gail rubbed a hand over her mouth. Her lipstick smeared. She was no longer looking at Ashley. She was looking through her. "I can't even go in that room. I can't go near that ... *thing*. I just...." Her words trailed into a low, meaningless murmur.

"Gail." Ashley gripped her shoulder, surprised by how hard, how bony it had become. When had she touched her last? "Gail." She hesitated, then forced the word past her lips: "*Mom*."

Gail stopped muttering. Her eyes shifted into focus.

"Tell me what's going on."

Gail tried to talk. "My throat is dry."

She left her mother on the couch and walked to the kitchenette. Menus for pizza places and Chinese restaurants and Mexican takeout covered the refrigerator door. Tara had pinned them in place with magnets she had collected from industry events—little squares advertising everything from Internet hosting services to box cover design. Ashley opened the fridge. Cold air drifted out.

The fridge was practically empty. There was a six-pack of Diet Coke, with one can gone, and some oranges in the fruit drawer. Ashley tugged two cans from the six-pack and carried them back to the living room.

Gail took hers gratefully. She popped the tab and sipped. Ashley watched tiny beads of carbonation fizz against the woman's upper lip.

"Is that better?"

Gail's throat pulsed as she drank. A few seconds passed and she wiped her mouth and nodded. "Thank you."

"You were saying something about … a thing?"

"Tara had a telephone cord wrapped around her neck. So tight it cut into her skin. And she was … hanging. From the back of that exercise thing."

"The Bowflex?" Nausea rose in Ashley's throat. She turned away. Took a swig of Diet Coke. The can was cold against her palm.

"The police came. They took pictures. And they … did things with Tara's body. Forensic stuff, I guess. They took her away in an ambulance. No siren."

Ashley tried to imagine this final, lonely ride in a silent ambulance. She couldn't.

"There was a detective," Gail said, "a woman who asked me a lot of questions. Yesterday she called me and told me that the coroner's office formally ruled the death a suicide. That's when I called you."

"*That's* when you called me? Two days after you found Tara dead?"

"I know how you feel about me. I was … afraid."

Ashley couldn't argue with that. She had cut off communication with her mother seven years ago, pretty much the day Tara graduated from high school. She and her sister had gotten into Ashley's car and left home and never looked back. Except Tara had looked back, apparently.

Ashley did not want to think about that.

"Have you ... made arrangements? For the burial and everything?"

Gail nodded. "The funeral service is tomorrow morning. I had some help planning it. A man named Kingsley Nast, someone who worked with Tara. Do you know him?"

Another name from the past, one that brought mixed emotions.

"A nice man," Gail continued. She shifted her weight and the couch released another cloud of Tara's perfume. "He contacted me. While Rob, that lowlife, didn't even call to offer his condolences."

"I'm glad you were able to make arrangements. I know that's what Tara would have wanted. I wish I could be there, but ... I'm flying home tonight. It's best that way, I think."

Gail's face whitened. "You're going to miss Tara's funeral?"

"This isn't my life anymore. I left it behind. I'd rather keep it behind me."

"Is that why you stopped calling her?"

Ashley feigned interest in her Diet Coke. "I guess so."

It was more complicated than that, of course. A hell of a lot more complicated. But why should she struggle to explain herself to this woman who had never understood her, who had never even tried to understand her?

Gail grabbed Ashley's wrist. The sudden movement surprised her. She jerked her arm away reflexively, but her mother's bony fingers held firm and drew Ashley's arm onto her lap. Her expression was pleading.

"I need you here. Please, Ashley. Just for a few days." She tugged Ashley closer. The scent of Tara's perfume gave way to Gail's sour breath.

"I can't." She tried to pry her mother's fingers off of her wrist. They were cold and damp from holding the soda can.

"I know you have a lot of anger," Gail said. "Tara did, too. But I made things right with her, didn't I? Maybe you and I—"

"First of all, there's nothing you could ever do to 'make things right.' And secondly, you're not the reason I can't stay."

"I wouldn't ask you if I had someone else. But I don't. So please just listen to me. You said yourself, Tara would never commit suicide. What if she didn't? What if, you know, someone else...."

"What?"

Gail took a deep breath. "I think Tara was murdered."

Ashley looked more closely at her mother's taut face. Studied her eyes. Her pupils. "Are you ... are you using?"

Gail flinched away from her. The couch springs creaked. "How could you even ask me that?"

"What you're saying—"

"I've been clean for almost a year. Tara helped me. That's what your sister does. She helps people. I mean, did. That's what she did. Tara didn't turn her back on people. She wasn't like you."

"I never turned my back on Tara."

"Then why did you leave?"

So—Tara might have reconciled with their mother, but she had never betrayed Ashley's secret. A rush of love for her sister cut through her guilt.

"You don't have the right to ask me questions."

For a second, Gail looked ready to make an acidic reply, but then she deflated and sank against the couch cushions. "I didn't call you thinking we would make up and live happily ever after. I called you because of Tara. You need to help me convince the police of the truth."

"The police are a lot more experienced than you or me in determining whether a death is a suicide or a murder."

"I don't need experience and neither do you."

Ashley brought her can of Diet Coke to her mouth and drank, not because she was thirsty, but to hide the uncertainty she was certain showed on her face. Surely what Gail was saying was crazy. How could the LAPD and the coroner's office mistake a murder for a suicide?

"Tara wasn't depressed," Gail said. "She had no reason to kill herself."

"You told me Rob dumped her."

"She got over it."

"They lived together for years."

"She didn't need Rob anymore. She was accomplishing things. She was happy. If he hadn't broken up with her, she probably would have done it herself."

"People can fake happiness. They do it all the time."

A phlegmy rattle came from Gail's throat. "She wasn't faking it. And there was no note. Explain that. Explain why Tara wouldn't leave a note."

"What do you want me to do, Gail? Meet with this detective and tell her that Tara would never hang herself? You think my opinion matters to the LAPD?"

Ashley rose from the couch. She put her empty Diet Coke can on an end table, then picked it up again, looking for a trash can. She headed for the kitchen.

"She had a stalker," Gail called after her. Ashley froze. "He's been following her for months. Once or twice a week she would notice him. Watching her."

"She told you this?"

"And I saw him once. Tara and I were having lunch at Olive Garden. She pointed him out."

"Did you tell the police?"

"Of course."

"And?"

Gail shrugged. "They didn't think it was relevant."

Ashley paced back and forth over the pale square of carpet where the TV stand had stood. She had had some stalkers in her time. Few things were scarier for a girl in the industry.

"The funeral service is tomorrow morning," Gail said. "After the burial, you can go meet the detective." She reached into the pocket of her slacks and pulled out a business card. "Detective Heather Collins," Gail read. "Devonshire Area Detective Division. She'll listen to you."

Ashley took the business card. The cardboard was soft and warm, its corners bent. She wondered how long her mother had been carrying it.

"How can I go to the funeral?" Ashley said. "I don't even have a suit. I didn't pack one."

"Tara has suits in the bedroom closet."

"I can't." The thought of wearing her sister's suit to her funeral brought another rush of nausea.

"You girls always shared your clothes. If it bothers you, you can return it after the burial. Here, I have an extra key to the apartment."

Ashley took the key with a hand that felt numb.

"One day," Ashley said. "But I'm doing it for Tara. Not for you."

3

A SIGN in the funeral home lobby directed Ashley and Gail to a large, wood-paneled room where muted lighting revealed rows of pews facing a casket and lectern. Gail let out a little gasp when she saw the crowd. The pews teemed with mourners. People sat shoulder-to-shoulder while others stood against the back wall. Other mourners inched forward in a long line to pay respects at the open casket. Ashley was not surprised. The porn industry was composed of outcasts and misfits, and for more than a few of them, the industry was their only real family. Ashley knew how that felt. Even after two years living a new life, she felt the lure of her old one. It was one reason she wanted to leave town as quickly as possible.

Her heels sank into deep carpet. Soothing piano music piped into the room, but she could barely hear the notes over the murmur of conversation. She split from Gail and made her way to the end of the line, taking her place behind a man in a black suit. Everyone wore black. Except for the odd tattoo peeking from a shirt collar or jacket cuff, the people surrounding her could as easily be Mormons as porn stars. Death—especially suicide—was never taken lightly in this community.

She knew many of the people here, and they knew her. There was little chance that her return to LA would go unnoticed. Maybe by the bigwigs at Vivid and Wicked, but not by the rank-and-file she used to see on a daily basis. Not by Kingsley or Beth Baldwin or Mark Peter.

Or Rob Rourke.

She almost did not recognize Tara's ex. His face was leaner. His body looked more fit, too. The biggest difference was his shaved head. It gleamed beneath the funeral parlor's recessed lights and looked so natural on him that for a moment she could not remember what his hair had looked like.

He was gripping a woman's hand. She was young and tall and ridiculously skinny. When she pushed a lock of black hair away from her face, Ashley saw bright green eyes.

Bringing a date to your ex-girlfriend's funeral. Classy, Rob.

The line inched forward. The floral arrangements around the casket smelled overripe, too sweet. She continued to scan the crowd and the thought occurred to her that Tara's stalker might be here. Wasn't that a common thing, the killer checking out his victim's funeral? The cops should be here. That detective, Heather Collins, should be here. Taking pictures. Looking for suspicious behavior.

"Your mother told me you'd come. I didn't believe her."

She jumped, and the man standing behind her laughed.

"Kingsley."

Unlike Rob, Kingsley Nast had not changed at all.

He stood about five-five, but the way he carried himself always made him seem taller than that. Forceful. His body practically vibrated with coiled energy. Even his hair seemed active. Black tufts bulged from the cuffs of his suit coat and his goatee was so thick and dark that it looked like it was straining to grow. His face was lined and craggy, but his eyes, beaming at her, held the unbounded enthusiasm of a teenager. She hugged him and felt a rush of nostalgia.

"It's good to see you again," she said into his shoulder.

"I'm sorry for your loss. Is there anything I can do?"

"Walk with me to the casket?" Suddenly, the thought of facing Tara's body alone filled her with dread.

"Yeah, I can do that."

They stood side-by-side as the line advanced. A woman sobbed loudly.

"Have you ... seen her yet?" Ashley said.

"Yes. She looks good. They covered up the ... you know, the ligature marks."

Ashley shuddered. Kingsley took her arm. They approached the casket.

Kingsley was right. Tara looked good. Lifelike. Ashley could almost believe she was asleep. But a few seconds in front of the casket destroyed the illusion. Tara's white cotton dress lay unnaturally still over her chest. Her throat looked plastic, like a mannequin's. A faint chemical odor tickled Ashley's nostrils and settled unpleasantly on her tongue.

A sob took her by surprise. It ballooned in her chest and rocked her forward against the casket. Even with Kingsley's hand on her arm, she almost lost her balance. She let out a squeaky noise.

"Are you alright?" Kingsley put an arm across her back and gripped her shoulder. The hairs of his goatee scratched her cheek.

"Give me a minute alone with her, okay?"

"Sure."

He released her and stepped back. Ashley hesitated for a moment, then reached into the coffin and traced the curve of her sister's cheek. It was room temperature, stiff and rubbery. Ashley touched her hair—the same auburn color as Ashley's, but somehow softer, straighter—and then her arm. It was as if her fingertips refused to break contact with her sister. Finally, with an effort, she pulled away.

And left a smudge on Tara's arm.

Ashley looked more closely. She realized that she had not left the mark. She had uncovered it. Her fingers were sticky with flesh-colored grease. She had rubbed off the undertaker's makeup, and what was beneath looked like a bruise. A dark, splotchy bruise.

Was that normal? To bruise your arm when hanging yourself? She supposed that the tightening phone cord might have caused Tara to thrash her arms. She might have smacked the metal frame of the Bowflex.

Or someone else might have hurt her. Someone who manhandled her against the equipment, forced a noose around her neck, and kicked her feet out from under her.

Ashley felt her breath quicken. She resisted the urge to rub the rest of Tara's exposed skin in search of more bruises. A good three-dozen people stood behind her, waiting to pay their respects. This was Tara's final public moment.

Kingsley stood a few feet behind her, his hands clasped in front of him, his expression patient.

She stepped away from the casket. A blonde woman who could not be more than eighteen took her place. Ashley heard her murmur some words to the body in the casket. She had a high-pitched voice and sounded even younger than she looked. She was crying.

"You look like you could use a glass of water," Kingsley said. "Let me ask the funeral director—"

"I'm okay."

The line to the casket thinned. A man in a black suit positioned himself behind the lectern. The microphone let out a squeal of feedback.

"Are you planning to give a eulogy?" Kingsley asked her.

Ashley shook her head. "I don't think ... I don't think I could."

Kingsley nodded toward the lectern. Gail stood beside the man at the microphone. She had a three-by-five index card in her hand.

"Let's get out of here," Ashley said.

Kingsley glanced across the room. His wife Cheryl stood talking to two other women.

"Just for a few minutes," Ashley said. "I think there's a coffee shop down the street."

Kingsley rubbed his goatee and nodded. "I know the place."

The man in the black suit spoke into the microphone, beginning the service in a solemn baritone. Ashley led Kingsley along the wall to the door. The hallway beyond felt cool after the stuffy air of the crowded room. She took a cleansing breath, then strode through the funeral parlor's lobby to the double doors leading to the parking lot.

———

THE COFFEE SHOP was almost too bright after the dimness of the funeral parlor. Sunlight streamed through a wall of plate-glass windows and lit up the chrome counter. Ashley inhaled the aroma of bacon and freshly brewed coffee. The waitress arched an eyebrow before leading them to an empty booth and putting menus in their hands. She cocked a hip. "Let me guess. Taking a break from a funeral?"

"Is it that obvious?" Kingsley said.

"Happens every day, hon. You ever wonder why people serve food at a wake? Nothing stirs the appetite like death. It's a psychological reflex. Can I get you coffee? Soda?"

"Just water for me," Ashley said.

"Coffee," Kingsley said.

"You got it. And I'm sorry for your loss." She walked to the counter and pushed through the swinging doors to the kitchen. Ashley heard the crackle of sizzling grease.

"So how have you been?" she asked Kingsley. "How's the industry?"

"Not like it was when you left, I'll tell you that. Things have changed."

"What do you mean?" She leaned back against the overstuffed vinyl.

"Well, the bottom's dropped out of the DVD market, for one thing. Everyone wants their porn online now."

"I guess it had to happen sooner or later."

"I was hoping for later. We still don't have a good digital distribution strategy in place. Barely turned a profit last quarter, and that's with me cutting costs left and right," Kingsley said. "For a while I was shooting scenes in my living room."

"Cheryl must have loved that."

Kingsley dismissed the thought with a wave. "It's not an option anymore, anyway. School's out. The girls are home all day."

"How are Valerie and Kate?"

Kingsley's bushy face perked up. "They're good. They're doing really good."

"I'm glad to hear that."

"But business." He grunted. "Fucking Brewster's gone. Did you know that? He went to New York to work on independent films. So I had to hire a new editor."

Ashley sighed. If there was one person in LA who might have been able to help her through this, it would have been Brewster.

Kingsley watched her, then shook his head. "Jesus. Tara's dead at twenty-five and I'm complaining."

"It's okay. I like hearing you talk."

"Thanks, but it's not okay."

The waitress returned to their table and clunked down Kingsley's mug of coffee and her glass of water. Kingsley ordered a bacon, egg, and cheese sandwich on a hard roll. "Nothing for me," Ashley said, and the waitress clucked her tongue and glided to her next table. Ashley sipped her water. It was cloudy and it tasted sour. She pushed the glass aside.

"Who's the girl Rob brought to the funeral?" she said.

Kingsley smiled. "Hot body, right? She looks so skinny and delicate, like you could split her in half with your dick. But when she moves, it's with this ... I don't know. Aggressiveness. I think it's her hips. They're kind of straight, like a dude's. The contrast with her legs and tits, it's sexy as hell. She'll win Best New Starlet for sure. Her name is Selena Drake."

"What's she doing with a suitcase pimp like Rob Rourke?"

Kingsley blinked at her, then laughed.

"What's funny?"

"Rob Rourke is no suitcase pimp. Not anymore. He's a bona fide player now."

Ashley could not suppress her own laugh. "In what game?"

"I never liked the guy," Kingsley said, "but I have to give him credit. He saw the talent agency trend and he rode it like a fucked horse."

"Talent agency? Like West Modeling?"

Kingsley laughed again. "Ashley, West Modeling is history. Bobby Paradise retired. The landscape's changed. Agents are serious business now. Every girl has representation, and these agencies take themselves seriously. It's a huge pain in the ass for directors like me."

"And Rob has to do with that how?"

"Rob and Tara started their own agency. Pinnacle Talent. Pinnacle represents the hottest girls in the industry, Selena Drake included."

Ashley let this sink in. Gail had told her that Tara was accomplishing things. Apparently, that included starting a successful business with Rob.

"Let me get this straight. Tara and Rob were business partners? Even after they broke up?"

"No choice. They're equal partners in the company."

"So now that Tara is dead, who inherits her half of the company?"

Kingsley spread his hands. "I haven't seen any legal documents, but your mother doesn't seem too optimistic about the subject."

Ashley nodded. "She told me Tara left everything to Rob."

Kingsley studied her over the chipped rim of his coffee mug. His gaze was unsettling. She said, "What?"

"Nothing."

The door chimed and a woman walked in. A little boy gripped her hand. The waitress led them to a table. Ashley heard the waitress tell the boy how handsome he was.

"Gail thinks Tara was murdered by a stalker," Ashley said.

"She shared that theory with me, too."

"You don't believe her?"

Kingsley shrugged. "I'm aware that there are crazy guys out there and that sometimes girls have problems with fans. I just.... Tara never complained to me about a stalker. And I never noticed anyone following her or bothering her."

"Gail claims she saw the guy. She says Tara pointed him out to her, when they were at a restaurant."

Kingsley looked surprised. "She didn't mention *that* to me."

"And at the funeral, I saw ... a bruise. On Tara's right arm." She extended her arm, pushed up the sleeve of Tara's suit jacket, and touched her skin near the elbow. "It could mean that someone grabbed her, or pushed her. Maybe there was a struggle."

"Ashley, dead bodies are different than live ones. Maybe the blood gathered there after death and darkened the skin. Or maybe the coroner did something that left a mark. Or the undertaker."

"I know. I sound silly, right? Like I'm in denial. Like I can't accept that my sister committed suicide."

"That's understandable. I find it hard to accept, too. But murder? Someone would have had to enter her apartment, rig the telephone cord into a noose, maneuver Tara's neck into the noose, and then hang her, all without disturbing the neighbors."

The waitress arrived with his breakfast sandwich. The smell of bacon, egg, and cheese made her stomach rumble. She turned her eyes away from the food.

"I would feel guilty if I didn't at least talk to this cop and make sure she did a thorough investigation. There's no harm in meeting with her. After that, I'm out of here."

"And back to your new life," he said. There was nothing sarcastic or condescending in his tone. He took a bite of his sandwich.

"Yeah," she said. "Exactly."

But first, she wanted to talk to the person who had covered up Tara's bruise.

———

KINGSLEY WALKED into the funeral home. Ashley did not follow him. She sat in the Fiesta and waited. After ten minutes, a black man in a black suit backed a hearse up to the funeral parlor's entrance, parked, and opened the vehicle's back door. Another half-hour passed before the pallbearers emerged from the building. Ashley recognized three of them as performers from the industry. The coffin seemed to float above them, a plain casket. The pallbearers carried it to the waiting hearse. Behind them, mourners filed out of the building.

Ashley wondered which cemetery Gail had selected for the burial.

She stayed in the car until the hearse and its tailing procession of cars had left the parking lot.

The lights were bright in the room where the service had taken place. Without mourners, the space seemed enormous. A funeral parlor employee, still wearing his black suit, pushed a broom across the floor. At the front of the room, Ashley saw the raised platform on which the coffin had rested. She suppressed a shudder. The man noticed her and straightened up. He looked about forty. He regarded her with sad, brown eyes.

"Oh. I'm sorry, miss. The procession just left. May I offer you directions to the interment space?"

It took her a second to realize he was talking about the gravesite. His carefully modulated voice and delicate formality threw her.

"No. Thank you. Actually, I'd like to talk to the undertaker. If he's here."

"The undertaker?"

"I mean, the person who prepared my sister's—Tara's—body."

"That would be Wesley, the dermasurgeon. If you care to meet him, you'll need to return at another time. He's currently performing a preservative treatment downstairs in the preparation room. Perhaps I can help you? My name is Simon and I am a licensed bereavement counselor."

Ashley was pretty sure that Simon could not help her.

"I really need to talk to the, uh, dermasurgeon."

"Yes. Wesley is performing a—"

"He's working on a body. I get it. It's okay." She tried a flirtatious smile. "I have a strong stomach."

"Yes. It is our policy not to permit relatives or friends into the preparation room."

"I understand, but maybe you could make an exception."

"No."

She chewed her lip. "Okay. Can I have directions to the cemetery?"

"Certainly." He reached a hand into his breast pocket and withdrew a small square of cardboard. He handed it to her.

"Thanks."

She dropped the card into her purse and headed for the door. For a moment, she worried that Simon would try to escort her to the parking lot, but he retrieved his broom and went back to cleaning. The sound of the broom sweeping the floor echoed in the large room.

Simon had said that the preparation room was downstairs. In the hallway, she looked for a stairwell. She heard voices and hesitated outside a door labeled *Selection Room*. She peeked inside. Another funeral parlor employee stood with a man and a woman in a showroom full of coffins. She imagined Gail and Kingsley walking among the caskets and another shudder ran through her body. She stepped past the room.

She continued down the hallway. A narrower passage intersected it. A sign on the wall indicated that restrooms were in that direction. Instinctively, she followed it. She passed a women's room and a men's room. At the end of the hallway, she found an unmarked door.

She tried the handle. It was locked.

She was about to knock when the men's room door opened and a man stepped out. Another black suit. With his tall body and his sad, brown eyes, he could be Simon's clone. More likely his brother or his son. He looked to be in his twenties.

"May I assist you?"

"Yes." *Crap. Now what?* She remembered what Simon had said about relatives and friends not being permitted into the preparation room. She straightened the sleeves of Tara's suit jacket. Tossed her hair back. Lifted her chin. "I'm with the state licensing board. I'm here to see Wesley. I spoke to Simon, and he directed me to the preparation room, but I seem to have gotten turned around."

The man stared at her and frowned. She forced a bright smile. She fully expected to be booted from the premises.

Instead, the man withdrew a key from his suit pocket. "You're in the right place. Wesley locks the door during services." He turned the key in the lock and opened the door for her. "There you go, Ms...."

She had no time to think. She blurted, "Coleman." It was Sean's last name.

"Have you met Wesley before, Ms. Coleman?"

"No, first time."

"I see. Well, I trust you won't let his, ah, eccentricities reflect poorly upon our establishment. I can assure you that Wesley is very good at what he does. And he very rarely comes into contact with clients."

"I'll keep that in mind."

She slipped past him and through the door. The man called down to tell Wesley he had a visitor from the state licensing board, then closed the door. She descended. Her steps became less confident as a large, well-lit chamber came into view. A stainless steel table stood in the center of the room. What she could only describe as gutters ran down from its corners. The floor beneath the table funneled to a drain at its center. The drain was discolored, rusty brown. A man's body lay on the table. A chemical odor saturated the air and made her eyes water.

"Hello?" she said.

"He can't talk." A man waddled toward her from an equipment rack. He was short and round. Scraggly blond hair framed his face and tangled past his shoulders. "He's got a mouth-former jammed in there and his lips are sewed tight. Otherwise, I'm sure he'd be a model of social etiquette. I'm Wesley Gladstone. I'd shake your hand, but...." He wriggled his gloved fingers at her. Drops of fluid flew from his fingertips.

Ashley said, "My name is Ashley Coleman—"

"From the state licensing board," he finished for her. He laughed, snorted, hawked up a wad of phlegm, and spat it at the drain under the table. "Sorry. All of these chemicals wreak havoc with my sinuses. Grab one of those tall stools and sit down, Ms. Latner."

She did not move. "How did you know?"

"Do you have any idea how many hours I spent down here with

your sister? Wait. That sounds gross. But you know what I mean. So what is it you want?"

"I, uh, had some questions about Tara's body. You're the derma-surgeon —"

"The *what*?" He cackled. "You've been talking to Simon. With Simon, it's never a body. It's a *loved one*. It's never a burial. It's an *inter-ment*. I'm an embalmer. I pump corpses full of chemicals, stitch them up, pretty them up, and serve them up on a platter with flowers." He froze. Stared at her. "Oh. What I meant to say is, I'm deeply sorry for your loss. Very deeply sorry."

He looked at her with such anxiety that she had to laugh. "Thanks."

"I have a problem with empathy."

"Yeah, I see that."

"It's not my fault. It's the way my brain works."

"That's okay."

"So lay 'em on me."

"Lay...."

"Your questions."

"Oh. Right." She took a breath. "During my sister's service, I touched her arm. Some makeup came away on my hand, and under-neath, I think I saw a bruise. I mean, I know I did."

"Yes, the stiff—" He stopped himself. "The corpse was bruised in several places. First I used a bleaching agent, a compound of carbolic acid. There was still some discoloration, though, so I had to use wax and a flesh-pigmented paste, too. That's probably what you rubbed off with your finger. No biggie."

Ashley felt a coldness gather in her stomach. "She had more than one bruise?"

"Oh, yeah. Arms. Legs. Stomach. And of course the ligature marks on her neck. I've worked on car accident victims with fewer blem-ishes. Um. I mean. Not that she wasn't very, very peaceful-looking."

"Someone beat her," Ashley said. "That's what you're saying."

"Well, no. I mean, I'm not a doctor. No medical training. Although one time, my neighbor's boy, he fell out of a tree, cut his leg bad. I stitched it up. Barely any scar. Probably should have been a doctor, right? A surgeon."

Ashley willed herself to remain patient. "Do you think Tara was beaten?"

He shrugged. "She hanged herself, right? She could have thrashed around."

"Have you embalmed other hanging victims?"

"A few, sure."

"Were those bodies as bruised as Tara's?"

His brow furrowed. She waited while he tried to remember. "No, actually. They weren't as bad."

She felt a deepening sense of dread.

"You know she had a tattoo, right?" Wesley said. "Half of a heart. On her ankle. Very pretty."

Ashley used to have a matching tattoo, the other half of the heart. She had had a laser procedure to remove it a little over a year ago, though a very faint shadow remained on her skin.

She looked at her watch. She had made an appointment with the police detective this morning. If she did not leave here soon, she would miss it.

"Thanks for your help," she said. "I'll let you get back to work."

4

The Devonshire Area Community Police Station was on Etiwanda Avenue in Northridge. It looked like a school building, flat and low with concrete steps leading to the entrance. A breeze drifted against Ashley's face when she stepped out of the Fiesta, but the hot, sticky air overpowered it. She tugged at the open collar of Tara's dress shirt, then pushed through the doors into the police station.

The waiting area smelled like air-freshener and mildew. And it was quiet. She was not sure what she had expected—maybe a cacophony of ringing phones, angry shouts, and the protests of hand-cuffed men being rough-housed through the booking process—but this small room filled with bored-looking people waiting on benches wasn't it. The only noises were the gurgling of a baby sitting on his mother's lap and the low, aggravated voice of a woman arguing with the middle-aged officer at the desk at the front of the room. Ashley stood behind the woman's broad back and waited. Whatever the woman was arguing about, the officer did not look impressed. He yawned and glanced at a computer monitor on his desk. He rubbed his mustache and said, "Like I told you, ma'am, I can't help you."

The woman threw her arms up in the air. "Asshole!" She stormed out of the police station, almost knocking Ashley out of her way.

The officer's bored face perked up when Ashley stepped forward. He looked her over. His gaze lingered on her chest, accentuated by the sleek cut of Tara's suit jacket. "You an attorney?"

"No. My name is Ashley Latner. I have an appointment with Detective Collins." She waited for his gaze to lift to her face, then added, "I'm a little early." She shifted her weight from one leg to the other. Tara's suit fit her well, but her heels were killing her. Tara and her tiny feet.

The officer slurped coffee from an LAPD mug, then checked his computer screen. "Right. Ms. Latner. Have a seat. I'll let the detective know you're here." He tilted his chin at the waiting area behind her.

She chose an empty bench and sat down. The seat was hard and uncomfortable. She crossed her legs, then uncrossed them when an old man sitting across from her ogled her thigh. She wished she had brought a magazine. She checked her watch.

A young Latino bounced out of his seat across from her and dropped into the one to her left. "I know you from somewhere."

Wonderful. She remembered all the letters and e-mails she used to get from state prisons. Two years out of the business, and she could still enter any police station and meet a fan.

Ashley pretended to study the kid's lean face. "No, I don't think we've met."

"I'm sure of it."

She shrugged. "Sorry."

She could feel the kid's stare. "Do you ride the bus?" he said.

"I don't even live in LA."

"Hmm. Well, if we never met before, we may as well meet now, right?" He smiled and his dark eyebrows jumped. "How long will you be here? In LA? I know some good clubs."

"I'm sorry, I— You seem like a nice guy, but I kind of make it a rule not to meet men in police stations."

"Oh." He nodded. "I guess that makes sense."

She looked at her watch. Shifted uncomfortably in her seat. It was time for her appointment. Two minutes past time, actually. She tried to make eye-contact with the officer at the desk, but he had lost interest in her. He tilted back in his chair, reading *Variety*.

"No, wait." The kid looked excited now. "I knew I recognized you!"

Shit.

Ashley shook her head. "You're confusing me with someone else."

"You look a little different on the TV, but it's definitely you."

The woman with the baby on her lap turned to look at her. The baby started crying and the woman bounced him against her chest. A man with a tattoo of a spider on his biceps put down a form he had been filling out. The old geezer across from her continued to check out her legs. She touched her nylons, self-conscious.

"You're on a soap," the kid said. "*General Hospital*, right? My mom watches that shit every day."

Ashley let her jaw unclench. She looked at her watch again. "Excuse me."

She stood up and walked to the desk. The officer put his magazine down and frowned. "You waiting for something?"

"I have an appointment with Detective Collins, remember? I'm Ashley Latner."

The officer nodded slowly. "Right. You'll have to reschedule."

"What?"

"Detective Collins can't see you today."

"I've been waiting here for half an hour."

"I understand that. But Detective—"

"How do you know she can't meet with me? Did you speak to her? You haven't left this desk." His coffee mug was empty now. She could see a circle of brown crud at the bottom.

The officer shrugged. "Intercom—"

"Would you speak to her again? Please? Is she here in the building?"

"Yes, but she's leaving—"

"You know why I'm wearing this black suit in ninety-degree weather?"

"I figured you were a lawyer."

"I already told you I'm not a lawyer. I'm a mourner. I just buried my sister. I drove here from her funeral. And I'm flying home to New Jersey on a redeye tonight. So please, all I'm asking is that you double-check with Detective Collins to see if there's any possibility that she would be willing to honor the appointment she made with me."

The officer blew a stream of air past his mustache. Ashley smelled onions. "I'll see if she's still here." He picked up his phone and punched in an extension. She could hear faint ringing from the handset. When she leaned forward, he cupped a hand over the mouthpiece of the phone and said to her, "Please return to your seat, Ms. Latner. I'll call you over after I've spoken to the detective."

Ashley made an effort not to roll her eyes. "Thank you."

The Latino kid smiled at her. Instead of returning to the seat beside him, she sat alone in an empty cluster of chairs near the door. The kid pivoted as she walked past him, and for a moment she worried that he would follow her, but he only pulled a phone from the pocket of his jeans.

She heard him say, "Mom. You'll never guess who's here."

Her own phone was nestled in her handbag. Sean had not tried to call her since her dramatic exit from his parking lot two nights ago. She knew she should call him, let him know she was in Los Angeles and that her sister had died. But then she would need to explain the details, and they would have to talk about the industry, and he would say something that would piss her off, or vice versa, and their fight would get worse instead of better.

She decided she'd call him tomorrow morning, when her plane landed in Newark.

The officer waved his hand at her. "Ms. Latner?"

She returned to the desk.

"Detective Collins will meet with you, but she only has five minutes. She has to be in court—"

"Fine."

A door opened behind the desk and another uniformed officer beckoned her inside.

———

THE SECOND OFFICER escorted her down a hallway and up a fight of stairs, past a bullpen full of cubicles. She heard the clicking of fingers on keyboards, the voices of people talking into phones. The officer stopped at a solid metal door. He squinted at a ring of keys until he found the right one, then unlocked the door and ushered her inside. She hesitated in the doorway. Stared at the battered steel table, the two metal chairs.

An interrogation room.

"Detective Collins wanted to meet with you somewhere quiet, that's all. Take a seat. She'll join you in a minute."

Ashley wondered if that minute would count as one of the five she had been allotted.

"Thanks."

He left and closed the door behind him. She sat in one of the chairs. The metal was cold. She had been hot outside; now she shivered. After a few seconds, she gave up trying to find a comfortable sitting position. There was nothing to look at except the bare table and the blank walls. The cool air carried a familiar odor. It took her a few seconds to place it. Lysol.

A surveillance camera leered down from its perch near the ceiling. Self-consciousness wormed through her at the thought that someone might be watching her. She averted her gaze from the dark lens and tried to pretend the camera wasn't there.

The door banged open and a middle-aged woman shouldered into the room. She wore a navy blue pants-suit, shiny at the elbows and baggy enough to disguise any trace of the feminine in her figure.

"I'm sorry for your loss." There was something so obviously insincere about the woman's tone that Ashley felt blood rush to her cheeks. "I only have a few minutes." Instead of taking the empty chair, she leaned a hip against the table, forcing Ashley to look up at her.

"I was told you had five."

The detective's eyes narrowed, and Ashley immediately regretted the sarcastic tone.

"I have to testify at a trial, Ms. Latner. I don't control the court system. I'm doing you a favor meeting with you at all."

She had the clipped voice of a schoolmarm.

"Okay." Ashley sighed.

"So. You're the deceased's sister. And you have some questions."

She was pale—almost an albino, but with light blue eyes instead of pink. Her hair hung like a white sheet and ended in a razor-straight line above the shoulders of her suit-jacket. Hundreds of freckles spread out from her nose like a rash. And apparently she had something against the use of makeup. She smelled like soap.

"Don't you ... have a file or something?" Ashley said.

"I don't have a lot of time." The detective drummed her fingers against the surface of the table. Her nails were unpainted and trimmed close to the fingers.

"You mentioned that. But I came here to discuss some important details. I think you should get the file."

Collins sighed. "I know the details, Ms. Latner. I don't need the file. The deceased's body was found on Thursday, around noon, by Gail Latner, mother of the deceased. Based on several factors including the body's temperature and the state of rigor mortis, the coroner estimated the time of death to be sometime late the previous evening, Wednesday night. Cause of death was asphyxia resulting from the compression of the airways and the carotid arteries by a ligature. Pronounced paleness of the deceased's face and the purple tint of her tongue corroborate asphyxia as cause of death. Examination of the scene revealed that the deceased fashioned a noose from a telephone cord, anchored it to a component of her exercise equipment, and used her own body weight to pull the cord tight around her neck. Are there any other details you would like to know?"

Ashley stared at Collins. She could not understand the woman's hostility, but she was not about to back down. Collins broke eye-contact first, but only to glance impatiently at her watch.

Ashley said, "I'm not sure my sister's death was a suicide."

"The coroner's report confirmed it."

"What about Tara's stalker?"

Collins tilted her head. The skin between her eyes creased in a *let's get real* expression. "Do we really need to go through this?"

"Go through what?"

"You used to work in the pornography industry. You know the types of people that business attracts."

"Show business types?"

Collins snorted. "You people live in your own fantasyland."

"We people?"

"Just because you're in front of a camera when you get down on all fours doesn't mean you're an actress or a model."

Ashley gripped the chair's hard metal armrests. Now she understood the hostility. "Why don't you tell me what it means, Detective?"

The detective's stare hardened. "Porn is a sleazy business. If you choose to be a part of it, that's your choice. Your sister's choice. But this office doesn't have the resources to chase down every horny masturbator who might develop an unhealthy fixation."

"Did you at least look into the possibility that a stalker did this? My mother saw him. Did you sit my mother down with a ... a sketch artist?"

"'White male, thirties, tall and thin.' That's all she gave us. She couldn't even remember his hair color. A sketch artist can only work with the details a witness gives him. You've heard the phrase garbage in, garbage out?"

"Did you do anything?"

Collins shrugged. "We conducted a thorough investigation."

"Tara died five days ago. How thorough could you have been?"

"Tell me how this mystery killer accessed your sister's apartment. There were no signs of forced entry, and your mother admits that she had to unlock both the lock and the deadbolt the day she found the body."

"Maybe he went in and out through a window. Did you interview the neighbors?"

Collins looked at her watch. "The windows were locked when police arrived on the scene."

"Maybe he tricked her into opening the door. He could have posed as a plumber or something. A neighbor might have seen—"

"And then the killer borrowed a key so he could lock the deadbolt when he left?"

"He wanted it to look like a suicide. So that would make sense."

"It doesn't make sense, Ms. Latner, and I think you know that." Collins straightened up and stepped toward the door.

"Wait. Tara had bruises. At the funeral, I touched her arm, and some makeup rubbed off and there was a bruise underneath. I talked to the embalmer. He told me there were bruises all over her body."

Collins shrugged. "I'm glad to hear that the funeral home was able to cover them up."

Ashley felt a column of bile rise in her throat. "You're just ... you're just going to ignore the bruises?"

"According to the coroner, the bruising did not occur on the day of death. Your sister was bruised several days prior, probably Monday."

"You didn't think that was ... suspicious?" She sounded small, meek, like a frightened child.

"Pornography is a rough trade. You of all people should know that."

"It's not *that* rough."

"I really need to get going. It was nice meeting you. Have a safe flight home." Collins already had her hand on the doorknob.

"Wait. If the case is closed, then there's no reason for you to keep Tara's laptop. I want it back. You can do that for me, can't you?"

"Sure, I can do that," Collins said.

"Thank you."

Collins smirked. "I just can't tell you her password."

5

HER CAR HAD BEEN SOAKING up sun in the police station parking lot for almost an hour. Opening the driver's side door was like opening an oven. Hot air buffeted her face. She leaned far enough inside to insert the key in the ignition. Twisted it. The engine and the air-conditioner churned to life. She shut the door and backed away.

She had forgotten how quickly a car could broil during summer in the Valley.

She paced while she waited for the car to cool. Tara's laptop, slung under her arm, felt like it weighed twenty pounds. The sodden fabric of Tara's shirt clung to her back. The suit would be a wrinkled mess by the time she took it off.

After a deep sigh, she opened the car door, tossed the laptop on the passenger seat, and climbed inside. Still hot, but no longer deadly. She glanced at the laptop, a chunky Dell, and shook her head. It was useless without her sister's password. She leaned forward and singed her hands on the plastic steering wheel.

"Fuck!"

She pressed her palms to the air-conditioner vents.

And started to cry.

No, not now, Ash. This isn't the time or place.

Through a blur of tears she saw a man and woman walk past her car. Cops in uniform. Two hazy round faces turned to stare at her through the windshield. Then they were gone.

Get a hold of yourself.

She wiped her eyes. Breathed slowly in and out until her sobbing stopped. She was okay.

She shifted the car into reverse. Then put it back in park.

She was not okay.

Tara was dead. And beneath the embalmer's skillful paintjob, her body was bruised. Her arms, legs, and stomach. What had Wesley said? *I've worked on car accident victims with fewer blemishes.* And the police did not care.

They didn't care.

Tara was a porn star. To the outside world that made the bruises unsuspicious and the suicide unsurprising. Detective Collins had probably spent all of three hours on the case.

More tears gathered at the corners of her eyes. She shook her head. Sucked in a breath.

If she caught her redeye tonight, she would be home in New Jersey tomorrow morning. She could go back to work that day, tell the bank manager that it was easier to keep busy than to stay at home and grieve. She could call Sean. Make up with him. Meet for dinner. Go back to his place. Return to a normal life. Leave all of this behind her. Again.

But that was bullshit. She had never left anything behind her. Not really.

If she wanted to find out what had really happened to Tara, she would need to stay. She knew that. No one else was going to do anything. It had to be her.

She pulled out her phone, called United, and canceled her flight. It was difficult to hear over the whoosh from the vents, but she was not about to lower the A/C. She put her phone away and let the cold air blast her face and neck.

Ashley had asked Detective Collins twice whether she had interviewed Tara's neighbors. The detective had dodged her question both times. That meant she probably had not done it.

It was as good a place as any to start.

———

SHE KNEW AS SOON as she drove into the parking lot that she had made her first amateur's mistake. The BMWs and Mercedes and Lexuses she'd seen there the previous day were gone. Yesterday had been Sunday. Today was Monday. 2:45 PM. Everyone was at work.

She parked in the mostly empty lot and climbed out of the car. She shaded her eyes and squinted up at the two-story building. She was here. She might as well knock on some doors.

She moved Tara's laptop from the passenger seat to the trunk for safekeeping, then headed up the concrete steps to the second floor of the building.

First she let herself into Tara's apartment using the key Gail had given her. Yesterday, she had admired the apartment's quiet. It had seemed like evidence of her sister's success. No barking dogs or whirling helicopter blades here, nothing to disturb her sleep. But today the dead quiet of the place made Ashley uneasy. She wouldn't mind a little barking. At least the darkened rooms were cool.

The thought of entering the room with the Bowflex machine made her skin crawl. Someone had used the Bowflex's sturdy metal frame to support the noose. To "anchor" it, in Detective Collins's words. But the room was Tara's home office as well as her gym. If Tara had written down the password for her laptop, the home office was where Ashley would find it.

Just don't look at the thing.

Unlike traditional weight machines, the Bowflex used polymer bars to create resistance. Averting her gaze from the long, curving bars was more difficult than she had anticipated. They seemed to beckon to her from the corner of her vision, like long black fingers.

She moved quickly to the desk with the computer docking station on it.

One of the guys she worked with at the bank kept his password taped to the bottom of his keyboard. Thinking of that guy now, Ashley lifted Tara's keyboard and ran a hand underneath it. There was nothing there. The desk had two drawers. She opened the first one. The smell of pencils and erasers brought back childhood memories. She pushed pens and pencils and paperclips around the shallow drawer but did not find what she was looking for.

She tried the second drawer and found a sandwich-sized Ziploc bag stuffed with slips of paper. Lifting the bag from the drawer, Ashley felt like crying and laughing at the same time. Tara had not changed too much in the two years she had been gone. She still collected all of her Visa receipts so she could check them against her statement at the end of the month, a habit for which Ashley used to make fun of her.

Ashley stuffed the bag in her purse. It was not the password she had hoped to find, but the bag of receipts might prove useful. She would look through the receipts later, back at her motel room. Maybe they would yield some clues about the final days of Tara's life.

Okay. Time to canvas the neighborhood—as they say on TV.

She started with Tara's left-hand neighbor and continued in that direction, knocking on each door and waiting a moment before moving on. It was not long before she was feeling the heat of the thick Valley air. She could have ditched the suit at Tara's apartment— had planned to—but had decided to wear it a little longer. It gave her an air of authority that might come in handy.

Her knocks at the first three apartments drew no responses. She was considering the possibility of leaving and coming back later, when she heard a noise beyond the fourth apartment's door. She pressed her ear to the warm wood and heard the drone of a vacuum cleaner.

She knocked. The drone continued. She knocked again, louder this time. The drone cut off and she heard the patter of approaching footsteps. The door opened a crack and an olive-complexioned face peered out.

"Hi. My name is Ashley Latner. My sister lived four doors down from you." Ashley gestured to her right. "I just, uh, wanted to talk to you for a minute, if that's okay."

The woman pulled the door open wider and offered Ashley an awkward smile. "*Lo siento.* No speak English. I clean house."

She wore a tank-top and sweatpants and her black hair was tied back in a ponytail. The vacuum cleaner waited behind her, its cord trailing to an outlet on the wall. Ashley smelled cleaning products. The woman was young—nineteen or twenty—and had a good figure, and the first thing Ashley thought was that she could ditch this job and make thousands a month in porn.

God, she was already forgetting all of the reasons she'd left.

"Do you clean this apartment often?"

"Monday and Thursday."

"Have you seen a man acting strangely near the building?" She tried to remember what Detective Collins had said. "A white man in his thirties, tall and thin?"

The woman stared at her, puzzling through the words. Ashley sighed. Maybe with a pen and paper, she could make herself clear. With drawings.

"May I come inside?" She took a step closer and pressed her palm to the warm doorframe.

The woman shook her head quickly. "Must clean."

"I only want to talk to you for a minute."

"No."

"You won't let me in?"

"No."

Ashley gritted her teeth. She had taken Spanish in high school, and one of her best friends growing up had been Latina. But over the years she'd lost her ability to speak the language.

"Listen, my sister—*mi hermana*—is dead. *Muerto.* She lived in an apartment here. Apartment 2F. I think a man might have hurt her. Killed her. Have you seen a strange man here? *Un hombre?*"

The woman shook her head helplessly. "Must clean."

The door closed. Ashley heard the click of the lock.

She took a step back. There was one more apartment on her left.

After that, she would try the apartments to the right of Tara's. And after that, the apartments on the first floor. Maybe by then people would be returning home from work.

She was about to move on when a flicker to her right caught her eye. She had already knocked on the door of that apartment. No one had answered. But now she saw the mini-blinds in one of the windows tremble, as if recently disturbed. Someone was in there. Watching her.

Ashley hurried to the door and knocked on it. "Hello? Is someone in there? Please open the door. I just want to talk to you."

She pressed her ear to the door. Nothing.

"Please." She knocked again. "My sister was a neighbor of yours. Tara Latner. Did you know her?"

She was about to knock again when the door pulled inward and an old woman glared at her. The skin of her face looked like leather stretched over bone. She smelled like old paper. "Get out of here! It's dangerous!"

The door swung forward. Ashley shoved her shoulder against the wood before it could close. "Wait. Please. I just want to talk."

"It's too dangerous."

Ashley felt her heart racing. "Please. I just want to know what you're afraid of. Did someone hurt you?"

The woman seemed to consider for a second, then grabbed Ashley's arm. Her bony fingers closed in a surprisingly tight grip and tugged her roughly through the doorway.

"They probably already saw us talking."

"They?" Ashley rubbed her wrist. "More than one person? Who are you talking about—" Her voice died in her throat. In front of the closed mini-blinds, potted plants lined the windowsills. Dozens of them. They were pressed close together in a green tangle.

The old woman followed her gaze. "The heat they give off confuses the satellites," she whispered. "Photosynthesis."

Oh no.

The apartment's layout was a mirror image of Tara's. The woman pulled her into the kitchenette. On the countertop, she saw an array of translucent red bottles. Her enthusiasm deflated. She had thought she was finally close to getting some answers, but all she had done was step into the paranoid fantasies of a confused old woman.

The woman was studying her black suit. "You're one of them."

"What?" She lifted one of the pill bottles. The name of the medication was printed on the label, but it meant nothing to her.

"You're one of them!"

"I made a mistake coming here. I'm not one of them. Calm down, okay? Please don't be afraid."

The woman grabbed a phone off the wall and poked buttons. Calling 911. Ashley's breath stopped. But the woman pushed more than three numbers. She gripped the phone to her ear. Ashley could hear it ringing.

"They're here," the woman said into the phone. "They've come for me."

Ashley heard a panicked, female voice on the other end. She wanted to yell that everything was okay, but she thought that might scare the person on the other end of the line even more.

The woman hung up the phone and pointed a finger at Ashley. Her joints looked as big and round as jumbo gumballs. "My daughter's coming, so you may as well leave now."

That sounded like a good plan to Ashley. She took a backward step toward the door. "I don't know who you think I am, but—"

"You're Homeland Security. I've seen you watching me. In your car. You didn't think I saw you, but I did."

Ashley had crept two steps backward. Now her spine was to the door and her hand was on the knob. She did not turn it. "You saw someone watching you? In a car?"

"Homeland Security."

"Was there a man in the car? A tall white man, in his thirties?"

"It was *you* in the car," the old woman said. "That's why you made your windows dark. So I wouldn't see. I know about your tricks and your gadgets."

"The car had tinted windows?" Ashley knew that she was probably wasting her time. The car the old woman was talking about had as much likelihood of existing as the satellites and the evil Homeland Security agents. But what if this woman really had seen something? She probably never left her home. And Ashley had already caught her peering out her window. "What kind of car did you see?"

"You didn't realize I was watching," the old woman said. She was reaching under her sweater now, scratching herself. "You thought you were watching me, *but I was watching you.* I know all about you. Homeland Security. Spying on me in your black car, watching me from behind your dark windows."

Black car. Tinted windows.

Maybe it meant nothing. Maybe it was the vehicle in which Tara's killer had patiently waited for her to return home, so he could go upstairs and lynch her in her own apartment.

The woman's hand moved more vigorously beneath her sweater. Ashley could hear fingernails raking her skin.

"Please stop doing that. I don't want you to hurt yourself. I ... my mission is over, okay? I'm going to redirect the satellite. You're safe."

The door opened hard into her back and sent her staggering forward. When she turned she saw a middle-aged version of the old woman gaping at her.

"Who are you and what the hell do you think you're doing here?"

"My sister lives in this building. I mean, she used to. I was just asking your mother some questions."

"Are you a cop? Is this about the woman who hanged herself?"

"No. Yes. I mean—"

"Are you with the police or not?"

"No."

"Then you have no right to be here. My mother suffers from schizophrenia. She—"

"Do you live here with her? She was telling me about a car. A black car with tinted windows. Have you seen a car like that? Maybe it was idling in the parking lot?"

The woman held the door open for her. "Get out of here. Now."

"She's Homeland Security," the old woman said. "She admitted it."

"No." Ashley smiled weakly, apologetically, at the daughter. "I was just trying to put her at ease."

"She controls the satellite," the old woman said. "She said she would redirect it."

The daughter's face blanched. "What have you been telling my mother? How could you ... be so cruel?"

The daughter shoved a hand into her purse and came out with a dark blue canister.

A second passed before Ashley realized it was Mace.

6

"DON'T MOVE." The old woman's daughter held the canister of Mace in one hand and fished a phone from her purse with the other. "How dare you come in here and confuse a mentally disabled woman?" She tapped the phone's screen. Ashley's pulse quickened with each tap. The canister in the woman's other hand remained rock-steady, aimed at her eyes.

"I guess I'll leave now."

"You're not going anywhere until we talk to the police."

Great. That's all she needed—to face charges as a tormentor of old women.

"I'm sorry I said those things to your mother. She was scared. I was only trying to make her feel safe."

"By telling her that her nightmares are real?"

"I made a mistake."

"You sure did. Mom begged me to take her out of the hospital. Now, she'll probably have to go back."

The old woman's eyes widened and her jaw twisted with panic. "Janice, they did tests on me there. They corrupted my mitochondria!"

Ashley inched to her right. The windowsill was at her back. She caught the earthy aroma of all of those plants. Dry leaves rustled against Tara's suit jacket. Janice kept the canister trained on her. She finished dialing and clamped the phone to her ear.

"Listen," Ashley said. "My sister is dead. I'm not here to harass anyone. I just want to know if you've seen a suspicious man hanging around the building."

"The woman in 2F committed suicide. What does that have to do with suspicious men?"

"Tara was murdered. The killer made it look like a suicide."

Janice paused, then lowered her phone and studied Ashley with new interest. "What's your name?"

"Ashley Latner. I—"

"How do you know my mother? Did you meet at Dr. Zoller's office? Are you— Have you been taking your meds?"

Ashley stared at her, then thought, *Oh, God, she thinks I'm crazy.*

The Mace remained in the air, thrust out at arm's length, aimed at Ashley's face, but at least she'd lowered her phone. That was good.

"I'm going to leave now. I'm sorry if I caused any trouble."

Janice looked unsure of what to do. For the first time, the arm holding the Mace wavered. Ashley took that as a positive sign and stepped toward the door. Janice sighed and lowered the Mace and dropped the canister into her purse.

Ashley touched her hand to the doorknob. Turned it. And got the hell out of there.

———

ON THE OUTDOOR WALKWAY, she heard a car engine. She looked over the railing as a sedan pulled into the parking lot. It was not black and it did not have tinted windows. It was a silver Lexus. But she hurried down the stairs anyway and met the driver as he was hiking across the pavement.

"Excuse me," she said, out of breath.

He was wearing a gray suit. A leather attaché case swung from his arm. Sunglasses blocked his eyes. He lifted them off of his face as she jogged toward him. He was young. Early twenties. Good-looking. He seemed to think the same of her. A smile appeared on his face.

"What's up?" he said.

"Do you live here?"

He nodded. "I moved in three months ago. You?"

She shook her head. "My sister lived here. In apartment 2F. Her name was Tara Latner. Did you know her?"

"I haven't had a chance to meet many people. I was kind of hoping you'd be the first." He smiled again and shifted his attaché case to his left hand so he could extend his right. "My name is Todd Hadley."

She shook his hand. "Ashley Latner. Todd, this is going to sound like a weird question, but have you noticed a strange man loitering around the building? A tall, thin white guy in his thirties?"

"What do you mean by loitering?" Before she could elaborate, he said, "I haven't seen anyone. Listen, would you like to get a drink with me?"

This was not going as planned.

"What about a car?" she said. "A black car with tinted windows?" She was already edging away from him. She had more doors to knock on. There had to be someone in the complex with information about Tara's stalker.

"You mean the Hyundai?"

"There was a Hyndai here? Black, with tinted windows?"

"Yeah. The jerk was parked in my space. Just sitting in his car with the engine running. I had to honk like six times before he moved."

"What did he look like?"

Todd shrugged. "I couldn't get a good look at him through the tinted glass. Definitely a guy, though. I could see the shape of his head and shoulders."

"I don't suppose you remember the license plate number?"

His eyes narrowed. "Wait a second. Are you a cop?"

———

SHE WAITED until she was back in her car before she let herself smile. She had done it. She had found something. The police had access to all kinds of DMV databases. They could run a search and print up a list of every person in the area who owned a black Hyundai. She reached for her phone, called the Devonshire Police Station, and asked to speak to Detective Collins.

A gruff male voice responded. "What is this regarding?"

"One of her cases," Ashley said. She juggled the phone and the steering wheel and almost clipped the side-view mirror of a slow-moving Lincoln. She swerved. "It's important."

"Detective Collins is unavailable at the moment."

A glance at the dashboard clock told her that only about an hour had passed since she'd seen the detective leave for court. Maybe she was still at the courthouse.

"Ma'am? Would you like me to transfer you to her voicemail?"

"No thank you."

Ashley ended the call, then Googled the address of the San Fernando Courthouse. If she could not reach Detective Collins by phone, she'd ambush her in person.

———

THE SAN FERNANDO Courthouse turned out to be a cheerful-looking building surrounded by palm trees. Ashley parked in the lot, but before she opened her door, she saw Detective Collins and a man walk out of the building. She sank in her seat and waited until the detective and the man parted ways. The man climbed into a Toyota Camry and drove away. Detective Collins marched across the pavement in the direction of a black Crown Victoria.

Ashley climbed out of her car. "Detective Collins. I need to talk to you."

The detective flashed her an indignant frown and tried to step around her.

"Please," Ashley said. "I have information about my sister's case."

"We spoke less than an hour ago."

"But I've learned something new. I talked to two of my sister's neighbors. Just give me a few minutes to explain."

Detective Collins seemed to consider. Then she gestured toward the Crown Vic. "Get in. I'll give you two minutes, and that's it." She aimed a key at the car and unlocked it with a beep.

Ashley climbed into the passenger seat. Collins got in on the other side and started the engine and the air-conditioner. Warm air gusted from the vents and slowly dropped in temperature.

"Well?"

"I think I have a description of the suspect's car—"

Collins groaned and shifted in her seat. Her eyes looked tired in her pale, freckle-covered face. "What suspect?"

"The stalker. One of Tara's neighbors told me she noticed a suspicious car in the parking lot. It was idling there, as if the driver were waiting for someone." Ashley was conscious of the embellishments as she tossed them in, but figured she had little choice if she wanted the detective to take her seriously. "She said it was a black car with tinted windows."

"You're sitting in a black car with tinted windows. Am I a suspect?"

"Wait. Let me finish. I talked to another neighbor. He said that he came home one day and found a black Hyundai with tinted windows idling in his space. He's pretty sure a man was driving. He honked and the guy took off."

"What model Hyundai?"

Ashley shook her head. "He didn't remember."

"And the names of these neighbors...."

"The man's name is Todd Hadley. The woman...." Ashley wrung her hands. "I didn't get her name. You know, I don't have all that much experience with this kind of thing. But she lives in apartment 2I. And she has a daughter named Janice."

Collins nodded. "A daughter named Janice. Great work. Did you get the name of her goldfish, too?"

"Are you going to make fun of me, or are you going to look into this?"

"Neither. I'm going to go home and have a glass of wine."

Ashley wanted to scream. "Why?"

"Because my shift is over and I don't feel like explaining to my captain why I'm working on a closed case. Is that a good enough reason for you?"

"No, Detective, it isn't."

Collins laughed and shook her head, staring up at the ceiling of her car as if to show God her exasperation.

"You don't care about my sister's death at all, do you?" Ashley said.

Collins looked straight into her eyes. "An idling car isn't suspicious. Certainly not suspicious enough to justify disregarding a coroner's report and spending limited time and resources pursuing a closed case. If you want me to put my ass on the line, you'll need to bring me something a lot more convincing than that."

"In other words, you want me to do your job for you?"

"No, I want you to waste your time instead of mine. Your sister's death was a suicide. It's sad. But it happened. If you need to run around playing detective before you can accept it, then do what you need to do. But don't expect me to join in the fun."

"You're a bitch."

"And you're a whore."

The word hit Ashley like a slap to the face. Collins looked down at her hands and blushed. Ashley glared at her.

"I'm going to find Tara's killer, and when I do, I'm going to make sure you lose your job over this case."

She opened the car door, climbed out, and slammed it closed.

———

FROM BEHIND HER own steering wheel, she watched Detective Collins drive out of the courthouse parking lot. It wasn't until the black Crown Vic had merged with traffic and disappeared that Ashley realized she was holding her breath. She released it in an angry whoosh.

It was an unyielding, natural law that she had somehow forgotten in the two years she'd been gone. Most people outside the industry

—"squares," as Brewster used to call them—abhorred people in the industry. It didn't matter that the balance sheets proved that millions of people were spending billions of dollars on pornography every year. Porn was everybody's guilty secret. Everybody's favorite scapegoat.

Hypocrites.

Ashley had only been in the Valley for a couple of days and it seemed like she had already accomplished more than Detective Collins.

Okay. So what do I do now?

Tara had told Gail that the stalker had been following her for months. More people must have seen him. Other neighbors. Tara's friends. Her colleagues in the industry. If Ashley could piece together a more detailed description, and maybe confirm that the black Hyundai was the stalker's car, then she could go back to the police, to Collins's captain maybe, and force them to reopen the case.

Only one problem. The person closest to Tara was the last person Ashley wanted to see.

Rob Rourke.

7

PINNACLE TALENT WAS HEADQUARTERED in a one-story building in Chatsworth. The sun was beginning to set when Ashley pulled into the lot. She hurried from the car to the building. She was pretty sure that this place had been an optometry practice two years ago, but walking through the door, she saw that it bore no resemblance to one now. The reception room reeked of Rob Rourke's taste—or lack of thereof. All gloss and no warmth, every surface as shiny as his newly bald head. The floor was tiled in marble. It looked expensive but made the place feel cold. A young woman with a wireless earpiece smiled at her from behind a chrome and glass desk. On the wall behind her, the words *Pinnacle Talent* gleamed in metallic letters that rose almost to the ceiling. The phone on the desk was silent, but she heard others ringing beyond the wall.

A squeak of leather made her turn. Two people sat huddled together on one side of a long leather sofa, a young couple. The girl looked eighteen. She gnawed on a hangnail. Her boyfriend, twenty-something, had his hands clasped in his lap. Both of them wore tank-tops. They had matching tattoos on their shoulders. Celtic symbols, Ashley thought, inked recently. The skin beneath was still puffy and slightly bruised. In front of the couch, a low glass table offered a fanned-out selection of magazines. The tattooed couple seemed uninterested in reading.

Ashley didn't blame them. She remembered the rainy afternoon she and Tara had walked into the office of West Modeling in Van Nuys. Seven years ago, Bobby Paradise had been the closest thing the porn world had had to a talent agent. He had shot Polaroid photos of Ashley and Tara, in and out of their short-shorts and halter tops in an office that reeked of cigarette smoke. She still remembered the rain buffeting the window, the sound of distant thunder. After taking the photos, Bobby helped them choose their porn names. They had opted to keep their real first names because that's what Jenna Jameson had done. Two days later, Bobby had booked their first jobs.

This place was a palace compared to Bobby's dark and grimy storefront.

"Can I help you?" The woman behind the desk smiled. She had soft brown eyes and perfect teeth. Before Ashley could introduce herself, she said, "Oh. God. I'm sorry. I didn't recognize you—"

Ashley dismissed the apology with a wave. Her heels clicked on the marble as she approached the desk. "I haven't worked in the industry in years. I'm surprised you recognized me at all."

"Come on. You're Ashley Hale. You're, like, a legend." She blushed. "My name's Rachel Miller. I haven't come up with a, you know, performing name yet, but I'm planning to get into the business soon."

She extended her hand over the desk and Ashley shook it.

"I'm a big fan," Rachel said. "I used to watch your videos with my boyfriend. You know, back in high school. You're body is, like, amazing. And you always looked really into the sex, no matter how crazy it got. We used to look for DVDs with your picture on the box. We *loved* watching you."

Ashley shifted her weight. She appreciated the woman's compliments, but she was not in the right frame of mind for this particular trip down memory lane.

"You're one of the reasons I took this job," Rachel said. "I found out Tara was your sister, and I was like, cool. I'm answering phones for Ashley Hale's little sister." Rachel looked quickly down at her desktop. "I'm sorry. Is it insensitive to talk like that so soon after, you know—"

"It's alright."

"So can I, um, help you with something?"

"I'm here because of my sister, actually. I'm trying to find information about—" She sensed the gazes of the tattooed man and woman and lowered her voice. "About a fan. One who might have been a little overzealous."

Rachel's brow crinkled. Then she nodded, understanding. "She never mentioned a fan like that to me. But I started working here recently. We weren't that close."

"Is Rob around? I'm thinking if anyone would know, he would."

"Let me call him. Oh, actually, I'm supposed to call Max. Rob has a personal assistant now. I keep forgetting."

"Rob has a personal assistant? And it's a guy?"

Rachel laughed. "Rob hired him last week to keep his calendar, manage his contacts. You know. Rob's real busy."

His calendar? His contacts? The Rob that Ashley knew never worked a day in his life and would not have been qualified to wait tables at Macaroni Grill.

A door opened to Rachel's right and a man sauntered into the reception area. Skin-tight jeans and a ribbed T-shirt exaggerated his blade-thin figure. He looked Ashley over before giving her hand a brisk shake. "I'm Max. Rob's not here." He had an accent, but a pronounced lilt in his voice made it hard to identify. Russian? She suspected that the lilt was at least partly affected. Combined with his mannerisms, it broadcast his sexual orientation loud and clear.

He noticed the couple on the couch and said, "Jasmine is going to help you today. She'll be ready in a few minutes."

He turned back to Ashley and his smile disappeared. "I'll let Rob know you were looking for him." He started to guide her toward the exit. Her mind raced. She did not want to leave yet. Even if she could not talk to Rob, she might find something in this place, some clue to Tara's death. Maybe the password for her laptop.

"As long as I'm here, could you give me a quick tour? I'd really like to see the business my sister created."

"I don't give tours, sweetie. I have places to be."

"I could look around myself. I won't disturb anyone."

"Actually, I've been instructed to ask you to leave."

"What?" Ashley turned to Rachel, but the receptionist had suddenly become captivated by something on her computer screen. The tattooed couple pretended not to listen.

Max let out a theatrical sigh. "Rob left instructions with me that if you were to show up here looking for him, I was to ask you politely to leave. And to call our security firm if necessary."

"Is this a joke?"

"No, darling, it's not."

Before Ashley could form a response, the door behind Rachel's desk opened and another woman glided into the reception area. Ashley recognized her. She was the woman Rob had brought to Tara's funeral. The new starlet Kingsley had told her about at the coffee shop.

Dressed in a denim miniskirt and a tube-top, she looked even skinnier than Max. Ridges in her cotton tube-top outlined her ribcage. She was tall, too. At least six feet. Her breasts were large, but not huge. If they were fake, they had been expertly done. She had large, expressive green eyes, accented by black mascara and dusky eyeliner. A delicate mouth. Long black hair. Kingsley was right about her hips. They were straight rather than curvy, but as he'd told her, that slight deviation from the feminine ideal somehow made her look even better.

"You're Ashley Hale." She extended a hand. Her fingers were long and slender, the nails painted dark red.

Ashley shook it. "And you're Selena Drake."

Selena did not seem surprised. Apparently, she expected to be recognized.

"I'm so sorry. I really loved Tara."

"Really? Is that why you're knocking boots with her boyfriend?"

Selena's head snapped back as if she'd been struck. Her face whitened and her lips parted. "We ... Rob and I ... we didn't get together until after he broke up with Tara. I would never—"

Max stepped between them. "You don't need to explain yourself, Selena-baby. This woman was just leaving."

"But I want to explain myself."

Max frowned at her stern tone, but said nothing.

"No, it's my fault," Ashley said. "It's been a long day. I'm frustrated. I shouldn't have taken it out on you. Is Rob here? I really need to talk to him."

Selena shook her head. "He's been down in San Diego all day. Two of our girls were booked with a company called Freeze Frame. Brand new. When Rob's not familiar with a producer, he likes to escort the talent to the set, make sure everything is legit, and get payment in advance. Sometimes he hangs around, just to keep an eye on things."

"That sounds ... responsible." *And not at all like Rob.*

"It was Tara's policy."

"Ah."

"She's always been focused on helping the girls," Selena said. "Guiding them."

Max was glaring at her now. Ashley wanted to get away from him. She said to Selena, "Hey, maybe you could give me a tour of the building."

"Absolutely not," Max said.

Selena laughed and gripped Max's shoulder. "Someone needs a massage."

"I do not need a massage," Max said. He yanked his knife-thin shoulder blade from Selena's hand. "I need you to stop talking to this ... woman."

"Two years ago, this 'woman' was one of the biggest names in porn. And she's Tara's sister. I'd like to give her a tour. I don't see why that's a problem."

"Rob said—"

Selena grinned. "I'll deal with Rob, Max. Don't worry about that."

Max threw his arms up and shook his head, clearly disgusted. "Fine. Whatever. I was only trying to do my job."

"Come on," Selena said. She took Ashley's hand and tugged her toward the door. "I can't stay too long, though. Someone's waiting for me."

Ashley followed her into a dim hallway. Framed headshots of women—clients, Ashley assumed—lined one wall. New performers Ashley did not recognize. Doors lined the other wall. They were open. Ashley looked inside the small, dark rooms. They had been set up as offices even though there was barely enough room for a desk and a chair in each of them. They had probably been examination rooms when this building had been used by optometrists. She saw a young woman talking into a phone while making notes on a pad of paper.

"Sorry about that," Selena said. "I don't know what Rob was thinking when he hired Max. The guy has some kind of a gay Napoleon complex."

Ashley was tempted to voice her opinion of Rob, then thought better of it. Selena was helping her. Why sour the relationship by slamming her boyfriend? They walked past an office with a middle-aged man working at a keyboard.

"Are all of these people employees?"

"Pinnacle's Web site is handled internally," Selena said, following her gaze. "We've got three guys, that's all they do. The site gets updated all of the time. New girls join. Some get fired. And girls are always changing their mind on what they are and aren't available to do." She gave Ashley a mischievous grin. "I do everything, but not every girl is like me. Rob hired some sales people, too. He says this business is all about contacts."

"Uh-huh."

Selena glanced at her. "So why did you leave the industry? I mean, most girls would kill for a career like yours."

"Ask me that another time. It's kind of a long story."

"If you ever decide to come back, you should definitely sign with Pinnacle. The agency manages over seventy girls."

"Wow."

"Yeah, it's nuts. But it's important. Pinnacle and the other agencies have really changed the industry." Selena paused at a doorway near the end of the hallway and reached inside to touch the light switch. "This one was Tara's."

The office was larger than the other rooms. The furniture was a little nicer, too. There was a desk and chair at one end of the room, a tall file cabinet in the corner. A large window filled most of one wall. Ashley looked out at a view of three palm trees and the wall of the building next door. She touched the glass and tried to imagine Tara standing at this window and gazing at those rattling palms.

"No one has cleaned her stuff out yet," Selena said. "It's hard to accept, you know? That she's never coming back."

Ashley walked around the desk and sat in the swivel chair. The desk had a monitor, keyboard, mouse, and docking station—the same setup Ashley had found in Tara's apartment.

Selena watched her. "Are you looking for something?"

Ashley considered telling her the truth. Selena might even know where to find Tara's password. But as friendly as Selena seemed, there was no way in hell that Ashley was going to trust Rob Rourke's girlfriend.

"No. I just ... I don't know. It makes me feel closer to Tara to sit in her chair, behind her desk."

She checked under the keyboard. Nothing. She opened the desk drawers and found pens, highlighters, paperclips, and some hanging folders. She pulled out the folders and opened them on the desk. One held a marked-up draft of a document. It looked like a manual, a how-to guide for working in the industry. The other folders held other documents related to the agency. A PowerPoint presentation about STDs. Printouts of the Web site. No password.

Selena leaned her hip against the doorframe. She looked uncomfortable. "I'm not sure if you should be looking at that stuff."

"It's okay," Ashley said. She turned to the file cabinet.

"I'm not sure that it is."

Ashley sighed and stood up. "Okay. Can we finish the tour?"

Selena's smile returned. She led Ashley back to the hallway. The last three doors were closed. "Pinnacle has three sets. Professional quality. Producers can rent them by the hour. There's a pool hall, a barn, and a medieval-looking dungeon. The last one was Rob's big idea. He said the agency could market it for features and S&M. But the pool hall is the one that gets the most bookings. It must be a male fantasy, I guess, banging a girl on a pool table." She opened the first door. Ashley saw a pool table. Balls were racked in a triangle on its surface. "Sometimes Rob shoots pool in here. The table's real, but the felt has been warped by, you know, fluids."

Ashley could imagine. Even after Selena closed the door, the smell of lube lingered. "When do you expect Rob back from San Diego?"

"I don't know. He probably hasn't left yet. He usually calls me from the road."

They walked back to the reception area. The couch was empty. Ashley wondered if the tattooed couple had fled or if they were in a room somewhere, the boyfriend standing in a corner while a Pinnacle employee snapped naked photos of the girl. Rachel remained behind the reception desk. She saw them and clicked her mouse. A game of solitaire vanished from her monitor.

"I'll see you around?" Selena said.

Ashley looked at her watch. "Let me buy you dinner. We can talk about the industry. And about Tara."

Selena frowned. "I can't. I have ... plans. Another time? Here, let me give you my mobile number."

"Okay." Ashley chewed her lip. She waited while Selena wrote her number on a pad of paper on Rachel's desk. "Selena, did my sister ever mention anything to you about a stalker?"

"A stalker?"

"There was a man who was following her. I think he might have had something to do with her death."

"I thought she killed herself." She ripped the sheet of paper off the pad and handed it to Ashley. She had printed her phone number in small, neat handwriting.

"Maybe."

Selena's face paled as the import of Ashley's words hit her. "You think someone killed her?"

"I don't know yet. Not for sure. But if there's anything you can tell me about this stalker, it would be a big help."

"Tara never mentioned anything."

"She never told you that a man was following her?"

"No." Selena shook her head.

"Did you ever notice anyone strange hanging around places that Tara went? A white guy? Thirties? Tall and thin?"

"No."

"What about a black Hyundai with tinted windows? Have you noticed one lurking in the parking lot?"

"A black Hyundai? I don't think so, but I wasn't, you know, looking out for one."

Ashley sighed. "Rob never mentioned anything about a stalker?"

"No."

"Tara's body was covered in bruises. The coroner determined that they were inflicted days before her death. I think maybe this guy, this stalker, attacked her or something."

Selena shook her head. "She got the bruises on set."

"On set?"

"Julia James—she's one of Pinnacle's girls—was scheduled to do a pretty rough scene last week. You know. Slapping, choking, that kind of stuff. At the last minute she freaked out. She came here and told Tara she didn't want to do it. So Tara went in her place. I guess it was pretty rough. She came back all banged up."

"Tara told you this?"

"Well, she told Rob. He told me."

"Jesus." Ashley understood that part of the appeal of porn was the transfer of power. The fantasy of a man dominating a beautiful woman, or being dominated by one, or one woman dominating another. But when the power fantasy overshadowed the actual sex, and all you were watching was one person abusing another, she could no longer see the appeal. Who wants to watch some thug hit a woman?

"That's why she had the bruises," Selena said. "She wasn't, you know, jumped by some crazy guy or anything."

"Do you remember the exact date?"

Selena shook her head. "Maybe Rachel can look it up."

"No problem," Rachel said. She moved her mouse. Tapped her keyboard. "It was ... this past Monday."

The same day the coroner had estimated, according to Detective Collins. Ashley crossed her arms over her chest. "So who shot this rough scene?" There were plenty of bottom-feeding assholes in the industry who felt no compunction profiting from their performers' pain. "Anyone I know?"

"Yeah, I think you know him," Selena said. "Kingsley Nast."

8

————————

SHE WAS NOT sure which upset her more—the idea that Kingsley had shot a scene in which some brute had beaten the shit out of Tara, or the knowledge that bruises that had once looked like evidence of a stalker now supported Detective Collins's conclusion. That pornography was a rough trade and a sleazy business. That Tara had committed suicide.

She sat on the edge of her motel room bed. The mattress springs creaked. She ran her fingers through her hair. She had ordered a pizza. It would be here soon. Her stomach rumbled. She opened her purse to get her wallet and saw the plastic Ziploc bag she had taken from Tara's apartment. She had forgotten all about it.

The receipts formed a pile when she shook them out onto the bedspread. Tara must have been near the end of her billing cycle. Ashley plucked them from the bed at random, not sure what she was looking for. There were gas receipts. Sunoco. Exxon. She realized with a frown that she did not even know what kind of car Tara drove. There were some department store receipts. Some receipts from fancier places. Two weeks ago, Tara had spent three-hundred dollars at a boutique shoe store on Rodeo Drive. Not bad for a girl who used to count her change at the Wal-Mart in Tarzana.

There were a few restaurant receipts. Ashley put those in a separate pile. Maybe she would visit the restaurants and try to find out who Tara had been dining with. It was a long-shot, but if she got desperate enough....

She was about to add another restaurant receipt to the pile, but the date stamped on the receipt made her look more closely at it. Tuesday, 8:52 PM. According to Detective Collins, Tara had been killed one night later.

The receipt was from a place called Rosie's in West Hollywood. A bar? Tara didn't drink. Had she met someone there? Did this mean something? Was it important?

She considered calling Detective Collins, but she knew Collins would only dismiss this latest discovery as unimportant. And could Ashley really argue with that? It was a receipt from a bar. It probably meant nothing.

She could almost hear the detective's voice in her head. *Your sister spent a few bucks at a bar the night before she died. So what? Maybe she went to the bar because she was depressed. People do that sometimes. It's a cliché, but hey, she was a porn star, right? Cliché city.*

Ashley massaged her temples. Her appetite was gone. The thought of pizza made her feel sick now. But it was too late to cancel her order. What she really wanted to do was go home. The urge to get out of here, to return to the normal life she had been forging in New Jersey, drove her across the room to her phone. She picked it up and called Sean.

It rang twice before he answered.

"Ashley?"

The thickness of his voice reminded her that it was three hours later on the east coast. Almost midnight. The thought of him lying alone in his bed struck an unexpected pang of homesickness in her breast. "Hey, Sean." She leaned back on the motel bed and cradled the phone against her ear. "I ... I'm sorry we fought."

"I am, too."

She smiled. Stretched out her arms and legs. The air-conditioning felt good on her skin. "So why didn't you call me?"

"I was planning to. I just wanted to get my thoughts in order first."

"I've been ordering my thoughts, too."

She heard a faint crackling noise and imagined him pushing his blanket aside and climbing out of bed. "There's something we need to talk about."

"There's a lot we need to talk about," she agreed.

"Why don't you come over. Or I can drive to your place—"

"I'm in LA."

The line went silent. "LA?"

"My sister is dead. Tara."

More silence. She listened to the rhythm of his breathing. "What happened?"

"She was murdered. I think."

"What?" There was no grogginess in his voice now.

"She was in the industry. Apparently there was a guy stalking her. And—"

"Jesus Christ, Ashley."

She thought she could hear him pacing now. Or maybe she just knew him too well. Knew that he had thrown on his robe and was circling the bedroom, barefoot and agitated. "I should have called you days ago," he said.

"You didn't know."

"I guess we should wait to have our conversation when you come back. I mean, it sounds like you've got a lot to deal with right now."

A thread of discomfort twisted through her. "What conversation?"

"Never mind. Just ... do what you need to do in California. When you get home, we'll talk."

"Sean, what conversation?"

She heard him swallow, and this time, there was no chance she was imagining it. He always swallowed and licked his lips after saying more than he intended to.

"You're planning to break up with me," she said. All of the frustration, sadness, and rage that had built up during the long, hot day came barreling out of her and into the phone. "You motherfucker."

"Ashley—"

"I cannot believe you, Sean."

"Ashley, please, we don't need to do this right now—"

"What kind of person goes out and buys an engagement ring and then doesn't propose, and then dumps his girlfriend over the phone from the other side of the country two days after she learns her sister is dead?"

"The timing could have been better—"

"And *I* had to call *you*! To get dumped!"

"I'm sorry. It's just that I've been doing a lot of thinking. And I don't think I can get used to, you know—"

"Fuck you!"

She threw her phone across the room. It banged off the wall and tumbled on the carpet. By some stroke of luck, it remained in one piece. The distant squeak of Sean's voice trickled from its speaker.

——————

She did not retrieve it from the floor until the next morning. By then, the battery was dead. She plugged in the charger and padded to the table and sat down. The table wobbled under her elbows. She opened the cardboard pizza box she had left there the night before and ate a breakfast of cold, greasy leftovers.

She couldn't stop thinking about Kingsley. About how he had sat in the coffee shop with a sympathetic expression on his face while she told him about the bruise she'd discovered on Tara's body. A bruise he had put there.

The smart thing to do was stick to her original plan. Find Rob. Maybe talk to more of Tara's neighbors. Someone must have seen the stalker. But she knew she would not be able to focus on anything else until she faced Kingsley. She wiped tomato sauce from her lip and picked up the motel room's phone.

She still remembered the number.

She could not hold back a smile when Angela's motherly voice greeted her. At least one thing had not changed during the two years

Ashley had been gone. Good old Angela still manned the phones at Tyrant Productions.

"It's Ashley Hale." Her porn name rolled off her tongue as if she had never stopped using it.

"Ashley, dear!" Angela clucked delightedly. "You scurried out of the funeral home before I had the chance to say hello and offer my condolences. I am so sorry about Tara. I didn't realize you were still in town."

"There are a few things I need to straighten out before I leave."

"Well, I certainly hope you'll drop by the office. My grandson bought me the most heavenly Earl Grey tea for my birthday."

"Are you trying to bribe me?"

"Humor a lonely woman."

Ashley grinned. If there was one thing Angela was not, it was lonely. Her eccentric career had made her a minor celebrity among the other women who lived in her over-fifty community. Ashley could only hope to be as popular someday.

"I'll bring the scones." Ashley twisted the rubber phone cord between her fingers. "The reason I'm calling is I'm trying to find Kingsley."

"He's shooting three scenes for *Ass Bangers 22* today." Hearing Angela pronounce Kingsley's titles in her prim and proper voice never failed to amuse her. "I know he'll be thrilled if you stop by."

Don't be too sure.

"Where is he shooting?"

"A house in Granada Hills. Hold on. I'll get you the address."

———

PORN HOUSES WERE EVERYWHERE in the Valley if you knew what to look for.

She followed Angela's directions to a tree-lined road in the middle of sunny suburbia. She had to shake her head as she cruised past single-family homes with tricycles in their driveways, SUVs with *My Child Is An Honor Student* and soccer ball bumper stickers, and dogs moping in the heat. Add some white picket fences and you'd have the perfect textbook suburbia. How could these people not realize that one of their neighbors was supplementing his income by renting his house as a location for pornographic video shoots?

She found the house and parked along the curb in front of it. The driveway was already clogged with cars. Two women, one of them dressed, the other wearing nothing but a short terrycloth robe, stood outside the front door smoking cigarettes. All of the first-floor window shades were pulled down.

Ashley inhaled the scent of freshly-mowed lawn before stepping into the cloud of cigarette smoke. She did not recognize either of the women, but they seemed to recognize her. The one in the robe smiled widely. She had lipstick on her teeth. "Ashley Hale! Oh my God. You're back in the jizz biz?"

The girl's gaze roamed up and down Ashley's body and smiled approvingly. Ashley blushed. When she had thrown on a miniskirt and tank-top this morning, looking provocative had been the furthest thing from her mind. All she'd been interested in was beating the heat.

"I'm just visiting old friends," she said. She fanned cigarette smoke away from her face. She still had not decided how to confront Kingsley—whether to burst in and call him a liar, or be more subtle and allow him to trap himself in more lies. She looked up and down the peaceful street. A bird hopped across the lawn, turned a beady eye on her, chirped once, and flapped away.

"I'm Crystal Blue." The woman in the robe stuck out her hand. "I'm such a big fan, I can't tell you. Are you here to hang out on the set? King's setting up to shoot my scene next. It's a three-way."

"I'm Jenna Flame," the other smoker said.

"Nice to meet both of you."

Crystal opened the door for her. She heard yelling inside. Kingsley's voice. Crystal made a face and pulled her robe tighter around her body. "One of the guys who's supposed to be in my scene is new."

"He's having problems with wood?" Ashley said.

"No. Documentation."

"King is *pissed*," Jenna said.

Kingsley's voice careened through the house. Ashley followed it through a large, modern kitchen and into a living room where several tripod-mounted lights had been set up and aimed at a couch. Two Sony digital cameras sat unused on the seat of a matching recliner. Kingsley stood near one of the shade-covered windows. He was breathing heavily. Beads of sweat glistened where his black tangle of hair met his forehead. He was glaring at a steroid-pumped kid, and even though the kid was twice Kingsley's size, the kid cowered. The set's sparse crew had gathered at the corners of the room.

"You're sorry? Jesus Christ, you've cost me a whole fucking day! Do you know what that translates to in lost profits, you dick-brained fuck-up?"

The kid had a wallet in his hands, the nylon and Velcro kind that Ashley had not seen since high school. He ripped back the Velcro. His hands shook so badly that Ashley expected him to drop the thing. He managed to wrestled a laminated card out of one of the pockets. He shoved it toward Kingsley.

"Is this okay?"

Kingsley knocked it out of his hand. "I can't use your student ID, you fucking moron. Didn't Susan explain anything to you before she sent you over here?" He shook his head, a look of disgust on his face. "You know what? Just go home. Just go the fuck home."

Kingsley turned his back on the kid and pulled a phone from the holster on his belt.

Ashley scanned the room for a familiar face and found Beth Baldwin, a makeup artist that Kingsley had been using since before Ashley had entered the business. Beth was in her forties, but she had not allowed her age to change her style. Her hair was still blue and spiky, and she wore a studded choker around her neck. Ashley tapped her narrow shoulder and had to smile at the beam that lit her face. They exchanged cheek-pecks, then Beth gripped her in a bear-hug that cut off her breath. She smelled like hairspray and makeup.

"What's going on?" Ashley said.

Beth rolled her eyes. "Schmuck didn't bring his driver's license.

Kingsley is real anal about papers now. He has to be, with the FBI inspections and everything."

"FBI?" Ashley wasn't sure if Beth was joking or serious.

"You've been away for awhile. The government has dropped its 2257 inspections for now, but politicians still hate the industry. The FBI has teams of agents inspecting Kingsley's records. It's a colossal pain in the ass. Kingsley even hired a college kid as a part-time records keeper just to ensure that Tyrant's documents are in order."

"What are they looking for? Underage performers?" The kid who had just taken the brunt of Kingsley's anger looked at least twenty, but you never knew for sure. Any industry vet who'd been around during the Traci Lords fiasco would tell you that.

"They're looking to make trouble, that's all," a man said. Ashley turned to scowl at the eavesdropper, then did a double-take. Beth noted her reaction and grinned.

"Sorry to interrupt," the guy said. "I recognized you, wanted to say hi. I'm Kingsley's editor. Zack Cutter."

When Kingsley had told her about having to replace Brewster, he had failed to mention that the replacement was hot enough to be an underwear model. Zack Cutter was tall and lean. His frame carried just the right amount of muscle to show that he knew his way around a gym but was not obsessed with his own figure. His black hair was cropped short. And he had a roguish smile that lit up his dark blue eyes and dimpled his clean-shaven cheeks.

She realized she was staring. "I'm Ashley Hale." She shook his hand. His grip was warm and strong. "Cutter is a strange porn name."

His smile turned from impish to shy. "It's a film geek thing. Cutter, you know, like an editor cuts film? Not that I actually physically cut any film. It's all digital now. But—"

"I get it. It's cute."

His smile deepened. "You're Tara Rose's sister, right?"

"Yes."

"I'm sorry for your loss. Tara was great. And she ran a hell of a talent agency. Not like the jokers who sent this kid over." He tilted his chin toward the steroid-abuser Kingsley had just reamed out.

"Yeah, no shit," Beth agreed. "Mischief Modeling. It's run by Susan Jacoby. Do you remember her, Ash? She was a suit at Vivid back in your time. Now she's got her own business. She represents male and female talent, and she ties them together in packages. If you want one of her hot-off-the-bus girls, you have to book one of her dud guys, too. That's why this kid—his name is Chaz—is here instead of one of Kingsley's regular cocks."

Ashley tried to look sympathetic, but it was difficult to care about Kingsley's casting issues. Her gaze shifted past Beth's shoulder and she watched Kingsley mutter into his phone. Looking at him, her anger returned.

"I need to talk to him."

"You might want to wait," Beth said. "He's pretty pissed off."

So am I.

She left Zack and Beth and walked across the room. The moment Kingsley put down his phone, she made sure that she was the first thing he saw. The bastard actually smiled at her. "Angela sent me a text message that you were dropping by. How are you holding up?"

"Let's talk somewhere private."

"Give me a minute. I'm trying to figure out a way to salvage a big fucking mess."

She glanced at Chaz. "I heard."

"The scene was originally going to be two guys—Mark Peter and Chaz here—with Crystal Blue. Now ... I don't know. Mark's ready to go. But the idea of straight boy-girl doesn't thrill me, even with the anal."

"What does thrill you, King? Slapping? Choking? Maybe a few kicks and punches?"

The skin between his eyes creased and his goatee shifted as he frowned. "What?"

She glanced at Zack and Beth and the rest of the crew. No one was paying any attention to their conversation—yet. She kept her voice low. "Kingsley, we can have this conversation somewhere private, or we can have it here. Your choice."

"What conversation?"

"The one where we talk about the bruises all over my sister's body."

He blinked. "Ashley, I have no idea what you're talking about."

"I thought you were her friend. I thought you were my friend." So much for keeping her voice low. She felt hot tears well in her eyes seconds before they spilled down her face. She wiped them, but too late. Everyone in the room had turned to stare at them. Including Chaz, who looked relieved to no longer be the focus of Kingsley's attention.

"I am your friend," Kingsley said.

She shoved him. He staggered back against the window and banged the shade sideways. Sunshine flashed into the room.

"Does it sell well, Kingsley? Does rough sex help your bottom line?"

"Ashley, I'm not going to deny that Tyrant puts out a line of rough sex titles. It's called *Through the Wringer*, and yeah, the series does well. But it's not real, okay? No one leaves here with bruises."

"Obviously Tara did."

"Tara? She's never performed in the series. I haven't shot Tara in ... what? A year, at least."

Ashley stared at him. The hurt and confusion twisting his face looked genuine. She felt foolish all of a sudden.

"Where is this coming from?" Kingsley said. "Who fed you this bullshit?"

"Never mind. It's not important."

"It's important to me. If someone tried to convince you that I would hurt Tara, I want to know who it was. Come on." He took her arm. "Let's have that private conversation."

He led her through the kitchen, where a laundry basket full of dildos rested on the granite countertop next to a fresh pot of coffee. She smelled French roast as he drew her past the counter and into a small den. Someone's jeans were draped over a chair. Various pieces of fetish wear—thigh-high boots, a latex corset, a butt-plug with a horsetail coming out of it—were strewn across the couch. A makeshift dressing room.

"Okay," Kingsley said. "Start from the beginning."

The hurt and confusion had disappeared from his face, replaced by a hard, angry glint in his eyes.

"Selena Drake told me that Tara replaced another girl on one of your shoots, and that Tara came back covered in bruises."

Kingsley's eyebrows popped upward. "Selena Drake said that?"

"Yesterday, at Pinnacle."

"Did she claim to know this firsthand, or was she telling you something she heard from someone else?"

"I think she said Rob told her." Ashley shook her head. "Why does that matter?"

"It matters because Selena's a sweet girl and I can't imagine her slandering me. But Rob…. That fucker."

She had never seen Kingsley like this. Coiled so tightly. His body seemed to vibrate with stress and tension. His eyes were fierce but tired, harried. The Kingsley Nast that Ashley had known two years ago had been a happy man, quick to smile and laugh, a man who had loved his work and his family and his life. This Kingsley Nast looked on the verge of a nervous breakdown.

"You're telling me he's lying?" Ashley said. "I know Rob's an asshole, but what would he have to gain by spreading rumors about you? He makes money off of Tyrant, right? Agency fees and a piece of his girls' scene rates. It's in his best interest to have a good relationship with you."

Kingsley barked out a laugh. "Are you kidding? The wolves are at the fucking door, Ash. You have no idea."

Ashley shook her head. She did not know who to believe.

"I told you yesterday," Kingsley said, "the industry has changed." He looked at her now with almost fatherly concern. "You should go home. Go back to your new life, Ashley, your fresh start. You don't want to be in the Valley anymore."

"I'm not leaving until I find out what happened to Tara. I was hoping, you know, that I still had one friend here. But now I can't even trust you."

"Don't say that."

"It's true. It's like I'm the only one who cares that Tara might have been murdered. There's a stalker out there—"

He let out another short, rough laugh.

"What?" she said.

"It's just ... the way you talk about this stalker. This mystery man."

"There's no mystery. Gail saw him."

Kingsley shrugged. "Half the girls in the industry have overzealous fans. It's the nature of the beast. But most of these guys are just shy and socially inept. Harmless. And the ones who aren't harmless—they're nuts. And a nut doesn't carry out a perfect murder. He doesn't carefully stage a suicide. A nut goes in there and he makes a mess."

"You can't generalize like that."

He put his hand on her shoulder and leaned closer. "Listen to me, Ashley. The world's not as complicated as we like to believe. Things are usually what they look like. If a woman is found hanging from her Bowflex machine, chances are pretty damn good she did it to herself." She started to protest, but he held up a hand. "If Tara *was* murdered—and I don't think she was—then I'm telling you it wasn't a stalker."

"No one else would want to kill her."

"Are you sure about that? Why don't you talk to your mother again? This time, ask her about a conversation she had with Tara a few weeks ago."

"A conversation about what?"

"About changing her will."

9

ASHLEY HAD no trouble navigating the web of suburban streets that led to her childhood home, a drab ranch-style house on a small patch of unkempt lawn in the foothills of the Santa Monica Mountains. Her internal GPS delivered her to the house as if she'd been driving there every day for years.

She climbed the familiar slate stepping stones that led from the curb to the front door. They were old and cracked and wobbled under her high heels. She wished that Gail had replaced them. They brought a surge of memories of games she and Tara used to play out here as kids.

She rang the bell and heard footsteps in the house. Gail looked surprised to see her.

"Hi Gail," Ashley said.

Gail smiled sadly. "So we're back to that? 'Mom' was a one-time thing?"

"May I come in?"

"I was hoping you would visit. I didn't think you would."

The house's odors caught her off guard—aquarium water, old carpet, mothballs—and lanced deep into her memory banks before she could prepare herself. Pieces of her past that she had not thought about in a decade shook loose. Her throat tightened. Jesus. Her mother had not changed the place at all. The same inane knickknacks adorned the foyer walls. Through the doorway on her left, she saw that the family room still boasted the worn and sagging couch that she and Tara had jumped on as children, the nineteen-inch boob-tube on which they had watched cartoons—and later *Dawson's Creek*. She knew that the bedrooms down the hall would be unchanged, too. She wouldn't go anywhere near there, not even with a gun to her head.

"Did you talk to that detective?" Gail said.

"Yeah. Nice woman," she said, surprised by her own sarcastic tone.

Ashley stepped into the family room. The carpet had worn thin. The mini-blinds on the window were twisted shut. The only light came from the lamp in the foyer and from Gail's fifty-five gallon aquarium, which stood on a wrought-iron stand against the far wall. She walked closer to the tank, drawn by the bubbling sound of its filter and the warm, wet smell that rose from the oily surface of the water. Fat, colorful fish glided back and forth while smaller ones sucked up against the glass walls or slid along the gravel floor.

No matter how run-down the rest of the house became, the aquarium would always be clean and well-maintained. Gail had always been fastidious when it came to her fish. During Ashley's childhood, Gail had cleaned the thing at least once a week. More if she was on meth.

She came to Ashley's side now. "She blew you off, didn't she?"

"Yes." Ashley noticed a seahorse bobbing among the underwater flora.

"I guess you came to say goodbye. I don't blame you for giving up."

Ashley peeled her gaze from the tank and turned to face her mother. "I'm not giving up. And I didn't come here to say goodbye. I came here to get some straight answers from you."

"Answers about what?"

"Did you tell Kingsley Nast that a few weeks before she died, Tara told you she'd decided to change her will?"

Gail's gaze shifted away from Ashley's. She backed up a step, then walked to the window and opened the blinds. Sunlight filtered into the room. She stood at the window for a moment and stared out at the overgrown lawn and the street, where the little yellow Fiesta baked in the sun.

"Yes."

"And you didn't bother to tell me because...."

Gail turned to face her. "I was afraid that you would think I was only after Tara's money. And that's not true."

"And you told Kingsley because he's a good listener?"

"Tara trusted him. They were friends. She was always going over to his house. And he was so helpful with the funeral arrangements. I needed someone to talk to."

"Well, now you can talk to me. What was the revised will going to say?"

Gail crossed the room and sat on the couch. "Tara said she was going to leave her half of the talent agency to me. After Rob left her, Tara and I got closer. It was hard at first. She felt a lot of resentment toward me because of, you know, the way I was when you two were growing up. But we spent time together and ... we healed our relationship."

Ashley chewed her lip.

"I know you're skeptical," Gail said.

"So what are you doing about this? You're just going to let Rob inherit Tara's half of Pinnacle without a fight? I've only been in LA for a few days and I already know that Tara put her heart and soul into that company."

"After Tara died, I went to see her lawyer. He didn't have any idea what I was talking about. He said Tara never approached him about changing the will. I got the feeling he was, you know, not coming right out and saying it, but implying that I was a liar. So I got my own lawyer."

"That's good," Ashley said.

"But he says that without evidence, there's nothing we can do. And I haven't found any evidence. No marked-up copy of the old will, no letters to or from her lawyer, nothing."

Ashley thought of the laptop. If she could access its files, she might find something there. At least she understood now what Kingsley had been trying to tell her. Rob Rourke had benefited directly from Tara's death.

She tried to imagine the argument that would have flared if Rob had discovered Tara's intention to leave half of their company to a middle-aged woman who knew nothing about the industry. He would have felt betrayed, furious. Maybe he would have hit her a few times. Caused some bruises.

How far would he go to protect the only success he'd ever enjoyed?

She remembered Kingsley's words and her stomach sank. *I'm telling you it wasn't a stalker.*

"Are you still staying at that Travel Inn? How many nights has it been? It must be costing you a fortune."

"I have a job, Gail. I built up some savings in New Jersey."

"And the rental car. That's got to be what? Twenty dollars a day? Why don't you stay here? You can sleep in your old bedroom."

Ashley headed for the door. Gail jumped up from the couch and pursued her. "Where are you going?"

"To get more answers."

"It's ten to twelve. Stay for lunch."

Ashley reached the front door, then turned back to look at her mother. "Maybe you found a way to 'heal' your relationship with Tara. Maybe she was lonely after Rob left her, and sad, and vulnerable, and you swooped in. Don't think you can make that happen with me."

"I'm your mom."

"No. It's too late for that, Gail. Way too late."

She opened the door and let herself out.

———

Yesterday, she had believed that as her business partner and ex-boyfriend, Rob was the person most likely to know something about Tara's stalker. Now, she wondered if the stalker even mattered. Rob had a motive for wanting her dead. He probably still had his key to her apartment. He had instructed his personal assistant to keep Ashley away from him. And he had tried to use Selena to throw suspicion on Kingsley.

It was time to talk to Rob face-to-face.

The thought of returning to Pinnacle Talent and dealing with Max made her hands tighten into fists on the Fiesta's warm plastic steering wheel. She was not going to spend half the day arguing with Rob's flunky. She pulled out her phone and called the number Selena Drake had given her instead.

"Hey Ashley!" Selena sounded excited to hear from her. "What's up?"

"I really need to talk to Rob. Do you know where he is?"

"Sure. He's at home today."

Ashley smiled. *Bingo.* "And where's home?"

"He moved in with me, a few months ago." Selena gave her an address in Van Nuys.

"Thanks."

The drive did not take long. Selena and Rob lived in a powder-blue, two-story townhouse that could only be described as cute. No one answered when Ashley clacked the door's metal knocker, but she could hear a man's voice inside and recognized the cadence immediately. Rapid-fire bullshit. Rob was home.

She made a fist and banged the door until the wood vibrated.

A shouted curse rewarded her effort. She heard angry footsteps, then the door flew open. Rob stood in the doorway. His eyes widened in surprise when he saw her.

She could feel her own lips form a surprised pucker. She had expected to confront the old Rob Rourke, the suitcase pimp who had favored tight jeans, cowboy boots, loud shirts, and cheap jewelry. Sometime during the two years of her absence, he had developed a fashion sense—or a personal shopper. He wore an expensive-looking, lightweight suit with his shirt open at the collar. He had ditched his gold chain and bulky rings. His only jewelry was a watch. A ray of sunlight from outside made his bald head shine.

He eyed her warily and said into his phone, "I'll call you back, D." He ended the call and slipped his phone into a pants pocket. He did not step back from the doorway or invite her inside.

"Surprised?" she said.

"I knew I couldn't avoid you forever."

"But you hoped."

His shifty smile had not changed at all. It spread slowly across his face. The way he leered at her made her regret wearing the miniskirt, but it was so damn hot out. "What can I do for you, Ashley? You thinking about getting back in the biz? Miss the feel of a nice big cock up your ass?"

"Not really. I guess I never liked that feeling as much as you do."

His smile only widened. "Then you're a very good actress."

"You must have some acting skills, too, if you've managed to convince anyone that you have the brains to run a company."

"You'd be surprised. I could probably even find a gig for you. The MILF niche is huge right now."

"I'm not interested in helping you pay your rent."

"I pay a mortgage, Ashley. And I don't need your help."

"But you probably need Selena's. I'm surprised she doesn't object to sharing her house with a parasite."

"Tara didn't mind, either."

Hearing him speak Tara's name felt like a punch to the gut. Her breath caught in her throat.

"I'm attracted to successful women," Rob said with a shrug, "and I like living with them."

"You're a creature of habit."

"I guess so."

"Or just a creature. Are you going to invite me in?"

"I wasn't planning to."

"Plans change." She stepped forward and was gratified when he stepped back. He smiled, shook his head, and closed the door. The small entryway opened directly on a staircase. There was a kitchen to the left and a TV room to the right. She saw the big-screen TV and thought of the pale square of carpet in Tara's apartment.

"What exactly do you want, Ashley?"

"I want to know what happened to my sister."

He leaned against the wall. "That's easy. She croaked."

She bit back her anger. "Convenient timing for you, from what I understand."

"What's that supposed to mean?"

"She was planning to revise her will. Leave her half of Pinnacle to Gail. But she died before she could make the changes."

Rob shrugged. "News to me. I guess I was born under a lucky star."

She looked directly into his eyes and held his stare until he glanced away. "If you had anything to do with Tara's death, you're going to need more than luck to save your ass from me."

"Interesting."

"What is?"

"Just that I always thought Tara was the overprotective sister, and you were the flake that up and disappeared two years ago without even saying goodbye."

She tried not to let him see that his words had struck home, but the hurt must have been visible on her face. He smirked.

"It's been real swell catching up. Now please leave my house."

"You know, I always knew you were a douche bag, but I never thought you were a truly bad person. I never thought you were capable of murder." Her voice broke. "I should have insisted she leave you. You bastard. I should have fucking run you down in my car."

His gaze ticked to the right and a worried expression fell over his face. Ashley turned and saw a woman standing on the staircase. She was huge. Six feet tall and at least three-hundred pounds. Somehow she had managed to come halfway down the stairs without making a sound. She looked from Ashley to Rob. Her facial features were flat. Her eyes had an upward slant and her ears were too small for her head.

The woman said, "I want grilled cheese please."

"Not right now, Janie. Go back to your room, okay?"

"I want grilled cheese please."

Rob glanced at Ashley. His face was reddening. "Selena's sister lives with us. She's ... you know. Down syndrome." He turned his attention to Janie. "Grilled cheese is bad for you. You can have some carrots and celery if you want."

"I want grilled cheese please."

Rob muttered, "Jesus Christ." Then he smiled up at Janie and said, "Grilled cheese it is!"

Janie came down the stairs and stopped in front of Ashley. "They call me Janie." Her voice was husky, slightly slurred.

"They call me Ashley."

Rob rolled his eyes and led them into the kitchen. He placed a pan on the range and flicked on the heat, then lopped the end off a stick of butter and dropped it into the pan. The butter sizzled. Janie watched intently. "Careful. The stove gets hot." He pushed her back a step and grabbed a bag of white bread. Pulled out two slices. "One grilled cheese for Janie. You want one, too, Ash? Don't worry. If you put on some pounds, I can book you for a plumpers video."

Ashley opened her mouth, then closed it. She was not sure what to say. She did not want to continue their verbal battle with Janie's big, innocent eyes watching her.

"We need to talk, Rob. Alone."

"There's nothing to talk about. What happened to Tara is sad, but if you think I had something to do with it, you're nuts."

"You don't seem particularly devastated by the loss."

"And that means I'm guilty?" He smiled and dropped Kraft singles onto the sizzling slices of bread. "Guess what? I'm not the only person who's happy she's gone. I'm just the only one honest enough to admit it."

"Is the grilled cheese almost ready?"

"Everyone liked her," Ashley said. She struggled to hold back her anger. "I know it and you know it."

"You know it how? Because people told you? What else are they going to say? You're her sister."

The smell of hot butter and melted cheese filled the kitchen.

"Why wouldn't they like her?"

"Oh, I don't know. Because she was a meddler? Because she was always in people's business? Always telling them how they should live their lives? 'Don't spend all your money. Don't do drugs. Don't hook on the side.' Acting like she was their fucking mother."

Janie squealed. "Robby said *fucking!*"

"No I didn't, Janie. I said *fudging*. You know, like chocolate." Rob glared at Ashley. "Thanks a lot. Now I'm going to get reamed by Selena."

"I like chocolate!"

"Tara was trying to help girls in the industry," Ashley said. "She was trying to steer them away from the usual traps and pitfalls and slime-bags like you."

Rob plucked a spatula from the countertop and scraped the sandwich from the pan. He slid it onto a paper plate. Janie hovered behind his shoulder. "She went over the top, especially with the Just Say No bullshit. I wouldn't be surprised if she was whacked by a drug dealer. Not yet, Janie. Still too hot."

"Is that how you tricked Selena Drake into thinking you were a human being? By pretending to care about her sister?"

"I know it's hard for you to believe, but I do care about Janie. And Selena and I are in love."

"Please, stop before I vomit." She looked at the sandwich cooling on the paper plate in his hand. "First you point the finger at Kingsley. Now you point it at a nameless drug dealer. But from where I stand, you're the one with the biggest motive, Rob."

He quirked an eyebrow. "Listen to yourself. Motive? What's next? Are you gonna cuff me, Sarge? Take me down to the station and beat me with a phonebook?"

He handed the plate to Janie. She tore into the grilled cheese sandwich with evident glee.

"Where were you the night Tara— Where were you Wednesday night, Rob?"

"You're asking if I have an alibi?" He laughed.

"That's another way to put it."

"I didn't know Tara was planning to change her will. So I didn't have a motive. And what are you talking about, pointing the finger at Kingsley? Kingsley Nast? When did I ever point a finger at that hairy jerk-off?"

"You told Selena that Tara was ... hurt during one of Kingsley's shoots. Kingsley says he hasn't shot Tara in a year."

"Then Kingsley's lying."

"No offense, Rob, but I'm more inclined to believe Kingsley than you."

"Then you're a bad judge of character. I may be a prick, but I'm not a liar. Let me show you something."

He turned off the range and walked past her. She followed him into the TV room. There was a cabinet against the wall next to the TV. He pulled a key-ring from his pants and unlocked the door on the cabinet. Three shelves were jam-packed with DVD and Blu-Ray cases. Their colorful spines formed a lurid rainbow.

"Selena's collection. We keep it locked, because of Janie."

"That's a lot of DVDs." Hundreds, she thought.

"Selena tries to keep one copy of every title she's in. There are a few missing, of course. And there's a ton of online and digital stuff— we don't have copies of everything. But what you see here is a pretty good overview of her career so far."

Janie wandered in with her sandwich. "Grilled cheese good."

Rob scanned the titles, then slid one out. He handed it to Ashley.

"What's this?"

"Look at it."

She did. It was a video called *Knockouts*. There were several women featured on the cover. One of them was Selena. "Okay."

"Look at the back."

She flipped the case over, then pulled it closer to her eyes. There were more pictures on the back, stills taken from the movie. One showed a beefy guy seizing a naked girl in a chokehold. Another showed a woman with a man's fingers squeezing her throat. The final still showed Selena Drake with a noose around her neck. The trademark purple banner of Tyrant Productions ran across the top. Kingsley had shot this title.

"I suggest you watch the bonus features," Rob said. "I think you'll find them particularly interesting."

"This doesn't mean anything."

"We went to a movie. Selena and me. The new one with Bruce Willis."

She stared at him, not following.

"That's my alibi," he said. "Does Kingsley have one?"

10

"DAMN, this is some sick and twisted shit."

"It sure is," she agreed.

She was sitting next to the young guy who manned the front desk at her motel. She had asked him to lend her a DVD player to use in her room, and he had insisted that she use the one in his office instead. Then he had hovered over her shoulder, smelling of Axe body spray, rubbing his hands together at the prospect of watching porn with a woman.

He was not rubbing his hands now.

The only sound was a fan creaking in the corner. "I'm going to watch it one more time." She selected the bonus feature from the DVD menu and played it again.

It was a lengthy behind-the-scenes clip shot with a handheld camera—a common "extra" that Kingsley included on Tyrant DVDs to help justify a higher price. Ashley fast-forwarded through shaky footage of porn starlets dressing and undressing and chatting to the camera about how turned on they were and how much they loved to fuck. When Kingsley's hairy face filled the wobbly frame, she dropped back to regular speed. The image zoomed out to reveal Kingsley standing beside Selena Drake on the set. He held a length of rope in his hand. While Selena gushed to the camera about how much it turned her on to be asphyxiated, Kingsley's fingers worked the knot. It took him maybe five seconds to form a perfect noose.

He was a fucking expert.

"People get off on girls being choked?" the guy said. He ran a hand through his greasy mop of hair. "I don't know if I'll ever get a hard-on again."

"Thanks for letting me use the DVD player." She was so angry, her jaw had clenched. She had to force the words through her teeth. "I need to get going."

He looked both disappointed and relieved when she stood up. "Hey, no problem."

———

ANGELA'S EYES lit up when Ashley stepped through the door of Tyrant's office-warehouse. The old woman was out of her chair and hugging Ashley in seconds. Her embrace was as warm and soft as Ashley remembered it. And she still smelled like fresh-steeped tea leaves. Ashley felt some of the tension leave her shoulders as she hugged the woman. They parted and Ashley got a better look at her. She had aged a lot in two years. The skin of her neck looked looser and was shaded with liver spots. There were new folds and creases on her face, wrinkles around her mouth. Gray hairs crowded the brown ones on her head.

"I was afraid you wouldn't stop by," she said.

Ashley felt a tremor of guilt. "Come on, Angela. You know I could never come to LA and not visit you."

Angela looked unconvinced, but she smiled anyway. They both knew that this building was the last place Ashley wanted to visit. You only needed to glance around the small lobby to see why. Framed, poster-sized reproductions of DVD box covers lined the walls, a showcase of Tyrant's bestselling titles. Ashley's image graced half of them.

Ass Bangers 6—She posed on her hands and knees, wearing

nothing but seven-inch, red platform heels, and grinned up at the camera with her lips parted and a hungry look in her eyes.

Taste the Paste II—Naked again, kneeling, and facing the camera with her lower lip caught in her teeth. One of her arms cradled her naked breasts and pushed them up. Her nipples were hard, pointy. In her other hand, she gripped the shaft of someone's cock.

Hale Storm—Reclining on a staircase, red hair fanned out behind her. She wore a black fishnet bodysuit. Her thighs were spread. Her eyes locked on the camera.

There were more posters. She averted her gaze from them.

"You look more beautiful now," Angela said.

"Thanks."

"Unlike me. Every year, I look a little more like Yoga from those space movies."

"You mean *Yoda*. And it's not true. You look great."

Angela blew a dismissive gust of air from the corner of her mouth. "You're sweet."

Ashley's gaze slid to the posters again.

"It's hard for you to be here, isn't it?" The phone on Angela's desk rang. She ignored it. Her steady gaze remained fixed on Ashley. "Let me pour you a cup of tea."

The rest of the lobby had not changed much during the last two years, either. The same beige chairs. The same china teacup on the same saucer next to the same mouse pad on Angela's chipped, wooden desk. Ashley stopped Angela before she could go to the small office kitchen down the hall.

"I'm not really in the mood for tea right now. Is Kingsley here?"

The memory of Kingsley tying a noose replayed in her mind and she felt a spike of anger.

Angela said, "Is everything okay?"

"I don't know. I need to talk to him."

"Well, he's in a meeting right now. His lawyers are here. It's more of this FBI nonsense." She snorted. "Used to be, the biggest legal worry we had was remembering not to ship product to Utah. Now,

Kingsley spends more time with lawyers than he does with performers."

"I heard a little about it from Beth Baldwin."

"The FBI. Can you imagine? Men in Brooks Brothers suits and short haircuts, just like on TV."

"Do you know when the meeting will be over?"

"Well, let's see." Angela wandered behind her desk, pulled a thick paper appointment book from a drawer, and flipped through its pages. "He has the whole afternoon marked off."

"I need to see him now."

Angela looked conflicted. "I can't disturb him now, dear. I just explained to you how serious this situation is. And Kingsley never likes to be disrupted when he's meeting with lawyers. They charge by the hour, you know."

Ashley did not want to get Angela in trouble, but she did not plan on spending her whole day waiting for Kingsley's meeting to end. She did not care how much his lawyers charged. She needed to talk to him now.

"I think I'll have some of that tea, after all."

Angela looked at her with a dubious expression. She glanced at the door. The hallway beyond it led to the kitchen, but also to the offices and warehouse space. "Do I need to lock the door behind me?"

"I'll be good. I promise."

Angela did not look convinced, but after a few seconds of hesitation, she relented. Ashley watched her go through the doorway, then gave her a few more seconds to reach the kitchen down the hall. After a deep breath, Ashley hurried forward and opened the door.

And bumped into Zack Cutter.

He leapt backward, then smacked his hand over his heart and laughed. "Are you auditioning for a haunted house or something?"

"Sorry. I didn't mean to pop out at you like that. I'm just kind of ... in a hurry." She peered guiltily down the hall toward the kitchen nook. Angela emerged from it with a delicate-looking cup and saucer in her hands. She saw Ashley and sighed. Her breath swirled the steam that wafted from the teacup. The cup rattled quietly in the saucer as she stepped closer.

"If you're here to see Kingsley," Zack said, "your timing's bad."

"So I've heard."

She let Zack and Angela guide her back into the lobby, then tried to ignore Angela's disappointed pout as she took her cup of tea and sat down in one of the beige chairs. She sipped, rolled the tea along her tongue. Angela was always on the prowl for excellent Earl Grey.

Zack dropped into the seat beside her. "So what now?" he said. "You're going to sit here, sip tea, and wait?"

She was struck again by his handsomeness. His tall, lean figure. His short black hair. And that smile that lit up his blue eyes. Damn, he was good-looking.

She crossed her legs. Blew on her tea. "What do you care?"

"I don't know." His smile appeared again, the dimpled, roguish grin. "It's just that I was heading out to grab some lunch and you look hungry."

She eyed him over her teacup. "I look hungry?"

"I figured we could have lunch together. By the time we get back, Kingsley should be almost done with his lawyers."

"Are you one of those people who can't stand to eat alone?"

"Maybe I just enjoy the company of a beautiful woman."

"You work in porn. I would think the appeal would have worn off a little by now."

His smile widened and he laughed. She saw straight, white teeth. "Every day, I walk through this room and see pictures of you on the walls. I guess it's made me a little curious."

"Looking at naked pictures of me gets you in the mood for lunch? You might want to talk to someone about that."

"Come on. I know the perfect place. Best omelets in the Valley."

"Sal's?"

He looked impressed. "Great stomachs think alike."

She had not felt hungry before, but now that Zack had put Sal's menu in her head, she felt the first rumblings of an appetite.

"Okay," she said. "I'll have lunch with you. But don't think this is a date or anything. I'm in LA because of Tara. This isn't a vacation." She glanced at the framed poster for *Hale Storm*. "And don't think for a second you're going to get acquainted with my screen persona. It'll be Ashley Latner eating a frittata, not Ashley Hale."

"See? I'm having fun already and we haven't even left."

––––––––

THEY TOOK THE FIESTA. She watched with amusement as he folded his long legs into the passenger seat. When he had settled in and drawn the seatbelt across his chest, his knees pressed against the glove compartment. He looked at her with weary resignation.

"Most girls beg to ride in my Corvette."

"Most girls are idiots. I don't even know you. I'm not getting in your car and letting you drive me off to God knows where."

She pulled out of the parking lot. Zack swayed in his seat. Denim rubbed plastic as his knees slid against the glove compartment. He squirmed, but he was smiling.

"You remember how to get there?" he said.

"I think so."

They drove in silence. She considered turning on the radio, but decided against it. The sound of tires on pavement soothed her. She felt the seductive pull of her former lifestyle—the sun and the palm trees and the boulevards and a hot guy in the passenger seat—and had to mentally fight against it. The lifestyle wasn't worth the price. She had learned that two years ago. The hard way.

"Don't panic or anything," Zack said, "but I think there's a car following you." His eyes were fixed on the side view mirror. His smile was gone.

Ashley started to twist in her seat. Zack's left hand shot across the gearshift and gripped her thigh.

"No. Don't look back. Keep driving."

She could not be sure if her turbo-charged heart rate was due to the idea that she was being followed or to the sensation of his dry, strong hand on her bare thigh. She listened to her own shallow breathing, then carefully lifted her gaze to the rearview mirror.

"Which car?"

"Make a right at this next corner."

"But I'm in the left lane."

"I know. Cut across. Do it quick."

She jerked the steering wheel to the right. The Fiesta was not the most responsive automobile she'd ever driven, but it held the road. A red Miata squealed to a sharp halt and blared its horn at her. She skated past it and around the turn. She found herself on a one-lane, one-way road.

"Take a left."

She did. The Fiesta took the turn too sharply. Zack's elbow slammed the passenger door. He grunted and rubbed his arm.

"Now what?" she said.

He turned to look through the rear windshield. "Pull over." She pulled up to the curve. The Fiesta idled. "I think we lost them," he said. "Let's go eat."

She would have thought that a car chase would kill her appetite, but it had the opposite effect. At Sal's, she pored over the laminated menu and wanted to eat everything.

The waitress tapped her pen against her pad.

"Why don't you just bring us two coffees for now," Zack said.

Once the woman had stalked away, Ashley dropped her menu on the table and said, "You want to tell me what just happened?"

"We sat down. We opened our menus."

"I mean before."

He sighed. "I happened to notice another car leave the Tyrant lot when we did. Then I noticed it again while you were driving. It's probably nothing." He looked down and a guilty smile crept across his face. "Okay, so maybe I went a little overboard. I was having fun, I guess. You know. Secret agent stuff."

"You were just playing James Bond? Jesus Christ. You scared the crap out of me." She let out a long breath and leaned back. The padded booth sank beneath her. "I suppose the car had machine guns mounted on its hood, too."

"And a missile-launcher in the sunroof, right? No, I don't think Hyundai offers those options."

"Hyundai?"

"Yeah. A Sonata, I think."

"Was it black?"

He nodded slowly. "Why?"

"Tinted windows?"

"Actually, I think it did have tinted windows."

"Did you get the license plate number?"

He laughed. "No, I ... Ashley, it was probably nothing."

She ran her hands through her hair. "Listen to me. This is important. Are you sure you can't remember the license plate number? Or at least part of it?"

"I was watching the car through the mirror, Ashley. Why are you so interested?"

She looked out the window at the diner's crowded parking lot. The air above the vehicles wavered with heat. "I don't think my sister really committed suicide. I think she was murdered."

Zack leaned back. "Wow."

"Before she died, Tara told my mother that she had a stalker following her. I asked Tara's neighbors about it. A few of them have seen a suspicious car sitting outside the apartment complex. A black Hyundai with tinted windows. I think it might be the stalker's car."

"And you think he murdered Tara?"

Ashley shook her head. "I'm not sure. I used to think that. Now, I don't know. There are other people who seem suspicious."

The waitress brought their coffee. "Are you ready to order?"

Zack waved her away. "Soon." When she left, he said, "Ashley, I'm just a film geek, but I'm pretty sure the goal is to narrow the list of suspects, not add to it."

She shook her head, then smiled. "I know. I'm a hell of a detective, right?"

"You know what? Rewind and start from the beginning. Tell me everything. Two minds are better than one, right? Let me help you figure this out."

She watched him warily. "This isn't a game. My sister is dead."

"I never would have goofed around if I had known there was a murderer out there." He gulped coffee. "Give me a chance to help. I'm a pretty smart guy."

She sighed. And told him everything she knew. She paused in her recounting of the last few days long enough to order an omelet when the waitress came back. By the time she finished telling the story, both of their plates were clean and her stomach felt stuffed.

"Okay," Zack said. "So we have a few possibilities. This stalker guy who may or may not drive a black Hyundai. Rob Rourke. And Kingsley Nast." His mouth twisted when he spoke Kingsley's name, and Ashley wondered if she'd made a mistake voicing those suspicions. Zack worked for Kingsley, probably liked and respected him.

"Don't forget the drug dealer," she said, trying to shift the conversation away from Kingsley. "Rob told me that Tara was campaigning against drug use in the industry. He thinks she might have pissed off a local dealer."

Zack nodded. "Okay. Stalker, Rob, Kingsley, drug dealer. Four theories. Five if you count the possibility that Tara's death might really have been a suicide." He held up a hand. "I know you don't believe that, but we haven't ruled it out yet."

"What do you mean, ruled it out?"

He drained his mug and sighed, then put his elbows on the table and leaned forward. "That's how professional investigators work," he said. Sunlight slanted through the window and sparkled in his blue eyes. "They come up with a list of theories, and then they shoot them down one by one until only one is left standing. The one that's true. You've already done the first part. You've gathered information and come up with ideas. Now we need to do the second part."

"Narrow the list," she said. It made sense. "How do you know all of this stuff?"

He smiled. "Back in film school, I wrote a few spec scripts. Cop movies. I never managed to sell any of them, or even get an agent. Guess I'm better with an editing bay than a typewriter."

"You'll have to let me read one of your scripts someday. I'll be the judge."

"Does that mean we're friends?" He extended his hand across the table.

She shook it. "Friends," she agreed.

"And you'll ride in my Corvette next time, so I won't need back surgery?"

"Deal."

"Great." He waved the waitress over with his empty cup. "Another refill, please."

"More coffee?" Ashley protested. "I need to get back to Tyrant. Kingsley might be finished with the lawyers."

"What do you think you're going to accomplish by talking to him? All you're doing is bouncing back and forth between Kingsley and Rob. Rob says Kingsley shot a rough sex scene in which Tara was hurt, Kingsley says he didn't. Before you talk to either of them again, you need to find out who's telling the truth."

"Okay, smart guy. How do I do that?"

A crafty smile flitted across his face. "If Kingsley shot a scene with Tara—which, for the record, he never showed me—it's on his computer somewhere. He backs up his digital footage religiously."

"What if he deleted it?"

Zack shrugged. "I'm sure he did, especially after you ambushed him on the set this morning. That doesn't mean it isn't still on his hard disk."

"I don't get it."

"It's the way computers work. When you create a file, whether it's video footage or a Word document or whatever, you're basically storing information on your computer's hard disk. The space where the information is stored is made up of data clusters—sections of storage space—and each data cluster has its own individual address in the hard disk that the computer keeps track of so it can find the information when it needs to. You following me so far?"

"I guess."

"Okay. So let's say you decide to delete a file. What you've actually done is you've told the computer that those data clusters are not important anymore. The computer is free to use them to store new information. But what most people don't realize is that the data in those clusters doesn't go anywhere until the computer actually fills those data clusters with new information. And that doesn't happen right away. The original data can sit on the hard disk for months, just waiting to be accessed by someone who knows how to find it."

"Okay. Now translate that into a language spoken on Earth."

"Let's assume Kingsley used Tara in a violent sex scene, then for whatever reason, decided to deny it ever happened. He goes onto his computer, finds the file containing the raw footage from his digital camera, and deletes the file. He thinks it's gone. But unless he saved a whole hell of a lot of new files between then and now, chances are good that the Tara file is still sitting in data clusters on his hard disk."

"And you know all of this because ... let me guess. You wrote a screenplay about hackers."

He laughed. Shook his head. "My dad is a security specialist up in Silicon Valley."

"Tara got the bruises on Monday of last week. That's what the police told me. And Pinnacle's receptionist said that Monday was the day Tara did a scene for Tyrant."

"Perfect. If Kingsley created the file that recently, it should still be recoverable. All I need to do is access his computer while he's not around."

"Is that all?"

A family at the table next to theirs stood up and moved toward the exit. A busboy hurried over with a spray bottle and a rag. He dumped the dirty plates and silverware into a plastic bucket, then sprayed the table and wiped it down. The odor of Windex drifted in the air.

"It's no big deal," Zack said. "I have free reign of Tyrant's offices. Meet me there tonight and we'll get one piece of this mystery solved."

She couldn't help smiling at his enthusiasm. "Is midnight good for you?"

"Sounds good. Don't use Kingsley's lot. Park at the fast food place across the street. Just in case." He turned to look out the window, his expression suddenly serious.

Despite the diner's poor air-conditioning, she felt a chill.

11
———————

ASHLEY PUT her lipstick down on the sink. It was pointless to deny that she found Zack Cutter attractive. But until she'd spent a solid fifteen minutes in front of a motel room mirror applying makeup as if she were going to a club instead of breaking into an office building, she had not realized just how much she wanted the feeling to be mutual. She looked at the tight, low-rise jeans she was wearing and the black T-shirt stretched across the swell of her chest and all she could do was shake her head.

It was Tuesday night. Traffic was sparse. She turned the Fiesta off of the boulevard and onto the asphalt in front of a 24-hour fast food restaurant. Zack was waiting there. She could see his dark form silhouetted against light from the restaurant. He stood beside the Corvette. He was waving at her. She felt a flutter in her stomach.

For God's sake, you don't even know his real name.

She parked next to him and climbed out of the rental car. Behind him, a line of cars snaked past the drive-through window. She heard a crackly voice ask a driver for his order. She smelled French fries.

"You ready?" Zack said.

"Let's do this."

———

THEY DARTED across the street to the deserted parking lot of Tyrant's office-warehouse. The building looked different at night, its low, squat form almost fortress-like in the gloom. Zack led her to the rear, where two padlocked garage doors faced a loading dock. She stepped around a pile of cigarette butts. There was a small plastic box mounted to the wall. Zack flipped it open and revealed a glowing keypad. She watched him tap in a code.

"Kingsley must really trust you," she said.

"I like to work at night, when there are fewer distractions. He gets that."

He knelt and fit a key into one of the padlocks. Ashley gripped a metal handle and helped him raise the garage door. It clattered upward. In the darkness she saw a vast space. Rows of boxes lit by dim red nightlights. Zack nudged her inside, then lowered the garage door behind them. It rattled to the ground. Then there was silence.

Without turning on the overhead fluorescents, he led her through the maze of Tyrant products. Boxes loomed on all sides of them. The smell of cardboard was familiar, but it set her teeth on edge. Zack gave her arm a gentle squeeze.

"You okay?"

"Yeah. It's just ... quiet."

They moved through the double doors leading to the office section of the building. Even in the dark, she could see that nothing had changed since the days when she used to hang out here with Kingsley and Brewster. They hurried down the carpeted hallway toward Kingsley's office. Zack went in first. He lowered the shade and turned on the desk lamp. Wooden shelves lined the walls, sagging under the weight of three-ring binders and books and a dusty Panasonic boom box. Kingsley had never cared about fancy offices. His real workplace was behind the camera.

Zack eased into the swivel chair behind the desk. It wobbled under his weight. He slid the mouse. Kingsley's desktop popped to life on the screen, accompanied by a barely audible hum.

"Okay. Let's see what we can find." He opened a window on the desktop. Started tapping keys. Ashley leaned over his shoulder and tried to follow along, but he worked too swiftly, opening and closing windows before she could absorb their contents. His fingers were a blur on the keyboard.

"Aha," Zack said.

"You found something?"

"Maybe. There was a file named TTR7TARA created last week."

"TTR7?"

"Could mean *Through the Wringer 7*. Maybe Kingsley named the file quickly and forgot that 'wringer' starts with a W."

"Can you play the video?"

"It's been deleted. I'll try to recover it."

She turned back to the shelves and caught a flash of light in the corner of her vision. She moved to the window and lifted the shade just enough to peek outside. A pair of headlights in the parking lot went black. She heard a car door open and close.

She let the shade drop back into place. "Someone's here."

"Shit."

Zack grabbed the mouse and started clicking. Windows vanished in a flurry, then the screen went black and the PC's humming ceased. He stood from the swivel chair and pushed it against the desk. His expression was pinched. Frustrated.

Ashley opened the door of Kingsley's closet. The space inside looked too small for one person, much less two, but the sound of a door opening limited their options. She took Zack's hand and pushed him inside, then squeezed against him and pulled the door shut. The closet smelled like Kingsley's jackets.

"Cozy," he said.

His breath was a warm puff against her ear. She could feel his heartbeat where his chest pressed against her back.

Outside the closet, she heard someone enter the office. Whoever it was turned on the light. It lit the edges of the closet door in a bright outline.

"Fucking morons." It was Kingsley's voice. "It's not enough the

Feds want to shut me down, my own employees forget to activate the alarm." She heard the swivel chair shudder and squeak, then the sound of the computer coming to life. She hoped Zack had had enough time to cover his tracks.

"Trash. Trash. Trash. Trash." He was sifting through his e-mails, she realized. He stopped talking to himself, apparently having found one that required his attention. She heard him sigh. Heard the slow clacking of the keyboard as he pecked out a response.

Ashley shifted her weight and tried to find a comfortable position. Her butt dragged against a hardness at the front of Zack's jeans. Jesus. She'd given him a hard-on. She almost laughed. She put her hand over her mouth just in case.

The swivel chair made a ratcheting sound. Kingsley's footsteps crossed the room and seemed to stop directly in front of the closet door. Ashley's breath caught in her throat. She felt Zack's body tense.

The light clicked off. A few minutes later, Ashley heard the distant tones of the alarm being set. Then the even more distant rumble of a car starting.

She opened the closet door and they practically tumbled out.

Zack grinned at her, his face ghostly in the darkness. "That was fun."

"Yeah, I could tell you were enjoying yourself by the rod pressed against my tailbone."

"You felt that?" He moved behind the desk and turned on the lamp. The cone of light revealed his embarrassed smile. "Sorry. I guess that wasn't very gentlemanly."

"Don't worry about it. I'll just take it as a compliment."

He waved the mouse and the computer monitor brightened. "Back to work." She saw his eyes narrow. He said, "Kingsley, you hairy devil."

"What happened?"

"He's more sophisticated than I thought. He used a program called Evidence Eradicator—it's designed to stop people like me." He frowned. "He must have installed it after he found out that the Feds were seeking a warrant to look at his files."

"What do you mean, it stops people like you?"

"Remember when I told you that deleted data clusters remain on the hard disk until they're overwritten with new data? Well, this program overwrites the clusters with random zeroes and ones. It also erases the hard disk's memory of the location of the original file."

"Can you still recover the file?"

He grinned at her. "Don't insult me."

"Well, stop bragging and do it. I haven't been alone in a closet with a boy since junior high. It was a lot more fun then."

"Now you're hurting my feelings."

His eyes were locked on the monitor and his easy smile gave way to thoughtful concentration. She watched his hands work the keyboard and mouse and wondered what it would be like to watch him at an editing bay. There had been many times when she had sat at Brewster's side and watched him tighten hours of dull footage into hot and edgy scenes. She wondered if Zack was as good.

"Got it."

Her heartbeat quickened. "Can you play the video now, on Kingsley's computer?"

"If you're sure you're ready to see it."

"I'm sure."

Zack tapped a command into the keyboard and a window opened at the center of Kingsley's screen. Shaky footage began to play. She guessed that Kingsley was holding the camera. There was a time-stamp at the bottom of the screen. It confirmed the date. Last Monday. Two days before Tara was killed.

The view panned around a typical suburban living room, one that did not look much different from the set Ashley had visited the day before. This one had some faux-marble columns, small tables with vases, a brown suede couch, and a big widescreen TV. Tara stepped into the frame and Ashley felt her chest tighten.

Tara wore skintight leather pants and a belly shirt that showed off her pierced navel. Her red hair was pulled back in a loose ponytail. Gold hoop earrings swung from her ears. She looked unsure of herself.

"Are you sure you're okay working with me?" Tara's voice sounded tinny filtered through Kingsley's computer speakers, but the familiar cadences lanced Ashley's heart. "If you're willing to reschedule, I can find another Pinnacle girl."

A sob climbed up Ashley's throat. Zack jumped from the swivel chair and put an arm around her shoulders—awkwardly at first, then with a stronger grip. She wanted to bury her face in his shoulder, but she could not tear her gaze from the video. Tara seemed so *alive*.

"And blow my budget?" Kingsley said. Ashley thought there was a disturbing flatness in his voice, one that could not be blamed on the lousy computer speakers. "Let's just get this done."

"Where is everybody?" Tara said.

"I'm cutting costs. It's just you, me, and Carl."

Ashley pushed away from Zack and sat down in the swivel chair. Another figure entered the frame. Carl Packer. Just looking at the wiry, tattooed ex-con made Ashley shudder. She had worked with him once, a long time ago. She had refused to work with him again.

"Tara only agreed to do this scene to protect one of her new girls," Ashley told Zack. "She knew what Carl was like."

But she did not look intimidated or even nervous. Kingsley brought the camera closer, swooped it around her, lingered on her ass, which looked amazing in the leather pants, then moved to her breasts, which strained against the thin cotton of the belly shirt. Had the video not been deleted, this footage would have formed the introductory part of the scene—the tease—a technique Kingsley always used. Ashley watched the scene widen again as the camera backed away from Tara. Then there was a moment of shaking as Kingsley mounted the camera on a tripod.

"You don't want me to strip?" Tara tucked her thumbs into her pants and playfully pushed them down an inch, then back up with a roll of her hips.

"Carl will strip you."

Her teasing smile faltered and she shot a nervous glance off-screen.

"Carl, I want you to come into the frame fast and angry. Grab Tara and twist her around. Paw her chest a little bit, then shove your hand down her pants. Then get her clothes off and push her down on her knees for the blowjob."

Zack looked at Ashley with a concerned expression. "This is, uh, not unusual for a *Through the Wringer* scene. But it's all, you know ... no one really gets hurt."

"Relax, Zack. I've performed in rough scenes. If it crosses the line, I'll know the difference."

Carl did as instructed, but apparently could not resist adding his own trademark flair. He did not just grab Tara. He grabbed her by the hair, whipped her around. Then he dug his fingers into her chest. When he jammed his hand down the front of her pants, Ashley had to look away.

She hated this kind of porn. It tarnished the whole industry and offered right-wing conservatives a handy excuse to instigate the types of investigations that Kingsley found so intrusive. But she had to admit that the scene playing on Kingsley's computer had not crossed the line yet. Scenes like this were shot every day in the Valley. Tara had done plenty of them. Ashley had done plenty of them. They were uncomfortable, but they didn't leave your body covered in bruises.

Carl thrust Tara to the floor.

"Throat-fuck her," Kingsley said.

Zack looked at Ashley. "Want me to run it at double-speed?"

"Yeah. Okay." Ashley felt a wave of relief when the sound cut off and the frame-rate accelerated. She rubbed her face. "I didn't think this would be so hard to watch."

"Is it easier now?"

"A little."

Moving in fast-forward, the scene looked less real. Ashley's breathing steadied and her muscles relaxed. She watched the scene continue in predictable fashion. Doggie-style. Reverse cowgirl. Pile-driver.

"Okay," Ashley said. She leaned forward and peered at the screen. "Put it back on normal speed."

Zack clicked the mouse. The frame-rate slowed and the sound

returned. Grunts and moans and curses and slaps and Kingsley's voice saying, "Rougher." In the video window, Carl gritted his teeth. His forehead, neck, and arms were slick with perspiration. Sweat oozed into his eyes and made them red.

"Looks like Carl's having about as much fun as Tara," Zack said.

"Probably the first time in his life he's been criticized for being too gentle."

She watched him buck his hips harder, then roll away from Tara. He had lost his wood. Tara took him in her mouth as if the scene had been choreographed that way. In seconds, he was hard again.

"Hit her," Kingsley said.

Carl shot a sidelong, questioning glance at the camera.

"You want to tell me how to direct this movie," Kingsley snapped, "or do you want to fucking do what I tell you?"

Carl bent over and, while Tara continued to use her lips and tongue, he slapped her hard on the ass. Tara let out a muffled yelp but did not stop performing. Carl's slap left a red handprint, clearly visible on the video before it slowly faded.

"Enough of this ass-spanking bullshit." Kingsley's voice grated in the speakers. "Every piece of shit porn scene has that."

Carl pulled away from Tara. He had gone limp again. He looked directly at the camera—at Kingsley—and threw his tattooed arms up in frustration. "What the fuck do you want me to do, King?"

"I want you to put her through the wringer. That's the name of the fucking video, isn't it?"

"I don't even know what that means." Carl was whining now. "What the fuck is a wringer, anyway?"

"Jesus Christ," Kingsley said, disgusted. "Hit her again, and this time hit her *hard*."

Carl just stared at him.

"It's okay," Tara said, looking up at him. The look of resignation on her face brought a physical ache to Ashley's chest. "Just, you know, pretend."

Carl shrugged, raised a hand, and whacked it against Tara's arm.

So much for the theory that the stalker had beaten her.

"Harder," Kingsley said.

He hit her again. This time, when his hand made contact with Tara's arm, she swayed sideways and almost lost her balance.

"Good," Kingsley said. "That's better."

Carl hit her a third time and tears jumped to her eyes.

"Now suck his cock while he hits you."

Ashley had seen enough. She swung out of the chair and staggered two steps away from the computer. "Turn it off."

Zack closed the video window. The soundtrack cut off. The computer's hard disk chugged, then quieted.

"Well," he said, "I guess we learned who the liar is. Do you want me to make a copy of the file? I brought a jump-drive."

Ashley nodded distractedly. "Sure."

12

THE LINE of cars at the fast food place's drive-through had not shortened. Ashley watched the drivers inch toward the window, listened to the squawks that burst periodically from the speaker, and breathed the smell of burgers and fries. Her brain seemed to have locked up. Zack watched her with a concerned expression.

"Are you sure you're okay to drive?"

"I'm just ... I guess it's an emotional daze or something."

"That's understandable."

"Seeing Tara like that. So alive. And then...." She opened the driver's-side door of the Fiesta.

"Hey. Listen. Give me a call when you get back to your motel. So I know you're okay."

"I don't know your number."

He pulled out his phone. "Give me yours and I'll call you, then you can save my number."

She told him. Watching him tap the screen of his phone, she thought of Tara's laptop. It was still in the Fiesta's trunk. If Zack could access Kingsley's deleted files, maybe he could work around Tara's password protection. She walked around the car and popped the trunk.

Her phone rang. She answered and disconnected, then saved Zack's number.

"What are you doing?" Zack jammed his phone in his pocket and joined her behind the car. She lifted the laptop out of the trunk and handed it to him.

"This is Tara's. It's password-protected. Do you think—"

"No problem. What are you looking for?"

"I don't know. E-mails. Documents. Anything that might give us a hint about who killed her. I'm also hoping to find evidence that Tara was planning to change her will."

"I'll see what I can find. Don't worry. We'll figure this out." He looked at her doubtfully. "You're sure you're okay to drive? You don't want to get a hamburger first? A milkshake?"

"Zack, I'm fine."

———

Don't worry. *We'll figure this out.*

Back in her motel room, she wished she had invited him to come home with her. Just to have someone else there, someone breathing beside her. Company. But she had not invited him, and he had not suggested it. All he had said, leaning into her car before closing the door, was that he'd see her soon. And not to worry.

Right.

She turned onto her side. The motel room's air-conditioning had chosen tonight to conk out. After a few hours of climbing in and out of bed to fiddle with the thermostat, she gave up and resigned herself to a sleepless night. She stared at the darkness until it started to look like a physical thing, a mesh of black particles. The occasional sweep of headlights against the wall opposite the window broke the illusion and made her blink her tired eyes and turn her face into the pillow.

The comforter lay in a heap on the floor, but she kept the top-sheet wrapped around her. She needed it, no matter how hot the room was. She could not bare to lie on the bed in just her panties, with nothing covering her.

She brought the sheet up past her neck, gripped a handful of fabric in a fist beneath her chin. The sheet carried the faintly unpleasant odor of mildew, but she didn't care. Her stomach felt like it had a worm burrowing through it, digging and poking. She changed her position, but the feeling would not go away.

Did Kingsley kill Tara?

She did not want to believe it, but she could not get the tight, angry voice from the video out of her head. Nor could she stop thinking about the things he had made Carl do. Or his attempt to delete the file.

Or his skill at tying a noose.

But why? What possible motive could he have? He was Tara's friend. He was Ashley's friend.

Was, she reminded herself. *Two years ago.* Things change.

She forced herself to think of something different. Tara's graduation day. The warm sun on her face. The buzz of insects. The valedictorian's voice, distorted by a cheap microphone, as she talked about vast horizons and boundless opportunities.

Ashley had stayed home for two whole years to make sure that Tara graduated from high school. She had worked shit jobs at the mall and used all of her income to keep Tara's life as normal as possible. Clothing, food, all of the stuff that the other kids at Taft High School took for granted. She had shielded Tara from Gail's mood swings, from her meth and heroin binges. It had all felt worth it the day she graduated. The day they finally left Gail alone with her drugs and her boyfriends and her tropical fucking fish.

And then you came up with the bright idea to become porn stars. What a terrific big sis you turned out to be.

———

ON WEDNESDAY MORNING, she headed back to Tyrant hoping to find Zack. The parking lot was barren when she arrived, but she recognized Kingsley's Lexus SUV parked near the entrance. She gritted her teeth. She heard the low rumble of an engine as a red Corvette parked in the space next to hers. Zack climbed out. She opened her car door and joined him in the parking lot.

"Hey," she said.

"Good morning." He studied her for a moment. "If you're here to confront Kingsley, try to keep my name out of it. I mean—"

"Don't worry. Kingsley Nast is the last person I want to see right now."

He let out a breath. "Good."

"Confronting people hasn't exactly been a winning strategy for me. I came to find you."

"Me?" His smile returned.

She stepped closer to him, lowered her voice. "I don't have enough facts yet. Kingsley looks guilty, but so does Rob. And there's still the stalker. If I confront Kingsley now, all I'll accomplish is letting him know that I suspect him—and that you messed with his computer. I have a better idea."

"I'm listening."

"I think we should continue to try to solve this thing together. I mean, I get that you barely know me, but we seem to make a good team, and—"

"I'm in."

"Really?"

"Ashley, I watched that video, too. Don't think it didn't affect me."

She nodded. "Thank you."

The sound of a car made both of them turn. It rolled around the corner of the building.

A black Hyundai Sonata.

A morning breeze lifted the Hyundai's exhaust and blew it across the lot. The hot grit filled her nose and made her eyes water. She was too stunned to fan it away. She could not see the driver through the car's tinted windows, but she could feel him looking at her. A second passed. The car's engine revved. It shot past them, out of the parking lot and onto the boulevard beyond.

Her hand flew to her mouth.

Zack was already pulling the Corvette's passenger door open. "Get in!"

She did not hesitate. She scrambled into his car and drew the door closed after her. She took a deep breath and the smell of the leather seats rushed into her nostrils. Zack slid into the cockpit and started the ignition. The engine roared.

"It's him. Tara's stalker." Her thoughts were still catching up with what she'd just seen. "What is he doing *here*? He and Kingsley must be connected."

"Looks that way."

Zack swung the car in a tight 180-degree turn, then shot forward. The front wheels bumped out of the parking lot. The car swerved into traffic. Ashley glimpsed the black Hyundai three cars ahead and one lane over. She pointed and Zack gunned the engine and weaved through traffic.

"Try to get the license plate number," Zack said. His voice was tight and controlled. She could see tension in his neck. He wrenched the wheel hard to the right and they blew past a minivan. "Ashley. The license plate number."

"Okay."

"There's a pad of paper and a pen in the glove box."

She opened the glove compartment. Papers and a car manual and a bag of breath mints and a pad of paper and several pens and markers spilled into her lap. She took the pad and a pen and crammed everything else back inside, then forced the door to click in place. The Hyundai was further away now.

"I can't see the plate."

"Damn it."

Zack worked the gearshift. The Corvette jumped forward. Ashley's head pushed back against the leather headrest and her heart bounced into her throat.

A rusty El Camino and a gray Mercedes blocked their path. The El Camino, in the left lane, maintained a maddeningly steady 40 miles per hour. Zack swung from the left lane to the right lane and back again, but the two cars remained exactly parallel. Passing was impossible. Ashley cringed when he nosed the Corvette right up to the El Camino's rear, close enough to tap the rust-speckled bumper. The driver should have gotten the message, but he didn't. Instead of speeding up, he extended a pudgy brown arm from the window and pumped his middle finger in the air.

"Look at this a-hole," Zack muttered.

Ashley watched helplessly as the sea of traffic between the Corvette and the Hyundai widened. Zack brought the Corvette even closer to the El Camino and Ashley braced herself for a jolt, but he let up on the gas just before the two cars could touch. He banged the heel of his hand against the horn and held it there. Its flat blare rang out. Zack's face wrenched with frustration.

"He's getting away," Ashley said. She lost the Hyundai in the crowd of cars, then picked it out again, a small black square in the distance.

The Mercedes in the right lane picked up speed and Zack slid the Corvette behind it. They managed to get alongside the El Camino. Ashley risked a glance at the driver. He was fat, middle-aged. His seat belt cut between his man-breasts. He scowled. A second later he was ahead of them again, matching the speed of the Mercedes.

"He's playing with us," Zack said. "I can't believe this." He swung back to the left lane, behind the El Camino.

"What are you doing?"

"I'm passing the motherfucker."

Before Ashley could inquire further, the Corvette leapt off the road and onto the grass bordering the boulevard's left-hand side. Her seat bumped beneath her. The engine protested. Zack's hand jerked the stick. They powered forward and drew even with the El Camino. The driver turned to glare at them.

"Give him the finger," Zack said.

"Oh, grow up."

Zack shifted gears again and the Corvette shot past the El Camino. She did not want to imagine the trail of ruined grass behind them, but judging by the noises she was hearing, it was not a pretty sight.

A palm tree loomed up, directly in front of them.

"Watch out!"

Zack's hand left the gearshift and flashed protectively across her chest. His left hand yanked the wheel hard to the right. The left corner of the Corvette clipped the tree's slender trunk. The tree swayed. Its fronds cast shaking shadows across the windshield. She heard the high-pitched whine of another car engine and looked out the window to her right. The bastard in the El Camino had sped up. They were approaching another tree. The Corvette lurched back onto the road and cleared the El Camino's front bumper by inches.

Zack retracted his arm from her chest. "Sorry about that."

The El Camino's horn blared, but the sound ebbed quickly as the Corvette left him behind and raced toward the next cluster of vehicles. Ashley spotted the black Hyundai in the right lane four cars ahead.

"You write screenplays, edit film, hack computers, and do your own stunts. You're a Hollywood renaissance man."

"Thanks. Can you read the license plate number yet?"

She watched as the Hyundai accelerated through an intersection just as the traffic light turned from green to yellow. "Shit. We're going to lose him."

"Hold on."

"To what?" Ashley gripped the edges of her leather seat.

The Corvette launched forward. Cars to the left and right dropped back as if their drivers had slammed on their brakes. Ashley glanced at the speedometer and saw the needle arc past 90. The traffic light turned red seconds before the Corvette roared into the intersection.

"We've got him now," Zack said.

He was staring straight ahead, too focused on the black Hyundai to see the car streaking into the intersection on their right. Ashley saw it first in her peripheral vision. When she turned her head, it was already on top of them. A blue Volvo. Its driver was clearly visible through its windshield, his mouth open in a scream. He had a travel mug in his hand and Ashley had time to see the brown liquid shoot up in a coffee geyser and then the stink of burnt rubber filled her nostrils and there was the sound of glass shattering and metal rending and an air bag punched her chest and shoved her back hard against her seat. The car spun across the intersection. The right side lifted off of the ground. For a heart-stopping moment, she thought the car was going to flip. Then its right side slammed down and the car rocked and skidded to a stop.

She coughed, got her door open, and spilled out. Traffic had stopped all around them. People stood outside their cars. Some had phones held to their faces, but most just stared. Ashley staggered around the Corvette. The smell of burnt rubber was everywhere. The back of the Corvette was a crushed mess. The Volvo must have struck the rear corner. Ashley stared at the twisted fiberglass. If the Volvo had hit them a foot closer to the passenger seat, she would not be walking right now.

She yanked the driver-side door open. Zack blinked at her from behind an airbag. Blood trickled from his nostril. "Are you okay?" she said.

"I think so."

She helped him out of the car and they staggered together over the skid marks. Sirens wailed in the distance.

A tall, blonde man stalked toward them. His button-down shirt had a huge wet spot on the chest and he reeked of coffee. "That was a red light!"

"I'm sorry." Zack sounded weak.

"You could have gotten us all killed!"

Ashley positioned herself between the Volvo driver and Zack. "Stop yelling. It was an accident. Let's just exchange information and call the police."

"You're damn right we're gonna call the police!"

"Hey!" Zack lumbered forward. "Don't talk to her like that."

Ashley grasped his arm and pulled him gently backward. "It's okay. Go get your insurance card."

Zack glared at the Volvo driver. The machismo in his face looked almost comical as he stumbled around the Corvette. He leaned down to reach through the open passenger-side door. While his back was turned, Ashley scanned the nearby cars. The closest one was a white Toyota Camry. Its driver, a middle-aged man wearing a straw hat and sunglasses, was standing outside the car and watching them.

You've done a lot of stupid things in your life, but this....

Ashley took a deep breath, then moved.

The guy in the straw hat looked surprised when she approached him. His white eyebrows arched up. She said, "I need to borrow your car."

He smiled uneasily. "What?" The word came out in a slow drawl.

He had left his Toyota idling. She could hear the purr of its engine, could smell the exhaust streaming out of its tailpipe.

Just do it.

She shoved the man out of her way. The straw hat flew off his head and he stumbled three steps away from her and the Camry before he caught his balance. It gave her all the time she needed. She slid behind the wheel and slammed the door shut.

"What are you doing?"

There was a woman in the passenger seat.

Ashley gaped at her, unable to speak for two long seconds. "I'm ... I need to use your car."

"What?"

A fist struck the window and she jumped. The man in the straw hat shouted at her through the window. Ashley did not pause to try to understand the muffled words. Her foot stomped the gas pedal and she pulled the seatbelt across her chest.

"Where are you taking me?" The woman's voice jumped in pitch as the Toyota barreled forward. The tires shrieked. She shot past Zack. He was standing next to the Volvo driver. He turned to stare at her with a look of panic.

Ashley concentrated on the road. She needed to find the Hyundai. The crash had seemed to go on for hours, but it could not have been more than a few minutes. The Hyundai could not have driven far.

"Listen to me, please," the woman said. "My name is Noelle

Lanier. I have two children, Michael and Daria." She smelled like suntan lotion.

Ashley spotted the black Hyundai and her heart lifted. She resisted the impulse to speed up. The driver had no way of knowing that she had switched cars. If she did not act suspicious, he might never notice the white Camry tailing him. She could follow him all the way home.

"Please don't kill me," the woman said. "My children—"

"I'm not going to kill you," Ashley said. "I'm not going to do anything to you. Relax, okay? I just need to use your car for a little while."

She made a right turn after the Hyundai, keeping two cars between them.

"Use my car? You stole it. You ... *carjacked* it."

"I didn't have a choice. Didn't you see the big accident back there? I was in the Corvette."

The woman stared at her without comprehension. "And ... what? You're late for a meeting? God, you have blood on your face."

Ashley took one hand off the wheel and touched her forehead. The skin was rough and raised. She must have cut herself during the accident. She wiped her bloody fingers on her jeans.

"I'm not late for a meeting. I'm trying to follow someone. It's important."

The Hyundai made another right. Its speed had dropped. Apparently, the driver believed that the threat had passed.

"Following someone?"

"See that Hyundai Sonata? The black one with tinted windows?"

The woman hesitated, then said, "Yes?"

"He's my ex-husband," she said. "He's a ... deadbeat. He owes me six months of child support. He's been hiding. I saw him in a store, and I need to follow him home, find out where he lives or works—"

"So you can tell your lawyer," the woman finished for her.

"Yeah. My lawyer's going to rip him a new one."

"Good for you."

Ashley glanced to her right and saw the woman smiling.

The black Hyundai turned off the road and into a parking structure. Ashley followed. The sunlight vanished and the Camry's headlights flashed on automatically. The sound of the engine echoed in the enclosed space. Ashley slowed the car. She watched the Hyundai climb the ramp to the next level. She drove after it.

"There he is." The woman pointed down the row of cars. The Hyundai slid into an empty spot and parked.

"Thanks for letting me use your car," Ashley said. She put the Camry in park. "You really helped me out."

"*That's* your ex-husband?"

Ashley followed the woman's stare. A man stood next to the black Hyundai, but for a moment Ashley refused to believe he had emerged from the car. He did not match the image she had had in her head—tall, white, thirty-something. This guy could not be an inch taller than five-five and looked like he weighed over two-hundred pounds. He was also Hispanic. And at least fifty-five years old.

"I, uh, was young and stupid. It was a rebellion thing."

The woman nodded as if she understood.

"Anyway, thanks for the ride. It would be really great if, you know—"

"I didn't press charges?"

"Right."

The woman touched Ashley's shoulder. "Hey, we moms have to stick together. Go get that worthless punk."

"I will."

13

ASHLEY NOTED the Hyundai's license plate number, then followed the driver inside a four-story office building. If the entryway was any indication, she was not going to find Los Angeles's top companies renting space there. The walls looked like they had once been white, but decades of cigarette smoke had stained them gray. She spotted more than one crack running from the ceiling to the grimy linoleum floor. And it was hot.

The Hyundai driver stepped into an elevator at the far end of the lobby. Ashley turned her face away from him. There was a directory on the wall. She pretended to consult it until she heard the elevator doors rattle closed.

There were numbers above the elevator. Number 2 brightened, then dimmed. Then number 4 brightened. Ashley turned to the directory again. There were only three names listed for the fourth floor. Howard Wiggins, C.P.A., Frank Mustard, Esq., and Cruz Lombilla.

She spoke the third name aloud. "Lombilla." It seemed to fit.

A series of clanks and chugs echoed within the elevator shaft, but she did not have the patience to wait for the car to make its slow downward trip. She pushed open a battered metal door to the fire stairwell.

The fourth floor hallway was as derelict as the lobby. It smelled like dust. Doors lined both walls, but most of the offices appeared to be vacant. The first one on her right had once belonged to Mustard, the lawyer, but he must have moved. Half of the black letters forming his name had peeled off the door's pebbled glass window and dust coated his doorknob.

She crept further down the hallway. Three doors past Mustard's abandoned office, she saw Howard Wiggins's name. The accountant. His office was dark, but if he had vacated the building like Mustard, then he had forgotten to leave a forwarding address. A huge pile of mail leaned against his door, supported on one side by a rectangular FedEx box. Ashley bent down and picked up the box. The pile of mail spilled across the floor.

The box was solid. She hefted it in her hands, tested its weight. Not the ideal weapon for self-defense against a killer, but better than nothing.

She wished Zack were here.

She stepped carefully around the scattered mail. She hurried her pace and saw his name on a door to her left. It was closed, but when she turned the knob, the door opened silently.

She saw his ass first, puffy and round in faded gray pants. He was leaning over his desk. His back, terraced with layers of fat, shifted and bunched beneath a brown dress shirt. He aimed an aerosol can at his computer keyboard and blasted one group of keys, then another.

She stood stock-still in the doorway. She did not dare to breathe even when her lungs started to burn. This was the guy. The driver of the Hyundai. The stalker.

Her grip dented the corner of the FedEx box. The cardboard let out a little squeak. The fat man swung around. His eyes widened with surprise. She brought the box upward. Nailed his chin. His head snapped back. The aerosol can flew out of his hand. She swung the box again. Hit his ear. His body wobbled backward. His ass slammed the desk hard enough to scrape grooves in the floor.

Ashley braced herself to hit him again.

But he didn't come at her. "Ashley Hale."

His small eyes stared at her from a dark, puffy face. He was sucking in air, his breaths ragged and sour-smelling. The bottom of his shirt had come out of his pants.

"Surprised to see me?" she said.

He rubbed his chin but did not answer.

"It's not fun when you're the one being followed, is it?"

"No."

"My name is Latner. Not Hale."

"I know." His voice sounded strained. "But it's proper etiquette in the industry to use a performer's professional name until she tells you otherwise. Isn't that how it works?"

"Put your hands up," she said.

"Or what? You'll hit me with the box again?" An ugly smile creased his pudgy face. "What the hell's in it, anyway? Rocks?"

She reared back and swung, but this time he blocked the blow with his arm. The box jolted out of her hands and dropped to the floor. Her purse slid off of her shoulder and fell near the box. Lombilla's hands were on her before she could pick either up. Big hands, with fingers that were long and sinewy. She could not break his grip. He twisted her around and threw an arm around her torso, crushing her breasts and locking her arms to her sides. She struggled but could not break free. She kicked at his shins.

"Stop it," he said. The calmness in his voice only drove her to struggle more.

"I'll scream!"

"Look." He pivoted to his left and turned her with him. She faced a wall now. A framed photograph hung there, a group portrait of young men and women in uniforms. A sign in front of them said Los Angeles Police Academy Class of 1987. "I'm in the third row," Lombilla said. "Fourth from the right."

"You're a cop?"

"I used to be. Are you starting to understand?"

"That's why the police were so quick to call Tara's death as a suicide. They're protecting one of their own."

"No. That's not what I'm saying. If you'll stand still for a minute, I'll explain."

"Stop struggling? Is that what you told Tara to do? When you held her up against the Bowflex and looped a telephone cord around her neck?"

"You think I murdered Tara Rose?"

"You were stalking her. That makes you a pretty obvious suspect."

"Jesus." His grip loosened. He released her. Blood rushed back into her arms and she clenched her teeth against the sensation of pins and needles. Lombilla bent over and picked the aerosol can up from the floor.

Ashley rubbed her arms. Took a step back, away from him.

He held out the can for her to see. "It's not a weapon. It shoots air. For cleaning electronics." He aimed it at the ceiling and pressed the trigger. Air puffed out.

She noticed for the first time how clean the office was, how unlike the rest of the building. Chemical odors of Windex and furniture polish hung in the air. Every surface gleamed.

"You're good at cleaning things up." She thought of Tara's apartment, the absence of evidence. "And as an ex-cop, you'd know just what to clean. Why did they kick you off the police force, anyway? Did you get a little too interested in one of your female colleagues?"

He tucked in his shirt. "They didn't kick me out. They stuck me behind a desk. Because of my disability. I quit because of the boredom."

"Disability?"

"Obsessive compulsive disorder. Though I prefer to call it attention to detail."

"You think an insanity plea is going to get you off?"

"I told you. I didn't hurt your sister."

He took a step toward her. She stepped back.

"How did you find me?" he said.

"Your car. Tara's neighbors saw it."

He looked disappointed, but not surprised. He dug a slim wallet from his pocket and tossed it to her. She caught it. The soft leather flapped open in her hands. She saw Lombilla's face on a laminated card. "I'm a private investigator. Look at my license."

She looked at it. "This doesn't mean anything."

"I wasn't stalking Tara. I was conducting surveillance."

"I'm sure."

"Listen to me." He took another step forward. She tried to step back again, but her butt bumped the door. It must have closed on its own, as silently as it had opened. She imagined the fat man obsessively oiling the hinges. Lombilla closed the distance between them. "I was working—"

His hand shot forward. Ashley jerked sideways. His hand grasped air. She kicked. Her knee caught him between the legs. The impact jolted up her thigh. His face contorted and his hands clutched his groin and his knees gave out. He cradled his testicles. A keening sound wheezed from his mouth.

She grabbed her purse off of the floor and pulled out her phone.

"Don't ... call the police." If his voice had sounded strained before, it sounded like a different person's now. High-pitched, squeaky. "I'm not ... on good terms."

"You mean you're a sleazebag and you're one step away from losing your license."

"Yes."

She dialed 9-1-1 and listened to the line ring once. Twice.

"Put the phone away. Please. Just let me explain. I didn't hurt Tara. I wasn't even following her—not directly. I was following someone else."

"But you can't tell me who, right?" She let her sarcastic tone hang in the air. The third ring burred in the phone's speaker. "Client confidentiality."

"Fuck that. Put away the phone and I'll tell you everything."

Ashley considered for a second. What did she have to lose? She ended the call. But she kept her finger near the phone's screen.

"I was hired ... a week and a half ago." He grimaced. "God, this hurts. I think I may need a doctor." He gasped. "A man hired me to follow his wife. He thought she was cheating on him. He was right. Happens all the time. This is LA."

"That's why you were parked at Tara's apartment complex. You were following someone else. This is all just a big coincidence."

He shook his head. "My client's wife ... was having an affair ... with your sister. With Tara."

"Nice try. My sister wasn't a lesbian—she just played one on TV. I'm calling the police."

"No. Please." He let go of his groin and held up his hands, desperate. "It's true. There are photographs. Look in the file cabinet. Second drawer. The Grayson file."

Ashley froze. Grayson was Kingsley's name. His real, non-porno one.

Lombilla saw the change in her posture. "Russell Grayson. He's my client. He hired me to follow—"

"Cheryl?"

The thought of Tara and Cheryl having an affair was ludicrous—but also strangely plausible.

"Yes!"

"You followed Cheryl and learned that she was having an affair with Tara." She wasn't really talking to him anymore—she was thinking out loud—but he nodded eagerly anyway. "You told Kingsley about the affair," she said. "Showed him the pictures. When? When did you show him the photos?"

"I don't know. A week ago, maybe?"

"A week ago meaning last Wednesday? Are you sure?"

Lombilla blinked a few times as he massaged his crotch. "No. Wait. We met on the weekend. Sunday."

"Last Sunday? Three days ago?"

That would mean that when Kingsley learned of the affair, Tara was already dead.

"No," Lombilla said. "The Sunday before. Two Sundays ago."

Ashley strained to put the dates into the proper sequence in her mind. "Two Sundays ago, you showed Kingsley the photos." She was thinking out loud again. "Kingsley shot footage for *Through the Wringer* the next day. That explains why he went overboard. He was furious." It was starting to make sense, in a fucked-up sort of way. "Sunday, Monday, and Tara was killed on Wednesday night. And then you started following me." She looked at him. "Why?"

He squirmed against the wall. "Grayson paid me to keep an eye on you."

Her body went cold.

"Okay?" Lombilla said. "Now you know everything. Are you happy?"

His tone tempted her to give him another kick to the nuts. She resisted the urge. "Let me see the photos."

He fetched them for her. For some reason, she expected something salacious, blurry black-and-whites filled with skin and sex. But the photos, a stack of color four-by-six prints, were almost painfully innocent. Tara and Cheryl holding hands in a bookstore. Laughing over big salads at an outdoor café. Kissing in front of Tara's apartment door.

"Don't tell Kingsley we had this meeting," Ashley said. She dropped the photos into her purse.

Lombilla's teeth unclenched and he let out a strained laugh. "Believe me, I'm not planning on ... telling anyone about this."

––––––––

SHE HURRIED BACK to the parking garage before she remembered that she had no car. A Hummer thundered past her on its way down the ramp. Its side-view mirror almost clipped her shoulder. She did not even jump, too dazed to even turn away from the exhaust fumes that gusted into her face. She coughed on the hot and grainy air.

Tara and Cheryl.

It was hard to believe, except that it fit. It explained things. She had already discovered Kingsley's ability with nooses, had already seen a display of his anger toward Tara. Now that she knew his motive, the picture was complete. Cheryl had cheated on Kingsley and Kingsley had taken revenge.

Another car passed her. Its tailpipe belched more exhaust fumes into the hot air. Gritty smoke filled her mouth. Her nose and throat burned. Her stomach heaved.

She had to get out of here.

She grabbed her phone and pulled up Zack's number, grateful now that he had given it to her the night before. He answered on the first ring.

"It's Ashley," she said. "I need you to pick me up." There was a squeal of brakes on the level above her and she missed his response. "What?"

"I said, your concern is heartwarming. Yes, I survived the accident. And since you don't seem to be calling from a jail cell, I'm guessing the couple whose car you stole decided not to report you."

His tone coaxed a small smile from her face. She leaned against the concrete wall and imagined his bemused grin, the crinkles around his dark blue eyes. Despite the nausea and the adrenaline, his voice had a calming effect.

"What did you say to them, anyway?" he said.

"I can be very charming."

An old station wagon rattled down the ramp. He said, "Where are you? Sounds like the Daytona 500."

She gave him the address of the office building. "How's the Corvette?" she said.

His response was an exaggerated groan.

"That bad?"

"It's being repaired. In the meantime, the auto body shop loaned me a lovely Impala."

"Styling."

"Speaking of cars, did you manage to get the Hyundai's plates?"

"Not just the plates. The driver, too."

She could sense his surprise. Seconds of silence crept past. Finally, with a forced-sounding cheerfulness, he said, "Mister Tall Blonde and Thirty-something?"

"Not exactly. I'll tell you in the car after you pick me up." She realized how presumptuous she sounded and added, "Assuming you don't mind chauffeuring me."

"Not at all. And where shall I drive you, ma'am? A restaurant, perhaps? One with a good wine list?"

"That sounds nice. But I was thinking of somewhere more along the lines of your boss's house."

"I thought you were done with confrontations."

"It's not Kingsley I want to see. It's Cheryl."

———

THE ACCIDENT HAD LEFT a bruise on Zack's neck, just above his collar, that made her think of Tara. She tried not to look at it during the drive to Kingsley's West Hills neighborhood. It took most of the ride to tell him the details of her encounter with Lombilla. He did not interrupt her, although when she reached the part about kicking Lombilla in the balls, he squirmed and pressed his thighs together.

"Zack, he was three times my size."

"I didn't say anything."

"I had to defend myself."

"I know."

"But you're empathizing with him."

He glanced at her and cringed. "Maybe I feel his pain. A little. Even though he deserved it."

"Damn straight he did."

He smiled. Then, abruptly, his expression turned serious. "So you think Kingsley murdered Tara."

"What else would I think?"

"I'm surprised you haven't already called the police."

"I almost did."

"What stopped you?"

She sighed and leaned back in her seat. The Impala's cloth interior was a let-down after the smooth leather of the Corvette, and the car smelled faintly of dog, but it was still a step-up from the Ford Fiesta. She stretched out her legs.

"Detective Collins—the cop in charge of Tara's case—doesn't take me seriously. To her, I'm just the grief-stricken sister of a suicide victim. She thinks I'm in denial. And she hates porn, so of course she assumes I'm a slut and an airhead."

"Then she's an idiot. They should strip her of her badge."

"Yeah, well, in a perfect world. I'm just hoping she'll listen to Cheryl."

Zack turned the Impala into Kingsley's circular drive. Kingsley lived in a four-bedroom house, the palatial but generic type that Sean would have called a McMansion back in New Jersey. It sat on three acres of beautifully landscaped property, and the driveway looped from the quiet street to the column-flanked front door. Zack parked the Impala, but neither of them moved.

Kingsley was still at the office. While waiting for Zack to pick her up from the parking garage, she had called Angela to make sure. Ashley imagined Cheryl inside, cooking or watching TV or talking to the girls.

"How do you know Cheryl will talk to the police?" Zack said.

"I'm going to convince her."

"This sounds like a woman thing. Want me to wait in the car?"

"I think that would be best."

She touched the door handle, but before she could lift it, a wave of anxiety rushed through her. The nausea she thought she had left behind at the parking garage returned with a vengeance.

"What's wrong?" Zack said. His eyes, dark blue, held steady on hers.

Gail's words came to her mind, unbidden. *Tara didn't turn her back on people. She wasn't like you.* "I stopped calling her," Ashley said, looking at Zack. "And I stopped answering her calls. I just ... I couldn't deal with this place anymore. This life." She felt tears brim in her eyes and blinked them away. "She changed so much, and I wasn't here."

Zack touched her arm. Tentatively at first, then with a strong, warm grip that seemed to somehow transmit his confidence to her. "Tara understood."

"How do you know?"

"She was your sister."

She mustered a half-smile and a resolute nod. "I'll be quick. Then we can drive Cheryl to the Devonshire police station. We'll let the professionals take over."

"You mean my chauffeur duties are coming to an end?"

She touched his hand. "I don't know if I could have done this without you, Zack. I can't tell you how much I appreciate everything."

Her voice trailed away and they sat in silence, looking at each other. She thought he might kiss her, but the moment passed and he ran a hand through his hair instead. "Good luck in there."

"Thanks."

She popped the door open and stepped into the afternoon heat.

14

"OH MY GOD! ASHLEY!"

The gawky adolescent girl standing in the doorway was Kingsley's older daughter Valerie. It took Ashley a moment to recognize her. The last time Ashley had seen her, Val had been a gap-toothed twelve-year-old. Now she was fourteen. She had shot up two or three inches and her forehead was pocked with pimples, but her smile was no less exuberant.

"It's good to see you too, Val."

"I can't believe you're here!" Val rushed forward and grabbed her in a bear-hug. For a skinny girl, she had a lot of strength. Ashley felt her ribs compress. She patted the girl's back, hoping she would let go, and cast a glance over her shoulder at the Impala. The sunlight reflecting off the windshield prevented her from seeing Zack's reaction.

"Why don't we go inside?" Ashley said.

Val released her from the hug. She grabbed both of Ashley's hands and pulled her into the house, then closed the door. The foyer had changed. The walls were beige now instead of light brown and the little desk that used to be next to the door had been replaced with a slim black table. A vase stood on the table's narrow surface. Daisies leaned on long stems. Ashley inhaled their light bouquet as Val tugged her into the house.

"Do you like New Jersey?" Val said. "What's it like there? Do you have a boyfriend?"

"Val." Ashley touched the girl's knobby shoulder. "I'll tell you all about New Jersey later, okay? I promise. But right now I really need to talk to your mom."

Val's smile morphed into a pout. "But you just got here."

"It's important."

"Well, okay, but Mom's doing her yoga. She doesn't like to be interrupted. It messes up her chi or something. If we go in there, she'll be peeved."

"I'll deal with it."

Val blew air past her lips and turned a pirouette. Her sock-clad feet squeaked on the hardwood. Ashley followed her from the foyer to the family room. A hip-hop video played on a widescreen TV, but the sound was muted. A girl poked her head up from the couch. Val's little sister Katie, who must be twelve now. Her face lit up. "Ashley!"

"Nice manners," Val said. "Don't get off the couch or anything." She rolled her eyes.

"Yeah, you're the manners expert, Miss Burp-at-the-dinner-table."

Val's face reddened. "I do not!"

"Miss Fart-while-you-brush-your-teeth."

"Shut up!"

Val looked ready to bound across the room and throttle her sister. Ashley grabbed her arm. Val turned to her with a hurt expression, and Ashley let go, worried she had gripped her too tightly.

"Why are you laughing?" Val said.

Ashley had not realized that she was. "I'm sorry. I wasn't laughing at you, Val. I guess watching the two of you reminded me of me and my own sister."

The two girls looked at each other, and a somber silence descended on the room.

"Why don't we go see your mother now?"

———

VAL LED Ashley to the sunroom at the back of the house. The couches and coffee table Ashley remembered were no longer there. The hardwood floor was bare except for a light blue yoga mat. Cheryl knelt at the room's center, facing away from the door. She wore pink leggings and a white tank-top. Her blonde hair was tied in a loose ponytail. Her arms looked as thin and smooth as a twenty-year-old's. It was hard to believe she was twice that age.

She did not turn or acknowledge Ashley's and Val's entrance. It was so quiet in the sunroom that Ashley could hear birds chirping outside, through the glass. She gripped the cool wood of the door-frame and watched. Cheryl leaned forward and placed her elbows and forearms flat on the yoga mat, palms down. She stretched her legs out behind her. Her bare feet rose until only her toes touched the floor. Then her toes came off the floor and her legs ascended straight above her head. She maintained this position for several seconds, then bent her knees and brought her feet downward until they hovered inches above her head. Her body formed a C.

"Mom?"

Cheryl tensed, and for a moment Ashley thought she would topple. Her limbs quivered but maintained their balance. Without responding to her daughter, Cheryl reversed her movements step by step until her body gracefully returned to its kneeling position.

She took a deep breath, stood up, and turned. "I asked you not to disturb—" She saw Ashley and said, "Oh."

"It's my fault, Cheryl. I told Val it would be okay to interrupt you."

"No, that's ... fine." Cheryl reached down for her towel and mopped sweat from her face. "I was just finishing up, anyway."

"What was that position called, that you just did?"

"The scorpion pose?"

"It was pretty incredible. I didn't know you were so flexible."

"Thanks. It's not as difficult as it looks."

Val circled around her, too excited to stand still. "Are you staying for dinner?"

"I can't tonight. I just came by to talk to your mom. In private."

"Remember how you used to show me how to put on makeup?" Val said.

"Valerie." Cheryl's flat tone deflated the girl's enthusiasm. "Why don't you go watch TV with Katie?"

Val rolled her eyes. "I don't want to hang out with *her*."

Cheryl did not respond. After a few seconds of silence, Val made a frustrated noise in her throat and retreated from the sunroom. A few seconds later, the sound of the girls arguing filtered down the hallway. Cheryl made a face. "They're always fighting."

"They're sisters."

Cheryl sighed. "Are you doing okay, Ashley? I'm so sorry for your loss."

"I'm sorry for yours."

"Mine?" Cheryl wiped her face with the towel again, but this time Ashley sensed that she was using it as a prop. "I'm not sure what you're talking about—"

"I know you and Tara were more than friends, Cheryl."

She stopped toweling herself. "What?"

"Tara told me."

Lying was a gamble, but Ashley did not have time to listen to Cheryl's denials.

Cheryl glanced worriedly past Ashley at the open doorway. "I think ... maybe we should have this conversation upstairs."

"I think that's a good idea."

Cheryl moved past her. The smell of her perspiration filled Ashley's nostrils, then faded as the woman padded barefoot toward the staircase. Ashley followed her. When they reached the master bedroom upstairs, Cheryl turned and met Ashley's gaze straight-on.

"If you think I'm going to apologize for what happened, I'm not."

The statement caught Ashley by surprise. "Why would I ask you to apologize?"

"If anyone should be apologizing, it's you." Cheryl closed the door. Turned the lock. "What kind of a sister leaves town and never calls?"

"I had my reasons. If I could go back in time—"

"You can't. God." Cheryl stepped past her and dropped onto the edge of the bed. The mattress creaked. "It's so hard to accept that she's gone."

"I know."

Close up, Cheryl's face showed her age. A hint of crows feet spread outward from her eyes.

"Sometimes," Cheryl said, "I think of something, you know, that I want to tell her. And I pull out my phone and I actually start calling her before I remember."

Ashley did not know what to say. She nodded and hoped Cheryl would take the gesture as encouragement to continue.

"I should have known she would tell you about us," Cheryl said. "She never believed you had left for good, you know. She always said you'd come back. She said that the industry was your home."

"She did?"

"It was definitely *her* home." Cheryl's lips tugged into a tight smile. "It's amazing. I've lived on the periphery of the industry for a long time, but Tara was like no one else I've ever met. She really believed in the industry. She wasn't blind to its dark side like some of the girls you meet. She wasn't naïve. She hated the scam artists and the drugs and all of the bullshit. But she was passionate about the positive things. She believed that with the right guidance, a young woman entering the industry could avoid the bad stuff and forge a real career. And she was proving it. Every day she was proving it with Pinnacle. You should have seen the things she was doing."

Ashley knew they had limited time, but she could not resist the chance to learn more about her sister. She sat down next to Cheryl on the bed. She sank her fingers in the plush comforter. "Can you give me an example?"

Cheryl's mouth quivered. Then she must have remembered something good, because she smiled. "Lots of agencies give lip service to keeping their girls off of drugs. But Tara didn't stop at discouraging drug use. If a Pinnacle girl got into trouble, the agency didn't just drop her. Tara would help her enroll in a rehab program. In a few cases, Pinnacle even footed the bill. There was a whole article about it in the March issue of AVN. I have a copy if you'd like to see it."

"I would."

Cheryl crossed the room, opened the drawer of a small table in the corner, and pulled out a thick copy of the industry trade magazine. She brought it back to the bed and handed it to Ashley. The article was easy to find. Cheryl had dog-eared the page. Ashley read the four paragraphs. Cheryl waited, quiet.

"How did it start?" Ashley said. She placed the magazine on the bedspread behind them. "Your affair."

"Tara didn't tell you that part?"

"No."

Cheryl looked away. Her tank-top hung loosely on her figure. Perspiration had dried to a sticky sheen on her face. "It's not a particularly interesting story."

"I'd like to hear it."

"Okay. Well, I had known her for years. You know that. Russell's always introduced people from the industry into our private life. People he trusts and likes. Tara. You. Brewster. A few others. I had always enjoyed Tara's company, I guess, but I didn't start to really notice her—*really notice her*—until she and Rob started the talent agency. The way she talked about the industry—how it could be so much better, so much safer and more fair.... I admired her ambition and her selflessness. We met for lunch a few times. Just as friends. But then one night when Val and Katie were at their grandmother's and Russell had to work late, I called her—" She stopped herself, then took a deep breath. "It's not as if I intended to be unfaithful to Russell. And I've never thought of myself as gay, or even bisexual."

A few seconds of silence passed. Cheryl lowered her head and fixed her gaze on her intertwined fingers.

"I'm glad you found each other," Ashley said, surprised by her own conviction. "I don't think Tara was ever with another person who really appreciated her. I'm glad she was finally able to experience that."

Cheryl nodded. She looked choked-up, unable to speak.

"Now you need to do one more thing for her," Ashley said. She reached down and clasped her hand over Cheryl's and squeezed. Cheryl's skin felt smooth, her fingers long and delicate. "You need to come with me now. To talk to the police."

Cheryl looked up, confused. "The police?"

"It's time to tell them the truth about how Tara died."

Cheryl jerked her hands out of Ashley's grip. "I don't know what you're talking about. Tara killed herself."

"We both know that's a lie."

"She hanged herself." Cheryl rose from the bed.

Ashley stood up, too. Cheryl flinched. Something about seeing her sister's lover stare at her with confusion and suspicion created a weariness that dragged at Ashley, but she refused to give in to it. "Kingsley murdered her, Cheryl. You're covering it up."

"No."

"Tara would never commit suicide. If you really knew her—if you really loved her—then you know that's true."

Cheryl's jaw bunched. Ashley watched her face twist as she fought her emotions. She regained her composure and said, "Maybe she didn't kill herself. God knows I'd like to believe that. But Russell did not murder her, Ashley."

"Did you know he hired a private investigator to follow you? I talked to the guy. Cruz Lombilla. He found out about your affair, Cheryl, and when he told Kingsley, Kingsley was furious. I could show you proof of his anger. Video footage of a scene he shot of Tara that was so violent he later tried to delete it."

Cheryl was shaking her head. Her mouth trembled and her features wrenched again. This time it looked like she might lose control.

Ashley did not give her a chance to speak. "Kingsley knew how to make a noose. Did you know that? One of your husband's many talents. And I bet you had a key to Tara's place, right? That explains how Kingsley got in and out and locked her deadbolt from the outside after he killed her."

Her phone rang. She swept it from her purse to silence it, but changed her mind when she saw the display. It was Zack. She pressed it to her ear.

"Hurry up." Zack's voice sounded strained. "He's coming."

"What?"

"Kingsley. He just called to remind me about some work I need to do on *Ass Bangers 22*. He said he was leaving the office. Going home."

Ashley felt a chill. She looked at Cheryl, who watched her with a mixture of concern and defiance.

"Hurry," he said again. The connection ended.

Cheryl said, "What's going on?"

"We need to go."

"I'm not going anywhere."

"Val's old enough to watch Katie."

"I know she is."

"Listen to me. I know you love your husband. But Tara's dead. You need to tell the police—"

"No. You listen to me." Cheryl took a step forward and this time it was Ashley who flinched. "You only know half of the story. Yes, Russell found out about the affair. And yes, he vented his anger in a horrible way. He took advantage of a situation and he hurt Tara. But he didn't murder her. Russell was with me Wednesday night. We were attending a fundraiser for Free Speech Now. There are at least a hundred people who saw us there."

"That doesn't matter. He could have hired someone to kill her, just like he hired Lombilla."

"You don't understand. When he came home on Monday, after shooting that scene, he spent the whole night throwing up. And on Tuesday, he begged Tara to forgive him. Begged. And because she's Tara, she forgave him."

"Maybe that's what he told you."

"It's what *Tara* told me. I was ready to leave him, believe me. Watching him throw up in the bathroom, hearing him describe what he'd done to her, I was ready to take the girls and go. But Tara convinced me not to. She told me that she had forgiven him and that if she could, then I could." Cheryl's breath hitched and tears welled in her eyes, then slid down her face. "She broke it off. On Tuesday. She told me we had to end it. That it wasn't right. That I had a family and that nothing was more important than that. That Russell was a good man. She broke up with me and then the next night, Wednesday night, she—"

"This is bullshit. Either Kingsley killed her, or he hired some goon—"

"Russell did not murder Tara."

Ashley lost control. The anger burst from her in a rush. *"How can you know that?"*

Cheryl hesitated, then took a deep breath. "Because he wouldn't ... he wouldn't do anything illegal right now. Russell is convinced he's being watched. That he's the subject of some kind of investigation. He's been like this for months. Totally paranoid. He doesn't take out the garbage without seeing an unmarked van. Here. Look." She crossed the room and yanked open the drawer of one of the night tables that flanked the bed. She pulled out the handset of a cordless phone and showed it to Ashley. The mouthpiece had been pried off. The circle of plastic dangled from wires. "He broke it, looking for bugs. Do you understand? Bugs. There is no way he would do anything illegal right now. He wouldn't jaywalk, much less hire a hitman."

Ashley stared at the mutilated phone. She thought about the FBI inspections. The meetings with lawyers.

"What about the *Through the Wringer* scene? He wasn't too paranoid to shoot that."

Cheryl shook her head and let out a sad laugh. "Are you kidding? He bought special software to delete it from his computer. He paid Carl Packer to deny working with him that night. I'm still not sure if he was throwing up because of a guilty conscience or because he was terrified that he would be arrested. But believe me, there is no way he would have committed a murder two nights later."

Ashley did not know what to say. Seconds passed. Finally, she said, "Here. Tara would want you to have these." And she pulled the stack of photos from her purse.

15

ZACK'S EYES widened in surprise when she climbed into the car without Cheryl. "Kingsley is going to be here in minutes," he said.

"Just drive."

"What happened? Where is she?"

"Kingsley didn't do it." She yanked the seatbelt across her chest. The sun was low in the sky and directly in front of them. She shaded her eyes. Even with the A/C on, the car was uncomfortably warm.

"All of the evidence points to him."

"He didn't do it. Let's go get something to eat. Okay? I'm tired and hungry."

Zack studied her for a moment, then shifted the car into drive. "What did Cheryl tell you?"

"She told me enough."

"Are you sure you can trust her? She may be lying to protect her husband."

"She's not." She looked at him and found his frustration touching. This wasn't his battle. He had barely known Tara. But he obviously cared. "Let's just get something to eat, okay?"

"You're upset. Are you sure you're up for a restaurant?"

"I'm sure."

"Because if you'd rather go somewhere quiet, my place isn't far."

This suggestion might have sounded like a pickup line coming from another man, but Zack sounded genuinely concerned.

"Let me guess," she said. "In addition to all of your other skills, you're a gourmet chef, too."

He threw her a sideways glance. The muscles in his jaw relaxed. "Only if you like frozen pizza." A second passed and then they both smiled. She felt some of her inner turmoil subside.

They drove in silence. She watched the sun descend. They drove to Reseda. Zack parked the Impala in front of a small, Spanish-style duplex. The street was quiet, lined with modest one- and two-family homes. A matronly Latina woman standing in front of the house lifted her head when they pulled up. They stepped out of the car. The woman abandoned a small flower garden and ambled toward them. Her face was wrinkled with concern.

"Your car is okay, no?"

"The Corvette?" Zack said. "It will be. I hope." He took Ashley's hand and brought her closer to the woman. "Maria, meet my friend Ashley. Ashley, this is Maria, my neighbor and landlord."

"Nice to meet you," Ashley said. "You have a beautiful garden."

Maria beamed. Zack led Ashley to the front door, unlocked it, and invited her inside. His place was a typical bachelor pad. The furniture was mismatched and clunky, with plenty of soft, comfortable places to sit, classic movie posters on the walls, and of course a big TV.

"Can't skimp on the necessities," he said. "Make yourself at home. Relax while I get the oven going. Then we'll talk this through."

"Talk it through?"

"Like Holmes and Watson."

"Right."

She sank into the overstuffed cushions of a couch that faced the TV. The noises that filtered back to her, a string of clangs and bumps that only a man in a kitchen could make, made her smile.

He returned and dropped onto the couch beside her. "Okay. What makes you so sure Kingsley didn't do it?"

She told him everything Cheryl had told her. When she

mentioned Kingsley's belief that he was under investigation and being watched, Zack leaned forward and the smile faded from his face.

"I knew the Feds were driving him crazy," he said, "but I didn't realize they were actively watching him."

"He's probably just paranoid."

"Maybe."

"Besides, it only matters that he thinks they are."

Zack seemed to mull that over, then nodded. "Kingsley is too smart to have murdered someone if he thought he was under surveillance."

Ashley pushed a stray strand of hair behind her ear. "I don't know why that disappoints me. Weird, right? But it does."

"You want closure. You want an end to this. It's natural."

"But Kingsley and I used to be close. We were friends. Him, me, Brewster ... Tara. Two years pass and I'm ready to accuse him of murder."

"A lot can change in two years. Maybe Kingsley has changed, and you sense that somehow."

"Maybe. What about Tara's laptop? Have you cracked the password yet?"

"I haven't had a chance. But I will."

The smell of pizza drifted into the room. They moved to the kitchen. Zack cleared a stack of magazines—Variety and Entertainment Weekly—from the kitchen table. Ashley sat down. The table wobbled when she rested her elbows on it, but she didn't care. Drooling was a real concern as she watched him deliver the pizza from the oven to the table. He carved the pie into slices with a steak knife.

"I used to have one of those pizza wheel things, but I lost it."

"I don't care. Just feed me."

He laughed and slid a slice onto a paper plate and placed it in front of her. "*Bon appetit.*"

She gobbled half of it down before the searing heat registered. Steam filled her mouth. She dropped the pizza and sucked in a breath. The roof of her mouth felt singed. She poked the ragged skin with her tongue. It took her a few seconds to realize that Zack was laughing at her. He held out a glass of ice water.

She took it and gulped. "Don't laugh at me."

"Sorry. I just ... you're funny."

She'd been called plenty of things—especially during her porn career—but funny had never been one of them.

"Hey." He took the water glass and rose from his chair. "Let me get you a beer."

"No. I mean, thanks, but I don't drink."

"Really?" He sat back down and lifted his own slice to his mouth.

"You look surprised," she said.

"Not really. I just didn't expect—"

"It's not a big deal."

"Okay."

She lifted her pizza to her mouth again. This time she ate more cautiously.

"So," he said, watching her chew, "what do we do now?"

She wiped her face with a napkin. "Now?"

"I have an extensive collection of films. Real ones, not, you know—"

"You want to watch a movie with me?"

"I mean, unless you're too tired."

She rose from her chair, and straddled his lap. He looked surprised at first, but when she lowered her mouth to his and kissed him, she felt his lips curve into a smile.

"I'm not tired."

"Oh," he said.

"But I'm not really in the mood for a movie."

"Fair enough."

She kissed him again. Ran her tongue along the smooth wall of his teeth, then pushed past them to the warmth of his tongue. The pain of her burned mouth was forgotten. His hands came up, traced the curves of her back and shoulders, and rose into her hair. The pressure of his fingers on the back of her neck sent a shiver through her body.

The tip of her nose touched his. Her mouth brushed his lips. "Is Zack your real name? If we're going to do this I need to know your real name." She was surprised by the huskiness in her own voice.

"It's Gabriel Robinson. Gabe."

"Gabe Robinson. I like that." She shifted on his lap. He groaned. Her teeth found his ear. She bit his earlobe, then kissed her way down his neck to the hollow of his throat, enjoying the taste of his skin. His pulse hummed against her lips. She kissed the ridge of his Adam's apple and worked the top button of his shirt open with her fingers.

His hands slid under her tank-top and moved slowly upward. Her stomach muscles fluttered when his fingers passed over her abdomen. He palmed her breasts. Her breathing came in uneven gasps.

She undid the final button on his shirt and parted it, then slid her hands under his white T-shirt. His breathing turned as erratic as hers. She hunted for the zipper on his fly and felt his hands scramble at her jeans. The house was quiet except for the sounds of their breathing and the rustle of their clothes. She got his fly open and tugged his jeans down his thighs. He was wearing maroon boxer-briefs.

"I think I have some condoms in my purse." She twisted around to look for her bag, then remembered she had left it in the TV room.

He kissed her. "I have a whole box in the bedroom."

He cupped her ass with both hands, then stood, lifting both of them from the chair. She draped her arms around his neck, happy to be carried. They walked that way to the staircase and up to the second floor. His bedroom door was open a crack. He kicked it the rest of the way, then took two lurching steps and tossed her onto the bed. She bounced once on the mattress.

He pulled off his shirt and T-shirt, then shrugged his jeans down his legs and kicked them off of his feet. When she started to unbutton her own clothes, he leaned forward and grabbed her hand.

"That's my job."

"Oh yeah?" She leaned back against the pillows.

He stripped her slowly and carefully, pausing to admire her. He kissed her throat, her breasts, her thighs. Her eyes drifted closed. The heat of his breath puffed between her legs. She shuddered.

Sometimes when she had sex with a man for the first time, she felt a need to perform. To live up to the Ashley Hale persona. To pose and tease and do things that looked better on video than they felt in real life. Tonight, she knew she could just close her eyes and be Ashley Latner.

He used his tongue and fingers until her back arched off the mattress. Then he was scrambling for the nightstand beside the bed. He rolled back to her with a box of Trojans in his hand. Together they tore it open.

Her whole body felt hot. She tried to climb on top of him, but he grabbed her wrists and flipped her back onto the bed.

He was slow and methodical and tender. She clung to him and met each thrust, lifting her hips from the bed. His hands gripped her ass. Her climax rolled through her like a hot wave. A moment later, his face scrunched and she could feel the pulse of his own orgasm. He rolled off of her with a satisfied, exhausted grunt.

"That was awesome," he said.

"So modest."

"I meant you. You're awesome."

She knocked the condom box off of the nightstand so she could see the clock. She stared at the digital display, shocked. They had made love for hours. It was 11:00 PM.

She twisted around to comment about this to Zack, but the slow, heavy rhythm of his breathing told her that he had already fallen asleep. She watched him, smiling at the peaceful, almost childlike expression on his face. Then she turned over to try to get some sleep herself.

She couldn't sleep. For one thing, her brain wouldn't settle down. Questions chirped in her mind, demanding her attention—questions about Zack and about Tara and about Kingsley, even about Sean. She rolled over, pressed her face into the pillow, but changing positions did nothing to quiet her mind.

The other thing keeping her awake was the temperature. Zack's bedroom was like a refrigerator. She had not noticed it before, but now that she was lying naked in bed, goose-bumps rose along her arms and a shiver swept through her body.

She climbed out of the bed, careful not to wake Zack. It was funny that she still thought of him as Zack, even after learning his real name. She had learned in the porn industry that the first name you associated with a person was often the one that stuck. She wondered if she would ever think of him as Gabe Robinson, or if he would always be Zack Cutter.

A dresser stood against one wall of his bedroom. She could see its shape as a ghostly outline in the darkness. The thought of a sweat-shirt packed in one of its drawers drew her across the chilly hard-wood floor. Guys like Zack always had a few sweatshirts in their wardrobes, right?

She started with the bottom drawer, but all she found were two neat piles of folded white T-shirts. The middle drawer held balled-up socks. The top one held underwear. Boxer-briefs in an assortment of colors. She was about to close the drawer and try his closet when something caught her attention.

There were three neat stacks of underwear, side by side, about four pairs of boxer-briefs to a stack. They smelled of fabric softener. What had caught her eye was the depth of the drawer. It looked shallow compared to the two below it. As a girl who had learned early not to trust her mother, she knew what this meant. She pushed her hands under Zack's boxer-briefs. The drawer had a false bottom.

All she could see of Zack in the darkness was a hazy lump on the bed. He did not appear to have changed position since she'd climbed off the mattress. She listened for the sound of his breathing. She heard slow inhalations, exhalations.

She returned her attention to the drawer.

16

ASHLEY HESITATED FOR A MOMENT, then pushed her hands past the neatly folded boxer-briefs to the false bottom of the drawer. It was made of cardboard. She probably would not have noticed it had she not constructed similar ones as a child. She slid her fingernails along the edges and pried it up. She tried to balance Zack's underwear on its surface, but a few pairs slid off. She placed the cardboard on top of the dresser and bent to retrieve them.

What was she doing?

She was invading his privacy—there was no question about that. It wasn't something she wanted to do. But the idea of a grown man hiding things in a secret drawer disturbed her. She would feel better after confirming that it was nothing sinister. A diary. Or maybe a really bad screenplay he was ashamed of but could not bare to throw away.

She risked another glance at the bed. In the dim light, she could see his shoulders rise and fall in time with his breathing.

She straightened up and peered into the drawer. The false bottom had been fitted in place to conceal a stack of paper. It was difficult to see details in the darkness. She picked up the top sheet, intending to raise it to the pale light filtering past the window shade, but her breath caught in her throat when she caught a glimpse of the page beneath it. The second sheet in the stack was recognizable even in the dark. It was a glossy eight-by-ten photo of Tara. A publicity still, the kind Tara had taken with her to sign at conventions and appearances. Ashley had seen it a thousand times.

Her eyes moved from the photo to the sheet of paper in her hand. It was a fire-exit floor-plan. Just like the one posted on the back of her motel room door. This one had not come from a motel. She recognized the arrangement of the units, and the numbers. It was Tara's apartment building, and her unit—2F—had been circled.

Oh shit.

All of a sudden, the air felt cooler. She hugged herself. Her clothes lay on the floor near the foot of the bed, where Zack had tossed them. Her jeans formed a small pyramid next to her shirt and underwear. She took a step toward the pile.

Zack turned and kicked the sheets away from his body. She froze. Moonlight traced the length of his naked leg, pale and lean and muscular. She held her breath. Zack smacked his lips. One second passed. Another. His breathing returned to its slow, even rhythm.

She let her breath slide out of her lungs. Approaching the bed and retrieving her clothes no longer seemed like such a good idea.

Run. Get the hell out of here.

She couldn't. Not yet. Not until she saw what else was in the drawer. She stuck her hands back in. Underneath the photo, she found a paper-clipped collection of AVN articles. Words jumped out at her as she flipped through the pages. *Pinnacle. Rob Rourke. Tara Rose.*

Beneath these pages was a Web site print-out, but it was not Tara's.

It was Ashley's.

She had taken it down when she left the industry. But she knew that sometimes even deleted Web sites could be accessed. And Zack had already demonstrated his skill at recovering deleted files.

She did not bother to put the false bottom back in the drawer. The sound of Zack's breathing remained steady, but that did not mean that he would not wake up at any moment. He had not bothered to close the door in his haste to get her into bed. She slipped through the doorway now, and followed the dim hallway to the stairs. She padded down them as quietly as she could. Her purse was in the TV room. Her phone was in her purse.

She grabbed the phone and almost dropped it before she pressed the button to wake it up.

The screen remained black.

She pushed the power button. Nothing happened.

The battery was dead.

She searched the room for a land-line. There wasn't one. She hurried to the kitchen, but did not find a phone in there, either.

She gripped the edge of the kitchen counter, unsure of what to do. The smell of cold pizza turned her stomach.

Maria, the neighbor.

Maria would have a phone.

She returned to the TV room with the hope of finding a blanket to wrap around her naked body. Zack kept a few pillows propped on the couch, but there was no blanket. She chewed her lip and tried to ignore her racing heartbeat.

He must have a coat closet.

She found it in the entryway. It had a flimsy sliding door. She edged it an inch sideways on its track. The squeak that emerged made her stop. In her ears, it had sounded like a shriek. She could not imagine Zack sleeping through it. But it was too late to stop now. She gritted her teeth and ground the door to the end of the track.

Coats and jackets hung from cheap wire hangers. Her hands went to a raincoat. It hung near the center of the closet, crammed between a leather jacket and a windbreaker. The raincoat was of the long, tan, trench-coat type. She pulled it off of its hanger and shrugged her arms through the sleeves. The coat felt natural against her bare skin, and she had to shake her head at the irony. A naked chick in a trench coat. It was a porn cliché.

She twisted the front door's deadbolt. It disengaged with a quiet *thunk*. The air outside felt steamy after the chill of Zack's house.

Maria's door was ten feet away. She skipped barefoot over moist grass and knocked. First quietly, then with more urgency, pounding on the wood.

Come on.

A light bloomed above her. She looked up, but her relief turned to dread when she saw that the glow came from the wrong side of the duplex. *Zack's* side. A shadow passed across his window.

A second later, Maria opened the door. She squinted at Ashley. Ashley gripped the raincoat's belt and cinched it tighter.

"I need to use your phone. Please. It's an emergency."

"Zack is hurt?"

"Please. I don't have time—"

"*Si, si.*" Maria took Ashley's hand and drew her into an entryway that was a mirror image of Zack's. Ashley locked the door, then let Maria lead the way to the kitchen. Ashley assumed that it also matched the one in Zack's unit, but she wouldn't have known that by looking. Zack's kitchen had been bare, while Maria's overflowed. Racks of spices. Vegetables. Breads. The room smelled like cilantro. Maria plucked a cordless phone from its charger beside a bowl of grapes and handed it to her.

Ashley punched 9-1-1 with a trembling finger.

"9-1-1. What is your emergency?"

She heard the click of a key in a lock. Maria heard it, too. She looked at Ashley and said, "I will go to help him."

Ashley grabbed her arm. "Zack has a key?"

"Of course."

"This is 9-1-1." A nasally, impatient voice.

"I need help," Ashley said. "I'm trapped in a house with a murderer. The address is—" She looked at Maria, but the woman only gaped at her. "Damn it, just trace the call!" She dropped the phone onto the kitchen counter and started opening drawers. The operator's voice continued to leak from the speaker. Ashley ignored it. "Maria, I need your biggest knife."

A door creaked. She heard footsteps.

"My biggest—"

"Knife, Maria. I need a knife."

Ashley's hands scattered silverware in the drawer under the counter. There were butter knives, but nothing sharper. She opened the drawer beneath it. Placemats, a can opener, a corkscrew. She grabbed the corkscrew and whirled around as Zack stepped into the kitchen.

He had not bothered to dress. He wore the maroon boxer-shorts and nothing else. The broad, flat muscles of his chest gleamed in the pale light. He held a gun. A black, ugly semi-automatic.

"You shouldn't have gone through my things."

"Don't come any closer." She brandished the corkscrew.

Maria looked from one of them to the other. Her expressed shifted from confusion to fear.

"Put that thing down," he said. "Let's talk."

"You can talk all you want. I already called the police."

He flinched, but managed to keep the gun level. "Maria, please tell me she's bluffing."

Maria shook her head. "She make call."

"Fuck."

"Were you planning to hang me, too?" Ashley said. "Or did you come up with something more creative?"

Sirens whined, a faint sound that quickly grew louder. She offered a silent thank-you to the LAPD. The cops had proven their worth after all.

Zack's eyes filled with uncertainty. He glanced at his gun, held at arms length and aimed at Ashley's chest. His arm wavered.

"If you're still pointing that thing at me when the police show up, they'll probably shoot you in the head," Ashley said. "You should drop it while you still can."

"Put away the corkscrew first."

"Are you afraid I'm going to lunge across the kitchen and bury it in your heart?"

"The thought crossed my mind."

The idea held some appeal, but not as much as she would have thought. Maybe it was because of their recent intimacy—or maybe she just wasn't bloodthirsty enough—but she did not want to see him dead. Led away in handcuffs, but not dead.

"Fine." Slowly, she slid Maria's drawer open and returned the corkscrew to its proper place.

Zack nodded and his finger moved along the side of the weapon. Engaging the safety. She let out a pent-up breath. The sum total of her experience with guns consisted of a few months of going to a firing range with one of her mother's more interesting boyfriends, back when she was fourteen. But she knew that with the safety on, the gun couldn't fire.

Zack crouched. Placed the gun on the floor. Slowly straightened up.

"I wasn't going to hurt you. I only brought the gun to stop you from calling the police."

"How'd that work out for you?"

A bang sounded in the entryway, followed by the thunder of shoes on hardwood. Zack raised his arms above his head as a phalanx of uniformed officers streamed into the kitchen and surrounded him.

———

AN HOUR LATER, Ashley sat in an interview room at the Devonshire Community Police Station. If it was not the same room in which she'd met Detective Collins, it might as well have been. Same battered steel table, same uncomfortable chair, same Lysol smell in the air. She waited for almost an hour, rubbing the scraped surface of the chair's metal armrests. It was not exactly a hero's welcome. At least they had given her a change of clothes. The LAPD sweatsuit was three sizes too big, but it was warm and it covered her a lot better than Zack's raincoat.

The door opened. Ashley was only mildly surprised to see Detective Heather Collins. Judging by her haggard expression, the detective had been roused from sleep for the occasion. She held two cardboard cups, one in each hand, and steam drifted up from them. The smell of coffee drifted across the table.

Collins put one cup in front of Ashley, then settled into the seat across from her and took a gulp from her own. "You don't give up, do you?"

Ashley thought she detected some grudging respect in the woman's voice.

"Tara wouldn't have given up on me."

Collins nodded. "I'm not even going to ask why you were wearing nothing but a raincoat."

"I appreciate that."

The sleeves of the LAPD sweatshirt extended almost to the tips of Ashley's fingers. She pushed them up, a gesture that made her feel like a child. The material was soft and warm.

Collins turned her pale face to the camera mounted near the ceiling. She nodded her head to whoever was watching them. Ashley thought her expression looked even more tired and put-upon than usual.

The door opened and Zack walked into the room.

Ashley had been reaching for her coffee cup. Her hand jerked and knocked the cup over. Hot coffee spilled across the table. She stood up, scrambled backward. Her chair screeched against the floor and then toppled on its side. She backpedaled until her shoulders hit the cold wall behind her.

He was no longer wearing handcuffs. In fact, the police must have sent someone back to his house to fetch him some clothes, because he was wearing a pair of jeans and a fresh, button-down shirt. He even had a watch on his wrist.

"What the hell is going on?" Ashley said.

She looked to Collins, but the detective was busy mopping up coffee with a paper napkin. Zack took another step into the room. He held his hands out in front of him.

"This man is a murderer!"

"No, he isn't," Collins said. She balled the napkin in her fist.

"Agent Foster, you asked us to hold her here so you could explain yourself. I suggest you hurry up."

"Agent Foster?"

Zack closed the distance between them and tried to take her hand. She circled away from him.

"I work for the FBI. I couldn't tell you, Ashley."

"He couldn't tell us either, apparently," Collins said with dry sarcasm.

Zack raised a hand to his forehead and massaged the skin at his temples. "Could you give us a few minutes alone, Detective?"

"Sure." Collins jammed the soggy napkin into her empty coffee cup and headed for the door.

Before she could open it, Zack added, "And turn off the video feed. Please."

Collins did not respond, but she closed the door behind her with a little more force than was necessary.

17

"I'M SORRY," Zack said. "This isn't the way I wanted you to find out."

"Find out what? That you're a lying, manipulative bastard?"

"I only told you what was necessary to maintain my cover."

"Was fucking me necessary, too?"

His face recoiled as if he'd been slapped. "Ashley."

"Just ... just leave me alone."

"My feelings—our connection—that was real."

"*Our connection.* Right."

"Listen, can we sit down? Have a conversation?" He righted her overturned chair. The metal legs hit the floor with a *clang* that reverberated, then faded to silence. He took a seat in the chair Collins had vacated. Ashley didn't move. She hugged herself in the oversized LAPD sweatshirt.

"Three minutes ago, you thought I was a maniacal killer," Zack said. "A liar is a step up from that, right?"

She watched him warily. He had a point. She stepped closer to the table and sat in the offered chair. At least she would get the truth out of him. "You want to have a conversation? Let's start with you telling me your name. Your real one this time. Your *real* real one."

"James Foster."

She tried to apply the name to his face. It didn't fit. "I liked Gabe Robinson better."

"Really? I'm partial to Zack Cutter. Sounds bad-ass."

He smiled—the loopy grin she had come to know so well in the last few days—and she felt her defenses weaken and she hated herself for it. She ran her fingers over the tabletop. The metal surface was still slick and smelled of coffee.

"What else do you want to know?" he said.

"I'm guessing you didn't really learn about investigatory technique by writing screenplays?"

"I was trained at Quantico."

"And your hacking skills?"

"A two-year stint in Cyber Crimes."

"Do you really have a father in northern California who works in computer security?"

"My dad lives in Connecticut. He's a tax lawyer."

She traced random patterns in the film of coffee. Her fingertip squeaked. "Where did you learn to edit digital video? You must be pretty good, for Kingsley to hire you."

"The Bureau gave me a crash course. Part of my prep work for this assignment."

"And what exactly *is* this assignment?"

"That's the question, isn't it?"

"Yeah," she said. "What's the answer?"

His tongue poked along his lower lip. He looked at the ceiling, then at her, then at his hands. "Ashley, I really shouldn't be telling you any of this. You understand that, right?"

"But you are. Why stop now?"

He leaned forward. "Let me put it this way. If Kingsley Nast thinks he's being watched, he's right. I'm the one who's watching him."

"What did he do?"

"Nothing I've been able to prove. In fact, the taskforce was debating whether to pull the plug on my investigation when you showed up in LA. I convinced them that you might be the key to unearthing Kingsley's dirty secrets."

"Like murder?"

"Like murder."

"But he didn't murder Tara. We know that now. He's innocent."

Zack shook his head. "Kingsley is involved with some very bad people. Just because he didn't kill Tara doesn't mean he's not a murderer. You were friends with Calvin Burkes, right? Known in the industry as Brewster?"

She felt a cold weight in her chest. "King said Brewster moved to New York to pursue an independent film project."

"That's the story. But no one has been able to find him. Nine months ago, Brewster disappeared off the face of the earth."

"And you think Kingsley killed him? That's crazy. They were inseparable."

The coldness in her chest did not lessen. It was hard to imagine Brewster leaving the industry. He loved his work.

"We think Brewster saw something he wasn't supposed to see," Zack said. "Either Kingsley killed him, or one of Kingsley's new business associates did."

"What are you talking about? What new business associates?"

Zack opened his mouth, then hesitated again.

"You said you wanted to explain," Ashley said. "I'm listening."

"I know. It's just ... it isn't a short story. I don't know how closely you've been following the industry lately, but the shift in demand from DVDs to streaming and downloadable video has been pretty drastic."

She nodded. "Kingsley told me that. The day of the funeral."

"Well, Tyrant pretty much built its business on DVD distribution. I mean, Kingsley has experimented with online partnerships here and there, but ninety-nine percent of Tyrant's revenue comes from shiny little discs. About a year ago, distributors started to balk at the prices they used to be happy to pay. Tyrant's profits took a dive. To save the company, Kingsley tried to expand into higher quality content. Big features, shot in HD and distributed on Blu-Ray. But big features require big budgets, real sets, scripts. So he looked for investors."

"And who did he find?"

"You mean, *who found him*. The Kazakov syndicate. Organized crime. Let's leave it at that."

She almost pressed him for details, then thought better of it. Kingsley was in league with the mob. That was the gist. Kingsley had gotten into trouble and he had killed Brewster. The cold feeling expanded and she tasted vomit in the back of her throat.

Zack watched her but said nothing. The nausea faded.

"None of this has anything to do with Tara," she said.

"Apparently not. But I didn't know that when I started helping you."

"Helping? Is that what you call it?"

"I shouldn't have slept with you. Not under false pretenses. That was wrong."

"You think?"

"I'm sorry. I used bad judgment. I let myself develop feelings for you and—"

She scraped her chair backward and stood up. "Can I leave now?"

"Ashley—"

"I'm tired. I want to go back to my motel room. What time is it, anyway?"

"First we need to talk about what you're going to do with the information you learned tonight."

"You're worried I'm going to rat you out to Kingsley?"

"Not intentionally. But maintaining cover—protecting the consistency of a fabricated identity—it's hard. One slipup and everything is lost."

"I lived as a fabricated identity for how many years when I was Ashley Hale? I think I've got it down."

"Ashley—"

"Goodnight, James."

She knocked on the door to be let out.

———

AT 3:00 AM, the Tyrant parking lot was desolate. Even the fast food place across the street had closed its drive-through window for the night. Detective Collins pulled her Crown Vic to a stop next to the Fiesta. The rental car had been waiting there since Ashley had abandoned it this morning to pursue Lombilla's Hyundai. She thought of how much had changed in one day.

"Thanks for the ride." She unbuckled her seatbelt.

"It looks so inconspicuous," Collins said. Ashley followed her gaze to the warehouse, its blocky edifice outlined in moonlight. "You'd never know it was a porn production company."

"Yeah." Ashley was in no mood to talk about the industry, especially not with Collins. She reached for the door handle and pulled the latch. The door popped open. Humid air and the smell of moist asphalt filled the car. She was about to climb out when a thought struck her. "Tell me something."

Collins glanced at the dashboard clock. "It's late—"

"If you were investigating my sister's murder—I know you're not, but if you were—what would you do next? I've talked to Tara's neighbors. I went to Pinnacle and talked to people there. I questioned Tara's ex-boyfriend and her ex-girlfriend. I just ... I don't know what to do next."

She felt her throat constrict and knew she was close to tears. She turned toward the open door and sucked in a lungful of warm air. She did not want the detective to see her cry. She needn't have worried. When she turned back, Collins had her eyes closed and her head tilted back against the headrest. In the glow from the dashboard, her pale face looked luminescent.

"You want my advice?"

"Yeah."

"Call your mother. You're both in a lot of pain. You lost a sister and a daughter. You need to work through your grief together. Tara committed suicide. You need to deal with that. You need to accept it. Playing detective is not going to bring her back to life."

Ashley was too tired—physically and emotionally—to argue. She climbed out of the car. Collins watched her. Before closing the door,

Ashley stuck her head in and thanked the detective again for the ride.

"You're going to ignore my advice, aren't you?" Collins said.

"Pretty much."

Collins sighed. "Drive safe."

————

THE FIRST THING she did back in her motel room was plug her phone into its charger. Then she collapsed onto the bed and slept.

She woke early and opened the blinds. Sunlight filled the room, but it did not lift her spirits. Thursday morning. Five days had passed since she had learned of Tara's death, and in that time, what had she accomplished? Something tugged at the back of her mind. Something she had learned. Something important. What?

She checked her phone, made sure it was fully charged, and dropped it into her purse. Then she reconsidered and fished it out again, remembering Detective Collins's advice.

Gail answered on the fourth ring. "Ashley?"

"Yeah, it's me. I just ... I thought I'd call and see how you're holding up."

"I'm walking out the door, actually. I have a meeting."

She heard a thump on Gail's side of the connection, then the sound of a car starting. She gripped the bedspread and squeezed the spongy comforter in her fingers. "What's going on?"

"Remember when I told you that Tara was planning to change her will? Well, my lawyer was able to convince Rob Rourke's lawyer that a settlement would be in everybody's best interest. We're finalizing the deal today."

"Why didn't you tell me about this?"

There was silence on the line. "I was going to tell you—"

"He's paying you off," Ashley said. "That's what you're telling me. Rob is paying you to go away, and you're—"

"It's a *settlement*, Ashley. It's in everybody's best interest."

Ashley opened the closet and pulled out Tara's suit. She clamped the phone between her shoulder and ear and got dressed. "Where is the meeting?"

———

SHE FOLLOWED Gail's directions to a high-rise in Century City. The lobby was marble and glass. A group of important-looking people strolled past her, some talking into phones, the others conversing with each other in low voices. A scent of shoe polish and leather lingered in their wake. She approached the security counter. A directory indicated that the law firm of Weldon Katz & Bishop occupied the top eight floors, but when she gave the security guard the name of Gail's lawyer—Alfred Mueller—he told her to take the elevator to the second floor. Apparently, Mueller was unaffiliated with the big firm upstairs. Not a surprise, considering Gail's resources. Ashley stepped out of the elevator into a modest office. A receptionist escorted her to a small conference room where Gail and Rob, and two men Ashley assumed were their lawyers, faced each other across a table. A white pitcher and four glasses of orange juice stood on the table, but the glass in front of Gail's lawyer was the only one that had been touched.

"Excuse us for a moment," Gail's lawyer said.

He and Gail rose from the table and joined Ashley in the hallway. The man extended his hand. "Alfred Mueller. You can call me Alf."

"Nice to meet you."

"Ashley, you don't need to be here," Gail said.

Ashley glanced past them into the conference room. Rob glared back at her. She turned her attention back to her mother. "You're making a mistake, Gail. If Tara wanted you to inherit her half of the company, then you owe it to her to fight for that. Don't just ... take a payoff and slink away."

"Hey," Alf said. "No one's slinking. I've negotiated a *very* attractive deal, believe me."

"What do I know about running a talent agency?" Gail said. She laughed awkwardly. "I'm better off taking the money."

"How much money?" Ashley said.

Alf lowered his voice. "One hundred-thousand dollars."

"It's not enough. Jesus, you're giving him exactly what he wants. Full ownership of Pinnacle. Tara created that company!"

"Please, lower your voice," Alf said. He leaned closer to her. She smelled citrus on his breath. "Trust me, your mother is lucky to be getting anything. We have no evidence besides your mother's word that Tara intended to change her will. If this case went to court, we would get creamed. Your mother would get nothing and possibly might even have to pay Rourke's costs."

"Give me a couple hours." Ashley looked at Alf, then at Gail. "Delay the deal until after lunch. I'll find evidence."

"How are you going to do that?" Alf said.

"I have Tara's laptop. A friend of mine is working to crack its password protection. Once he does, I'll be able to search her hard drive."

Alf looked dubious. He turned to Gail. "It's your call."

Gail's nostrils flared. Ashley could hear the air rustling in and out of them. "I guess a two-hour delay wouldn't hurt. But Ashley, if you don't find anything, I'm signing the papers."

Ashley nodded. "Don't worry."

She backtracked down the hallway. The receptionist was no longer at her desk. She must have gone to the bathroom or to the coffee maker. Ashley hurried to the elevator and pushed the button and waited. She heard footsteps behind her. She turned, expecting to see the receptionist returning to her desk.

Instead, Rob swaggered toward her.

"I didn't expect to see you this morning," he said. Ashley jabbed the elevator button again. "I thought you and Gail hated each other."

"Nothing brings people together like a common enemy."

"Is that how you think of me?" He raised an eyebrow. "Maybe I should ask my lawyer to seek restraining orders on both of you. I came here to put an end to Gail's harassment."

"You came here to bribe her."

"Some people only respond to money. Maybe you're more like your mother than I thought. Do you want a handout, too?"

"I want what Tara wanted."

He laughed. "You're really something, Ashley. You disappear from Tara's life for two years, then after she croaks you come back and act like you're the fucking authority on what she wanted. What Tara wanted was for Pinnacle to succeed. And it is succeeding. Our girls are the highest paid in the industry. And we've become so much more than a talent agency. Because of me, we're into ancillary revenue streams now." She watched him savor the buzzword.

"Pinnacle is Tara's company. Not yours."

"Tara left Pinnacle in my hands for a reason."

"The only reason I see is that she was murdered before she could change her will."

"She wasn't murdered. She committed suicide. And if she'd wanted to change her will, she had plenty of time to do it before she offed herself."

Ashley raised her hand to slap him. He caught her hand and bent her fingers backward. Pain flashed up her arm. She twisted and tried to yank her hand away from him. He tightened his grip and turned her around and shoved her against the steel doors of the elevator. Cold metal pressed her cheek.

"What the hell do I need to do to get you and your junkie mother off of my back?"

"I don't know, Rob. Kill us?"

Someone coughed behind them. Rob let go of her. She felt a wave of relief. Ashley turned, massaging her fingers. The receptionist stared at them. A second later, the elevator chimed and the doors opened. Ashley backed into the car but kept her eyes on Rob.

"I never understood what Tara saw in you," she said.

He tugged at his lapels and straightened his suit jacket. "Different strokes for different folks, Ash." He smiled.

The elevator doors closed and she descended.

18

STANDING in the lobby of the office building, she called Zack. He answered after one ring. "Ashley? I'm glad you called."

Her muscles unclenched and a wave of relief washed over her. She hated him for that. "Have you found a way around the password on my sister's laptop?"

"I broke through about fifteen minutes ago. I've been debating whether to call you. I thought, you know, you might not want to—"

"I need to see that computer *now*. It's an emergency."

"An emergency?"

"I'm in Century City." She walked out the door and scanned the street around the building. Amidst the towers and parking garages, she spotted a café. She watched a group of men in suits walk through the entrance. She gave Zack the name of the place and the number on the door. "How quickly can you get here?"

"What kind of emergency, Ashley?"

Even over the phone, she could hear the concern in his voice. It made her cringe. "Relax. I'm fine. It's my mother. She's about to accept a payoff from Rob Rourke. I need to find evidence that Tara intended to change her will. Gail agreed to give me two hours. So, you need to hurry."

"I'm leaving now."

––––––––

THE CAFÉ SMELLED like fresh bread, vinaigrette salad dressing, and French fries. They ordered coffee, no food. Zack placed Tara's laptop on the table and turned it to face her.

"The password was *All-In*," he said. "Was Tara a gambler? Because that could be significant." He saw her shaking her head. "Not a gambler?"

"*All In* was the title of her first video. And it wasn't about the World Series of Poker."

"Ah." He sipped his coffee. "Too bad. The gambling angle opened up some new possibilities."

Ashley looked at the PC. Zack had already turned it on and the desktop had loaded. She clicked to the Documents folder.

"I hope you don't mind," he said, "but I already reviewed the contents of her hard drive. I didn't find anything that seemed relevant to her death."

"And her will?" She heard him sigh. She looked up from the screen. "What? You found something?"

"I found something."

"And?"

"Let me put it this way. If you want to challenge Rob in court, you probably don't want to see it."

"All I want is the truth."

"Okay." He pulled the laptop back across the table. She listened to his fingertip tap the touchpad, then looked around at the lunching businessmen. There were almost as many computers, smart-phones, and tablets at the tables as there were people. At least they fit in. "Here," he said. He swung the computer around so she could see the screen again.

He had opened Microsoft Outlook. One of Tara's e-mails was displayed.

"After you called, I did a quick search for e-mails containing the word 'change.' I didn't find anything about changing a will, but I found this. It's an e-mail from Tara to Cheryl Grayson, saved in Tara's Sent folder. Look at the date."

"About two weeks before Tara's death." Ashley thought about the timeline Cheryl had given her. "That was way before Kingsley discovered the affair. Way before Tara broke off the relationship."

"Right."

She pulled the laptop closer. It was warm to the touch.

CHERYL,

*W*HAT *A DAY. I definitely need to see you tonite and get one of your patented back massages. ;-) Seriously. I just got home and guess who I found waiting for me in my apartment? For the third time this week! Why did I ever give her a key? Talk about a moment of weakness. Now I need to get my locks changed. Ever since Gail got a whiff of Pinnacle's success, she's been trying to wheedle money from me. I will never give that woman a cent. God, I wish Ashley were here. She'd know what to do. Anyway, I'll see you later.*

LOVE,

Tara

ZACK'S GAZE was fixed on her. "You okay?"

"No."

Gail had claimed that she and Tara reconciled, and Ashley had believed her. Why? There had been a photo in Tara's apartment, but it had been a portrait of Gail, not a picture of the two of them. Had she seen any real evidence of a reconciliation? Kingsley had helped Gail with the funeral arrangements, but that could have been because Cheryl did not trust Gail with the responsibility. If the reconciliation never happened, then neither had the lunch at Olive

Garden. That meant that Tara had never pointed out her stalker to Gail. There probably never was a stalker. And there had never been an intention to change the will, either.

It was all a big lie.

A cash register *chinged* at the front of the café. Zack put his elbows on the table and leaned toward her. She could tell by his expression that he had already come to the same conclusions. "When you called the police on me, I decided to make the best of the situation. I reviewed Detective Collins's case file. There wasn't much there, but one piece of information struck me as interesting. Your mother took out a life insurance policy on Tara six months ago."

"You mean, Gail received money when Tara died? What if Gail is, oh God—"

"No. Whoever killed Tara went to a lot of trouble to make it look like a suicide. That's the last thing Gail would do. Life insurance companies won't pay death benefits if the person commits suicide within two years of the policy taking effect. It's called a suicide clause."

Ashley let out a breath. "That explains why she called me and asked me to come to LA. And why she told me Tara had a stalker. She wanted me to convince the police that Tara had been murdered. That way, she could collect the insurance money." She shook her head, disgusted. "She's been manipulating me from day one."

"Not just you," Zack said. "How much money did you say Rob Rourke offered to pay her?"

"I need to go."

"Wait. I was hoping we could talk. About us." He put his hand over hers. His grip was gentle, but pain flared where Rob had pulled her fingers back.

She slipped her hand free. "I appreciate your help. I really do." She slung her bag over her shoulder. "But there is no us."

———

SHE RUSHED BACK to the law firm, but she was too late. Rob and his lawyer were gone. So was Gail. The receptionist informed Ashley that

Alf was out to lunch with another client. She seemed confused by Ashley's questions. The agreement had been signed minutes after Ashley had left the building, she said.

Gail had never intended to give Ashley two hours to find evidence on Tara's laptop, because she had known that none existed.

And now, Gail was a hundred-thousand dollars richer.

———

BACK IN HER MOTEL ROOM, Ashley tried to distract herself with TV and fast food. The sitcoms she'd once found funny failed to make her laugh today, and her Taco Bell dinner sat mostly uneaten in its plastic bag. Tara's suit lay on the bed beside her. She had intended to borrow an ironing board from the kid at the front desk, but that had been hours ago and she had not moved. The day darkened beyond her window.

A knock at the door made her jump. She climbed off of the bed, crossed the room, and looked through the peephole. It was Zack, blurry and distorted by the fisheye lens. She opened the door.

He sniffed the air. "Fire sauce?"

"What are you doing here?"

"We started an investigation. I'd like to complete it."

"There's nothing to complete. Gail was lying about the stalker. That means Tara probably *did* commit suicide."

"You don't believe that," Zack said.

"We've already followed every lead. The black Hyundai, the stalker, Kingsley and Rob. We've learned nothing."

"We've put together a fairly detailed picture of the last few days of Tara's life. I wouldn't dismiss that as nothing."

Ashley shook her head. Something was tugging at her brain again, some detail that her conscious mind had dismissed but that her unconscious mind had tagged as important. She tried but could not grasp it.

Zack turned sideways to edge past her into the room. Reluctantly, she let him in, then closed the door. When she turned, she felt a flash of embarrassment. A pile of dirty laundry covered the desk chair. Zack looked at Tara's suit on the bed, then at the Taco Bell bag.

"There's something we missed," Zack said. "There has to be."

"You're the expert." She turned off the TV as she walked past it.

"Let's think about motive again. Who had a reason to want Tara dead?"

"Haven't we been over this already?"

"Let's go over it again. Sometimes, when you repeat something enough times, it changes in a useful way."

"I guess they taught you that at Quantico?"

"Yeah, they did. But I've also seen it in the field."

"In the field," she said. The law enforcement jargon still seemed wrong coming out of Zack Cutter's mouth, like dialogue in a badly-cast cop movie.

"Fine," she said. "Gail made up the story about the stalker, so that's probably a dead end. Kingsley wouldn't have killed her, because he thought he was being watched. Rob had an alibi, plus now it turns out he had no motive to kill her anyway. Tara never intended to change her will."

"Good," Zack said. "We can rule those people out. Remember what I said at Sal's? First, you gather information. You come up with a list of theories. Then, you shoot them down one by one, until only the right one is left standing."

"That's great," Ashley said, "except that we've shot down *all* of the theories. No, wait. That's not true." She started to pace in front of him. "Rob said that an angry drug dealer might have come after Tara. I thought he was just trying to deflect suspicion from himself. But Cheryl told me that Tara was campaigning against drug use in the industry, even offering to pay for rehab in some instances."

Zack nodded. "When I was looking at the e-mails on Tara's computer, I saw something about a drug dealer. I was focused on her will, so I didn't think much of it at the time, but now...."

"What did it say?"

"It was an e-mail from Selena Drake. Tara had asked Selena where the girls were getting their drugs. Selena's reply was something like, 'How would I know? I already told you I'm not into that stuff.' It's difficult to judge tone in an e-mail, but she seemed defensive."

"You think the e-mail is significant?"

"I think we should talk to Selena."

Zack pulled out his phone. She guessed by his clipped tone that he was talking to someone at the FBI. A moment later he ended his call and said, "You better change your clothes."

"For what?"

"Selena Drake is feature dancing at Gloss."

"Tonight?"

He looked at his watch. "Gloss is in North Hollywood. If we leave now—"

"The FBI keeps tabs on Selena Drake's dance calendar?"

He sighed. "I asked them to run a search, try to locate her."

"Okay. Whatever."

She pulled a skirt and top from her suitcase and went into the bathroom. She fixed her hair. Applied fresh makeup. Gloss was a classy place—for a strip club. If she expected Selena to feel comfortable talking to her there, she would need to fit in. She dressed, then studied her reflection.

When she stepped out of the bathroom, Zack was looking down at the floor, his face pensive. She hunted for a pair of heels that complemented her outfit, fit her feet into them. Zack was watching her now. She said, "What?"

"Nothing. I— You look amazing."

"Well, enjoy the view. It's all you're going to get."

He pulled keys from his pocket. "I'll drive."

"I don't think so."

They took her car this time. He did not protest when she climbed behind the wheel. Whether he sensed her need to take back some control, or whether he just didn't feel like arguing, she didn't know. Or care.

19

GLOSS WAS JUST like Ashley remembered it—dark and vast, with high vaulted ceilings that lent the place a cavernous feel. Speakers and lights dipped from the ceiling like stalactites, while couches, chairs, and cocktail tables divided the floor into a series of paths that twisted around the three raised runways. Music thumped from speakers in every direction, the bass turned way up.

Zack started to shoulder past clumps of men. He was moving toward the center stage, a long runway sporting three poles. Ashley had a better idea. She took his arm and led him in the other direction. They circled around to the rear of the club, which was elevated and gave them a better vantage point to scan the room for Selena.

"You seem to know this place well," he said. She had to lean close to him to hear his voice over the rumbling bass-line.

"Don't pretend you didn't run some kind of background check on me," she said. "You know I used to feature at strip clubs."

He flashed her a cautious smile. "Ashley—"

"Just find Selena so we can talk to her and get out of here."

Since leaving this life behind her, she had not missed stripping, but neither had she forgotten the rush of striding across a stage in a g-string and platform heels. Just being here, inhaling the familiar strip club odors of baby powder and perfume, stirred a kind of nostalgia.

The dancers grinding and pole-dancing on the club's three stages were strangers to her. She scanned the floor, looking for Selena among the crowd. As her eyes adjusted to the dark, she picked out at least fifteen strippers moving among the tables and couches, trying to entice patrons to buy lap dances and trips to the VIP room. She didn't see Selena.

"Are you sure your FBI buddies know what they're talking about?" she asked Zack.

"She's here somewhere." He sounded confident, but she saw creases of concern around his eyes. "She wouldn't flake on an appearance. She's not the type. Too ambitious."

A Beyoncé song faded. Ashley watched a ripple cascade across the floor as strippers rose from men's laps all over the room. Wads of cash changed hands.

"Maybe she's in the dressing room," she said.

"It's possible—" The rest of Zack's response was obliterated by an explosion of music that Ashley felt as a physical pressure against her eardrums. She recognized the harsh guitar chords. *Antichrist Superstar*. Not exactly a burlesque classic, but she had done enough dancing to recognize its potential. Another ripple crossed the floor, but this time it was the men who were standing up. All attention focused on the center stage.

Selena Drake strutted down the runway. Hoots and cheers and whistles and pounding shoes drowned out the first few verses of Marilyn Manson's nineties anthem. Selena wore a black microskirt that barely covered her crotch and a black bra and black high-heeled boots. She smiled at the crowd. The noise swelled.

Ashley glanced at Zack. His stare was riveted to Selena's body and his usually loopy grin had gone slack.

Selena circled the pole a few times, touched it with an outstretched fingertip, teased it. Her legs seemed impossibly long, her waist impossibly slim. She cupped her breasts, lifted the bra partly off of them, and then pressed the cups back in place. She approached the pole, hooked a leg around it, and jumped into the air. Then she dropped in a slow, controlled spin until she was sitting on the stage floor.

She rolled away from the pole. On her back, she arched her body and hooked her thumbs under the waistline of the miniskirt. She pushed the skirt—slowly—past her thighs, over her knees, down her boot-clad calves. When her legs were free, she raised them straight above her and spread them in a V. Her g-string was a barely visible black line. She ran a hand down one leg and along her ass until her fingers touched her g-string. She tugged the sliver of fabric aside to give her audience a fleeting preview before crossing her legs and letting the g-string snap back into place. Then she rolled onto her hands and knees. Her hips swiveled in a series of tight figure-eights that made her ass gyrate and flex in time with the beat.

"We'll have to wait for her set to end," Zack said.

"Yeah, I can imagine how difficult that will be for you."

Selena crawled to the edge of the stage. A man in a beige business suit leaned forward on his stool. He had a bill clamped in his hand. From this distance, Ashley could not see the denomination. Selena squeezed the cups of her bra and the man pushed the bill into her cleavage. His fingers touched the cream-colored skin of her breasts and lingered there.

Selena pivoted on her knees and transferred the cash to a small clutch on the stage behind her, then slinked backward toward the man, arched her back, and brought her ass close to his face. She reached back and slapped her left cheek, hard enough that the sharp *clap* carried over the snarling music. Then she was on her feet again, walking the length of the runway.

Her hands swept up behind her back and unclasped her bra, but she held the cups in place with her elbows. She crushed the loose bra against her chest, drawing the moment out. It was obviously a practiced routine, but there was nothing artificial about the smile on her face. She was enjoying this as much as her audience was. She flung the bra to the stage floor.

Marilyn Manson faded into Ludacris. The shift from rock to hip-hop seemed to signal that she was getting down to business. Her fingers slid down the straight line of her torso to the black strings that ran from her hips to the slice of fabric between her legs. She lifted one string away from her hip, let it snap back against her skin. Lifted the other one, pulled it down her thigh, pulled it back up again.

Usually when Ashley watched other dancers perform, she felt like a magician watching a magic show. Knowing the mechanics behind the moves drained most of the spectacle. Watching Selena was different. Ashley could see why all of the porn directors wanted her in their videos and on their box covers.

Someone touched Ashley's shoulder and she jumped. A blonde had approached her and Zack from behind. Dark roots showed under her dyed hair, and even in the dim light, Ashley could see the creases beneath her makeup. Her breasts looked overstuffed and too spherical. She gave Ashley a vacant smile. Her left hand stayed on Ashley's shoulder. Her right was pressed to the space between Zack's shoulder blades.

"How about a dance?" Her breath, close to Ashley's face, smelled like stale peppermint.

"No thanks," Ashley said.

The woman's hand played across Ashley's shoulder and slipped under her hair. Her fingernail traced a line up the nape of her neck and gave her goose-bumps.

"I promise you'll like it."

Ashley felt a moment of sympathy. Strippers had to hustle to make good money, and there was no worse time to do that than when a feature dancer held the attention of the room. Especially a dancer like Selena Drake. But sympathy was one thing. Ashley had not come here for a lap dance and certainly not to watch Zack receive one.

She brushed the woman's hand away. "No."

The woman's eyes turned to the stage and her expression hardened. "The only reason she's such a big star is because she's fucking a big-time porn agent."

Zack laughed. "You're criticizing a porn star for fucking her way to the top?"

The woman shot him a stony look, then turned up her chin and stalked away.

On stage, Selena tossed her g-string over her shoulder. The sweep of her pelvic bones under her pale white skin seemed to emphasize the narrowness of her frame. She walked along the edge of the stage. Men craned their necks at painful-looking angles as she strode above them. She was naked except for the high-heeled boots. That was where the men stuffed their money.

She stopped in front of one lucky patron, squatted in front of him and spread her knees. From where Ashley stood, she could only see the back of the guy's head—big ears, wisps of brown hair circling a bald spot—but she would bet money that his eyes were fixed not on Selena's smiling face but on the area between her thighs. Selena planted one hand palm-down behind her for balance and slid the other one down the flat plane of her stomach to the space between her legs.

"She'll probably do one more song after this one," Ashley said, "then set up a table somewhere on the floor to sign autographs and take pictures. If we intercept her in the dressing room, we'll be able to get our answers and get out."

"You seem eager to leave," Zack said. "I guess this place must spark some unpleasant memories."

She didn't feel like explaining herself to him. She led the way forward, into the crowd. A cocktail waitress in a black corset bumped Ashley's elbow. Her tray tilted. Glasses swayed and clinked. Zack's hand shot forward and steadied the tray. The waitress mouthed a thank-you and hurried past.

"Showoff," Ashley said.

She did not remember the exact location of the door leading backstage, but it wasn't difficult to find. A seven-foot-tall, Slavic-looking man blocked a door marked *Private*. It opened and a brunette in a blue teddy and heels skipped out.

Ashley approached the man. His close-set eyes swept up and down her body and his forehead furrowed. She had to rise onto her tip-toes to get within six inches of his head. She could smell the after-shave he had splashed onto his jaw.

"We're friends of Selena," she said, shouting to be heard over the music. The word *we* seemed to make his body stiffen. He turned a skeptical look on Zack, who had sidled over to stand beside her. "Can we wait for her in the dressing room?"

The man's eyes lingered on Zack. He scowled and crossed his arms over his chest.

"No men backstage, except employees."

"He's okay," she said. "His name is Zack Cutter. He works for Tyrant Productions, in the Valley."

He looked at her but did not respond. The company name did not seem to mean anything to him. Ashley sighed and turned her attention back to the stage. The DJ had moved on to the third song in Selena's set, a hip-hop track that Ashley did not recognize. Her performance would be finished soon.

"Screw this guy," she said to Zack. "We'll catch her when she steps off the stage and she'll walk us past him."

She heard the giant grunt behind her, but whether he had heard her over the pounding music or was just experiencing gas, she didn't know. They waited, listening to the final thumping beats of the song. Over the rows of heads facing the stage, Selena rose to her feet. She gathered the cash from the stage and stuffed it into her clutch. There was so much money that the little handbag refused to stay closed. She gripped it at her side, open and brimming with crumpled green bills, and picked up her g-string, bra, halter top, and microskirt. After flashing her fans another smile, she descended from the stage, hopping down the short flight of steps as effortlessly as if she'd been wearing gym shoes instead of high-heeled boots. Her pale skin gleamed with beads of sweat, but she did not look tired. She headed toward the dressing room door, where Ashley and Zack waited.

She stopped short when she recognized Ashley. A smile lit her face. She closed the distance between them in three quick steps, then gave Ashley an awkward hug, pressing her naked breasts to Ashley's top and thumping the clothing and the clutch against Ashley's back.

"Wow. Have you been here long? Did you watch my whole performance?"

"You're very good," Ashley said.

Selena's eyes settled on Zack. "You're the new guy who works for Kingsley."

"That's me."

Selena's fans had discovered that she had not gone directly to the dressing room. They began to close in on all sides.

"Listen," Ashley said. "We didn't come here just to watch you dance. We need to talk to you about something. It's kind of important."

Selena looked nonplussed. "You mean, right now?"

"If you don't mind."

"I ... guess not. But only for a few minutes. The manager is counting on me to sell a lot of photos and DVDs."

She led the way past the Slavic-looking man and through the door marked *Private*.

For a second, Ashley was blinded. Then her eyes adjusted to the brightly-lit dressing room. She inhaled the scents of perfume and makeup. The room was as she remembered it. An old-fashioned row of light bulbs lined the wall-length mirror. A long counter bore makeup of every brand and type—powders, tubes, pastes—and every other available surface was littered with wispy lace or fake leather. Gleaming metal stools with plump, round cushions lined the counter. She made her way into the room. Her shoe accidentally kicked a garter belt and sent it spinning across the floor.

A tall Asian girl applied the finishing touches to her bright pink lipstick. She did not move when they entered the room, but her eyes found them in the mirror. She clicked the cap onto her lipstick tube and blotted her mouth with a tissue. She wore a tight mini-dress, hot pink to match her lips.

"Got 'em warmed up for me, Selena?"

Selena deposited her things on the counter, then pulled a sheer white robe from a hanger and slung her arms through its sleeves. She did not bother to close the front of the robe.

"They can't pull their dollars out of their wallets fast enough," she said.

"Cool." The girl hopped off the stool, offered Ashley and Zack a perfunctory smile, then hurried out of the room, leaving them alone with Selena.

Ashley pulled two of the stools close to a third and formed a triangle, then gestured for Zack and Selena to sit. Selena crossed one leg over the other. Her robe fell completely open. This was the first time that Ashley had seen her naked up close, and she remained impressed. Still, she could not help noticing that her breasts bore faint ridges along the undersides of the nipples. It was a subtle but tell-tale sign of surgery. She had to give Selena credit, though. For an eighteen-year-old entering the porn industry, she had shown amazing restraint. Her breasts were natural-looking and of average size, nothing like the double-D flotation devices so prevalent in the industry.

Selena caught her looking and smiled. "Did you want to talk about my tits?"

"No." Ashley forced a smile, but could not maintain it. "It's about Tara."

Selena glanced at the door. "Okay."

"The last time we spoke, you mentioned that some of the girls at Pinnacle resented Tara's attempts to steer them away from drugs. I was hoping you could tell me some more about that."

Selena shrugged. "Tara saw herself as a kind of den mother. Her heart was in the right place. But a lot of the girls who come to this industry are escaping from the domination of parents or religion or whatever. The last thing they want is a new mom watching over them and making rules."

"How about you?" Zack said. "Did you resent Tara's motherly attention?"

Selena looked from Ashley to Zack. A mischievous smile broke across her face. "Wait a second. Are you two, like, an item?"

"No," Ashley said—maybe too quickly. "He's just helping me

figure things out." She glanced at Zack. "He's good at this kind of thing."

"I read a lot of *Hardy Boys* as a kid," Zack said. "And *Encyclopedia Brown*." When Selena didn't seem to get the references, he said, "Boy stuff. You probably read *Nancy Drew*."

Selena looked embarrassed. "I've never been much of a reader."

It took Ashley a second to realize that Selena had dodged the question. "Did you resent Tara, too?"

"I wouldn't use that word. But I think of myself as pretty mature. I know what I want in life, you know? And how to get it. Plus, I've been taking care of my sister for as long as I can remember. I know the meaning of responsibility. So when Tara started talking to me like I was some naïve teenage party-girl, it irked me. Wait—am I, like, a suspect?"

Selena probably meant the word as a joke, but even without looking at Zack, Ashley could sense the abrupt tensing of his body. There was a moment of awkward silence. Then Zack said, "We're not the police, Selena. We're just trying to figure out what really happened to Tara."

"And then you'll tell the police," Selena said. She clicked her tongue. Her smile was gone.

"We didn't come here to accuse you of anything," Zack said. "We just want to know what you know. It might be important. We think Tara's murder may have had something to do with a drug dealer."

His explanation failed to put Selena at ease. For the first time, she seemed conscious of her nakedness. She pulled the robe closed over her breasts—not that they were any less visible through the diaphanous material—and rested her arms over her lap.

"I don't know what I could tell you," she said.

"Start with the names of the girls who Tara worried about and tried to help," Ashley said.

Selena's face pinched. "Chloe Raine. Tianna Cole. Once or twice she talked to Amber Valencia about alcohol."

"Anyone else?" Zack said.

Ashley was tired of playing games. She said, "What about you, Selena? Do you use drugs?"

Selena was silent for a moment. Ashley could feel the intensity of her stare. After a few seconds, she said, "No, I don't use drugs. But for some reason Tara thought I did. It was annoying."

Ashley considered telling her about the e-mail that Zack had found, then decided not to. Instead, she asked, "Was there any drug dealer who might have felt threatened by what Tara was doing?"

"You mean because Tara was telling people not to use?" Selena laughed. "We're talking about young, hot girls who fuck for a living. They don't even know dealers. They don't buy their own drugs. Maybe the real junkies—but Pinnacle doesn't represent them."

"Okay," Ashley said. "But *someone* has to give these girls their drugs, and those guys must buy from someone."

Selena's gaze dropped as she considered this. "There is one dealer. I heard him call Tara a retard-activist. I really hate that word."

"What's the dealer's name?"

Selena hesitated. "People call him Billboard Ben. I guess he's a has-been model or something, though it's hard to believe. The guy is seriously fugly."

Billboard Ben. Ashley did not remember anyone by that name from her days in the industry, but she supposed that the illegal drug trade's turnover was probably as high as the porn industry's. "Have you heard of him?" she asked Zack.

He shook his head.

"How can we find him?" she asked Selena.

"It's not like I have his number. I told you, I don't use."

"But you've seen him. Where?"

"I know I saw him once when I was shooting a scene for Wrath Pictures. Phil Singer was the director. He might know how to reach him."

"Phil Singer." Ashley tried to keep the distaste out of her voice. "He's still working in the industry?"

"Yeah, he's still around. He's shooting a scene tomorrow morning with Tessa Taylor—one of Pinnacle's girls. I was in Rob's office when he booked it."

"Could you give me the address?"

Selena smoothed the silky material of the robe against her thighs. "I'm not sure Rob would want me to share that kind of information with outsiders." She hesitated, then sighed. "But I will, if you think it will help. Tara annoyed me sometimes, but she also gave me my start in this business. I owe her a lot. I'll get the info early tomorrow morning and call you."

Ashley nodded. "Thanks."

They all stood up. Selena checked her reflection in the mirror, grabbed a tube of dark lipstick from the counter, uncapped it, and applied a fresh coat.

"Just curious," Zack said. "Do you have any idea why Tara would think you were using drugs?"

"I don't know." Selena brushed past him. She stepped into a black g-string and hung the robe back on its hook. Ashley could see the muscles and bones of her back clearly defined beneath her smooth white skin. When she turned to face them again, her self-consciousness had departed as quickly as it had appeared. She made no effort to cover her jutting breasts. "She made life difficult for me for a few weeks. She even harassed my sister, which is not cool. But whatever. It's beside the point now. She's dead and I really miss her."

She pasted a smile on her face and opened the dressing room door. There was an eruption of cheers and whistles. Apparently a crowd of men had been waiting for her outside the dressing room. She strutted into their midst.

20

ASHLEY SPENT a restless night in bed. Even though she was alone in her motel room, she kept waking, springing out of her bed with her heart slamming in her chest, sure that someone was in the room with her. She could even see him for a few seconds—a pale and hazy shape lurking between the door and the thermostat, watching her. Then her head would clear and the hazy shape would dissolve and she would crawl back onto the mattress, only to wake in terror an hour or two later.

When the sun brightened the outline of her window shade and she began to hear traffic outside, she felt like she had not slept at all. Her head ached and her eyes felt scratchy beneath their lids. She rolled out of the bed and hoped a long, hot shower would pound the exhaustion out of her. It didn't.

She needed coffee.

She had just changed into a skirt and top when Zack showed up with two steaming cups from The Coffee Bean.

He stood in the doorway, looking downright penitent. "There are muffins in the car."

"You brought me muffins?"

"And your clothes, from my place. But I only have two hands, and I thought you would want this most." He gave her one of the coffees. She took it gratefully.

"You're smarter than you look." The coffee warmed her palm through the cardboard cup. She sipped, then gulped. It tasted good and the caffeine hit was almost instant. "Thanks."

"Listen." He stepped into the room and closed the door. "You haven't given me a chance to explain—"

"You don't need to." She turned her back on him and grabbed her bag from the top of the dresser. She slung it over her shoulder. "You're helping me prove that Tara was murdered. That's all that matters."

She made a move for the door, but he did not step out of her way.

"I don't agree," he said. "I think we ... I don't know ... go well together."

"Sure, when you were pretending to be someone I liked. But I don't know James Foster. And I really didn't come to LA to meet people, you know? What happened that night happened, but even if you hadn't been lying to me, it probably would have been a mistake. So let's just forget it."

He laughed without smiling. "It's not that simple, Ashley."

"It is for me. I was a porn star, remember? I'm used to having sex with actors. The only difference is that you were better than most of them at staying in character."

He had been better than most of them at other things, too—like cradling her body in just the right way while he rocked against her—but those thoughts were as dangerously seductive as the nostalgia she'd felt at Gloss. Southern California itself was seductive and always had been. She needed to shut it out. She had one mission here. One task. And when it was done, she would leave. For good this time.

"I wasn't acting." She could see the hurt in his eyes. "Not about that."

She nudged him aside and opened the door. The hallway beyond was gloomy and smelled faintly of mildew. She started down it, but

Zack did not follow. He lingered in the doorway, one hand holding the door open and the other gripping his coffee cup.

"Shouldn't we talk about this in the privacy of your room?" he said.

"I don't think we should talk about it at all."

———

THEY TOOK HER CAR AGAIN. He held a sheet of motel stationery on which she'd scrawled, in the half-legible handwriting of the half-asleep, an address that Selena had given her over the phone in a hurried whisper.

She watched his face scrunch up as he tried to decipher it.

"Don't worry," she said. "I know how to get there."

"I'm not worried." He fished a folded sheet of paper from his jeans pocket and handed it to her. She unfolded it and stared at a puffy, bearded face framed by a shoulder-length halo of tangled hair. The image was black-and-white, blurred and slightly distorted. "Billboard Ben's mug shot," Zack said. "From an arrest three years ago in San Bernardino. It's a fax. That's why the quality is bad."

"You must have called the FBI to get this for you. In the middle of the night?"

"I like to know what I'm getting into," he said.

She studied him for a few seconds, then started the car and turned up the air-conditioning. Warm air burst from the vents, then slowly began to cool. The sheet of paper fluttered in her hand.

"And?"

"His full name is Benjamin Crowder. He's a hustler, a bullshit artist. Holds himself out as a kind of modern-day hippie."

"I thought he was a model."

"He's had a varied career."

"Was he ever arrested for hanging someone?"

"No." Zack leaned back and tried to arrange his legs so that his knees would not press against the glove compartment. He gave up.

"But he was arrested for breaking three of his wife's ribs with a tennis racket. Want to know why he did it?"

She waited for him to tell her.

"The wife checked her friend into rehab. And the friend was one of Ben's regular customers."

"Sounds like he has a low tolerance for women who screw with his business."

"My thought exactly."

The address Selena had given her turned out to be a ranch-style house set on about two acres of dead, brown lawn. The narrow driveway was already crammed with cars, so Ashley parked on the street. She climbed out of the car and stepped onto the brittle grass. It crunched under her shoes.

"Have you met Phil Singer?" she asked Zack.

"No, but I know who he is. Old school. Been in the business forever. Started as a performer in the eighties, now he directs."

"Wow. Your FBI handlers must have briefed you pretty thoroughly."

"Not about Singer. But I listen, you know? It's part of being an effective undercover agent. I start conversations, try to pick up information about different players in the industry."

"Did you 'pick up' that he's a raging asshat?"

That made him smile. "No. You think he'll give us a hard time about contacting Billboard Ben?"

"He's going to give us a hard time the second he sees my face."

Halfway to the house's front door, they heard voices coming from behind the house. She led the way around the corner and saw a glittering swimming pool. Two women sunbathed naked on lounge chairs. Both were blonde, leggy, tanned. She wondered which one was Tessa Taylor, the Pinnacle girl. Beyond them, four men sat at a shaded plastic table, drinking beers. A ceramic ashtray occupied the center of the table, along with a pack of cigarettes. Singer was the only one smoking. A half-consumed cigarette perched between two yellow fingers of his right hand. Smoke drifted upward from its glowing tip, slow to disperse. The air reeked of cigarette smoke and chlorine.

"Well sodomize me with a monkey's cock," Singer said. "Ashley fucking Hale."

His British accent, which she had always suspected he exaggerated because he thought it made him sound more intelligent than he really was, seemed even more smug than she remembered it.

"Hi, Phil."

"Back in black, eh? I suppose leaving the industry gave you that empty feeling. In your pussy, I mean."

He stuck his cigarette in his mouth, smirking. Sweat gleamed on his pale forehead. Except for a band of wiry gray hair, he was bald. In every other way, he was nondescript. Average build, ordinary face. The same could not be said of the motley crew that surrounded him. A short, fat man sat to his left, slumped low in his chair. His bare and hairy chest sagged over his belly, which itself sagged over the waist of his shorts. The man to Singer's right was a black man who was either very short or a midget. The fourth guy, a lanky man with tattoos covering every exposed surface, was flipping through the business section of the LA Times.

After a few seconds of silence, Singer plucked the cigarette from his mouth and said, "Who's your friend?"

"I'm Zack Cutter." Zack stepped forward and extended his hand, but Singer made no move to shake it. Neither did any of the other men. "I work for Tyrant—"

"Cutter. You edited *On Her Knees*. Decent work. So—" His attention swiveled back to Ashley. His eyes blinked lazily. "I assume you brought documentation?"

Christ. He thought she'd come here to beg for work.

"I like to think that if I decided to make a comeback, I wouldn't need to crash your porn set to land a role."

"Is that what you like to think? How old are you, Ash? Forty-two?"

She bit back her anger. Singer had always been like this. Even back when he worked in front of the camera. The old-timers used to tell her that he couldn't maintain his wood unless he was whispering venom into the ear of his partner.

"I'm twenty-seven."

His smirk broadened. "And you think people would pay to watch you suck a cock, when they could be watching an eighteen-year-old hard-body like Selena Drake?"

"What I think is that I have a lot more fans than you do. But that's beside the point. I didn't come here for validation of my attractiveness. I need you to help me get in contact with someone. A friend of yours."

He crushed his cigarette in the ashtray. "Tough break, then. I don't have any friends."

Self-deprecating humor was not Singer's natural mode. She felt her guard rise.

"I like you, Phil," said the short and hairy man to his left.

"You don't count, Ron. You like everybody."

The black midget snickered, then took a swig of beer, leaned back, and burped.

A trickle of sweat slid down Ashley's back. She glimpsed Zack beside her, practically vibrating with impatience. He said, "Maybe 'friend' was the wrong word."

Singer's lip curled. "Who's talking to you, pretty boy? Not me. I'm talking to the pig in the skirt. Isn't that right, *pig*?"

Ashley ground her nails into her palms and forced herself to maintain her composure. Men like Singer had a thousand names for women—pig, whore, slut, meat-socket—but no amount of name-calling changed the fact that they depended on women for their livelihoods.

"Watch your mouth," Zack said. "It won't be easy to smoke with a busted jaw."

Singer let out a whoop. "Ashley the professional cock sucker got herself a boyfriend. And a tough one, too. A tough talker, anyhow."

Singer was the tough talker. Zack could deck him with minimal effort, and Ashley was pretty sure that everyone around the table knew it. She wrapped her fingers around his wrist to stop him. "Let it go."

"He called you a *pig*."

Singer made a show of looking at his watch. "This has been a real pleasure, Ash, a genuine pleasure. But I have a video to make. So, if you would be so kind as to vacate my set—"

"We're trying to get in touch with Billboard Ben," she said, "and we've been told that you know how to reach him."

Singer lifted the box of cigarettes and shook one free. Instead of lighting it, he rolled it between his fingers. A contemplative expression pinched his face.

"Ashley Hale wants to get in touch with Billboard Ben. Strange. I was under the impression that you didn't use."

"I don't."

He pursed his lips. "This wouldn't have anything to do with your sister then, would it?"

Alarm bells clanged in her head.

"Why would you think that?" Zack said.

Ashley shot him a look, but it was too late. He had tipped their hand and confirmed whatever theory Singer had developed in his nicotine-fueled lizard brain. Singer's mouth contracted into a tight smile. He leaned forward and lit his cigarette, then took his time with the first puff. He smoked for what felt like minutes. Then he exhaled twin jets of smoke through his nostrils and said to Zack, "No reason."

"Are you going to help us or not?" Ashley said.

"To get in touch with Ben? Look, Ben isn't going to want to meet with two douche-bags who aren't looking to make a buy. He's a business man, not a grief counselor."

"Is that why he had a problem with Tara?" Ashley said. "Because she was bad for business?"

"Who said he had a problem with Tara?"

She felt her face warm as anger twisted through her, but she forced herself to stay calm. Zack seemed to be under control, too, although she could hear him pushing air through his nostrils like a bull in a Warner Bros. cartoon.

"We'll make the meeting worth his while," she said.

Singer shrugged. "First you need to make this one worth mine."

She reached for her purse. "How much do you want?"

He took a drag from the cigarette, blew smoke. "Ashley, Ashley, Ashley. I'm a pornographer, not a panhandler. I want a performance."

21

"I don't have documentation," Ashley said. "I haven't had an HIV test in years."

Singer dismissed her excuses with a wave of his cigarette. "The Feds don't care about that anymore. Take off your clothes."

All eyes were on her now. Even the two sunbathing starlets sat up to watch this confrontation play out.

Zack said, "That's enough."

"I'm not going to perform," she told Singer. "I don't do that anymore."

The statement only seemed to increase his amusement. He plucked the cigarette from his mouth and smiled. "You don't have to fuck anybody. Just take off your clothes, bend over, and spread your cheeks for me. Tell you what—I won't even film it."

"Then what's the point?"

He smiled. Smoke trailed from his cigarette. She tried not to breathe in the pungent air. He wasn't going to give her an answer. And she didn't need one. The point was domination. Humiliation.

She turned on her heel and walked away. In her peripheral vision, she saw Zack hesitate, then follow her. His shoes crunched the grass as he jogged to catch up with her. "We're just going to leave?" he said.

"I'm sure Phil Singer is not the only person who knows how to reach Billboard Ben."

"But as soon as we mentioned Ben, he brought up Tara. He knows something."

"Anyone would have made that connection. Why else would I have come back to LA?"

"Ashley, I can make him talk."

"How? By beating the shit out of him?"

"I have training—"

"I need to think, okay? Just give me a few seconds to think."

They turned the corner of the house. Sunlight flared from the windshield of the Fiesta. Even though she knew it was going be a hundred degrees inside the car, she couldn't wait to seal herself inside it. She felt anger and nausea, a mix of emotions she had tried to leave behind her two years ago.

She pulled open the driver's side door. Zack grabbed her arm before she could slide into the car. His firm grip brought her back to the moment.

"You're just going to let that asshole scare you off?"

"I'm not scared." She yanked her arm free. "There's no reason to subject ourselves to his bullshit."

"Then why did we come here?"

She rubbed her arm. "I guess I forgot how big an asshole he is."

"I'm good at dealing with—"

Zack closed his mouth abruptly. Ashley followed his gaze. One of the sunbathers had pursued them to the front of the house. She walked gingerly on her bare feet, tip-toeing across the dead lawn.

She had thrown on a long T-shirt that barely covered her naked body. Her nipples poked against a Corona logo emblazoned on the front of the shirt. Ashley turned to look up and down the street. It was quiet. No one was around. In the distance, heat shimmered above the road.

"You are Ashley Hale, yes?" The woman's accent was eastern European. "You are wanting to get high?"

Ashley closed the car door and took a step closer to the woman.

A mingled scent of tanning lotion and sweat clung to her skin. There were beads of perspiration on her throat. She had bright green eyes.

"I'm looking for Billboard Ben," Ashley said. "Do you know him?"

The woman made a dismissive *tsk*-ing sound and tossed her crinkly blonde hair. "No need Ben. I share mine. Speed, yes? You tell me tips. About industry? I arrive two weeks ago. I think ... I think I may be having unfair pay. My name is Marta."

Ashley had known plenty of Martas, girls "fresh off the bus" in industry lingo. They came to Los Angeles with dreams of being models or actresses. Instead, they wound up doing DPs and gang-bangs for substandard rates. Tara had created Pinnacle to protect people like Marta. Ashley didn't have time to be so altruistic.

"I don't—I'm not really looking for drugs. I need to talk to Ben. Do you know how to reach him?"

"Oh yes, I know. In my phone." Marta turned, then gestured for Ashley to follow her back around the house. Ashley exchanged a glance with Zack, then followed Marta to the swimming pool, where the girl squatted beside a large purse and rummaged through it. Singer was still working on his cigarette. He grinned when he saw them.

"Changed your mind, did you?" he called from the table. "Ready to show me that famous stink-hole?"

Ashley ignored him. She kept her gaze on Marta. The other sunbather—Tessa Taylor, she guessed—was now watching her with open curiosity.

Singer laughed. "Would you rather see mine? Maybe taste it a little?"

Zack crossed the yard before she could stop him. Singer's cronies responded with slack-jawed surprise, but Singer bounced out of his chair and back-pedaled. His shoulders hit a palm tree. The fronds rattled. He threw up his hands. Zack's fist sailed past them and caught his chin. Singer's head snapped back. Bounced off the tree. Bark broke loose and clattered to the ground. Blood welled in Singer's mouth. He touched his lip, stared at the smear of red on his fingertips, then stuck the cigarette back in his mouth and sucked in a deep drag.

Zack shook his head and turned away from him, a look of disgust on his face. "Let's get out of—"

Singer launched himself forward. His stocky body collided with Zack from behind and knocked them both to the ground. The other guys at the table finally broke their stupor and stood up, but only to crane their necks and gawk.

Marta took Ashley's arm. The woman's fingers were hot and slick with lotion. Ashley watched her uncap a pen with her teeth. She spread her palm and Marta wrote a phone number across it, digging the ballpoint into her skin. Marta capped the pen and grinned at the two men fighting on the ground. She whispered, "He is very handsome."

"Zack?" Ashley looked at the numbers scrawled across the creases of her palm, then flexed her hand. "We're just friends."

"God, why?"

Singer's buddies clapped and whooped. Ashley could not tell who they were rooting for. Probably for violence itself. Singer had lost his cigarette. His hands were twisted in Zack's hair. He looked like he was trying to rip the hairs out by their roots. Zack punched Singer's gut. He pressed his other arm across Singer's throat. The cigarette was smoldering in the grass a few feet away. Ashley ground it out under her shoe. It released a final tendril of smoke.

"Hey." She crouched next to the men and tapped Zack's shoulder. "You can stop fighting for my honor now."

"Honor?" Singer sneered at her, but his voice, pinched by the arm across his throat, was barely audible. "I'm surprised ... a whore ... is familiar with the concept."

"That's it."

She plucked the shoe from her right foot, flipped it so the heel pointed down, and drove the point hard into the back of one of Singer's hands. He screamed and released his grip on Zack's hair.

"You bitch!"

Ashley aimed for his other hand, but he let go with that one before she needed to use the shoe. He rolled away from Zack. Her heel had scraped an ugly red gouge from Singer's knuckles to the middle of his hand. He poked at the wound and glared at her.

"You can get up," Ashley said to Zack. She showed him the writing on her palm. "We're good."

Zack rose to one knee, then stretched shakily to his full height. His hair was a mess. He brushed dead grass from his jeans.

Singer watched him. "I've been working in the jizz biz for a long time. I could make problems for you."

"Not as many as I could make for you." Without elaborating, Zack headed toward the front of the house and the car. Ashley walked at his side. This time she was the one hurrying to keep up with his pace.

"That was stupid," she said. "Fighting with that jerk. What's the point?" She tried to sweep dirt from his sleeve, but only managed to leave a smear on his shirt.

A grin brightened his face. "It's not a total loss. At least I got a free haircut."

"Funny."

"Hey." He opened the car door for her. "Don't be upset. It's like you said—we got what we came for."

She slid behind the wheel and waited for him to drop into the passenger seat. When he clicked his seatbelt in place, she started the car. "You're right. I just hate dealing with Singer. And I didn't like seeing him, you know—"

"Pull my hair like a little girl?"

"I was going to say 'hurt you.'"

"He didn't hurt me."

"Right." She gave him a sidelong glance. "Mister Tough Guy."

"I prefer Captain Indestructible."

"I'm still trying to get used to James." She expected him to laugh, but when she glanced at him, he was frowning. "What?"

"Nothing. Just ... you shouldn't use that name. Even kidding around. It isn't safe."

"We're in a car. It's just the two of us."

"I know, but if you start using the name in private, chances are you'll slip up and say it in front of someone."

"Your confidence in me is overwhelming."

"I have every confidence in you. I'm just giving you advice."

"Whatever, James."

She turned from one suburban street to the next, trying to retrace her path out of the development. She must have taken a wrong turn somewhere. All of the houses looked similar, a repeating pattern of the same two or three models in different colors.

"I'm serious," he said.

"McCarter Road. Does that sound familiar to you?"

"Not really."

"Thanks for your help, James."

His hand squeezed her shoulder. "Ashley. Please."

The middle-class suburban landscape deteriorated to an older area. She drove past convenience stores with lottery signs in their windows. Then liquor stores and laundromats began to appear. She heard the rhythmic honks of a car alarm in the distance.

"I need to turn around."

She pulled into the parking lot of a convenience store. Before she could get the car turned around, Zack asked her to stop. "I need to get a bottle of water. You want anything?"

"I'll go in with you."

She parked the car and they walked across the small lot. A bell dinged when Zack pushed the door open. The store smelled like crackers and stale pastries. There was no one inside except for a sleepy-looking kid behind the counter. Most of his face was hidden behind a copy of *PC Gamer*. Zack headed for the refrigerators along the back wall. Something about his stride told her he was still irritated.

She was not sure why she felt compelled to tease him. If it was a way of venting her anger, it was pretty immature, but she did not think that that was the reason. It had more to do with his actions at Singer's set.

He came back before she had a chance to fully puzzle it out. "You want anything?" he said.

"No thanks."

The kid behind the counter sighed, reluctant to put down his magazine. Zack put the bottle of water on the counter and tugged his wallet from the back pocket of his grass-stained jeans.

Back in the car, she said, "So do you go by Jimmy or Jim, or do people actually call you James?"

He stuck his water bottle in the console's cup-holder and turned to her with a frustrated look. "Ashley—"

"James is kind of pretentious, isn't it? I'm guessing your friends call you Jim. Or Jimbo."

"You're trying to make me angry. And it's working." He glared at her. "It's hot. Start the car."

It was hot. The heat had settled around them, a smothering blanket. But she did not reach for the ignition. She stared at Zack, then looked past him through the window. A blue Jetta shot past the parking lot. Then the street was quiet.

"Ashley. Start the car—"

She kissed him. It was not an action she had planned. He did not seem to mind. She pushed her tongue into his mouth. His right hand curved behind her back and edged her closer.

They kissed again, longer this time. She pulled back for a few seconds, just long enough to gasp in a breath, then climbed over the center console so she was on his lap, straddling him. He stared up at her with surprise. The sound of their breathing filled the car.

He shifted his legs. The feel of the denim against her thighs made her stomach flutter.

She kissed his forehead, then found his mouth again. She caught his lower lip between her teeth and bit down gently. His hands ran up and down her sides, then settled on her waist. His fingers felt cool against her warm skin.

"Someone could see us," he said. "The cashier in there—"

"Who cares?"

She cupped a hand behind his head. His hair and the back of his neck were damp. Her body was slick with perspiration, too. She could feel it gathering between her breasts and at the small of her back.

She reached down and unbuttoned the fly of his jeans.

"Ashley!"

He was laughing now. He made no move to intercept her hand. When her fingers pushed into his pants, he leaned his head back against the seat.

"I've never done it in a car," she said.

"Really?" He looked surprised. "Even, you know, professionally?"

She rocked against him. "Filming in cars is a hassle. The angle is too close." She reached for her purse, pretty sure there were a few condoms at the bottom. She fished around until she found one. "Put this on."

Zack hurriedly complied.

She pressed her face to his neck and breathed in the smells of grass and sweat. The head of his cock poked the inside of her thigh. She reached down and, with one motion, tugged her panties to one side and guided him inside her. She gasped as his full length entered her.

"I can't believe we're doing this." Zack gasped in her ear. "If the cashier walks outside for a smoke—"

"Shut up and fuck me."

His hips bucked upward. She let him set the pace, then matched his rhythm. She pressed her hands flat to his chest and rode him. The car filled with grunts and the slap of skin on skin. His head strained toward her, and when she leaned down, his lips brushed her throat, her cheek, her mouth. His head jerked backward. Muscles stood out in his neck. She felt his climax and the sensation triggered her own.

When the last spasm faded, she climbed off of him and settled into the driver's seat. He didn't move. The condom glistening in the sunlight.

"You might want to put that thing away now," she said.

"Wow. I never thought of myself as an exhibitionist, but ... wow."

She started the car and got the air-conditioner blowing. Her whole body felt slick and sticky. Her hair was a mess. She leaned forward and ran her fingers through it, then pushed it back behind her shoulders.

Zack reached across the console and took her hand. "I'm sorry I couldn't tell you who I really was. Believe me, I wanted to. I—"

She squeezed his hand. "It's okay."

"If there's anything you want to know—*anything*—ask me. No questions are off-limits."

"Just tell me you're not married."

"I'm not married."

She turned and smiled at him. "I was almost engaged. I mean, if we're telling each other everything, I guess I should tell you that. A week ago, I was pretty serious with a guy in New Jersey. I was ready to spend the rest of my life with him."

"What happened?"

"He turned out to be a jerk. But, the more I think about it, I don't know that I ever really loved him. I think I was just … I don't know … trying so hard to start a new life, a normal life. I would have married just about anyone."

"Why did you leave the industry?" Zack said. "No one seems to know."

"That's because I didn't tell anyone. Except Tara."

He watched her with his dark blue eyes. His face was serious now. He said, "If you don't want to tell me, that's okay."

"No." She squeezed his hand again. "I do want to tell you."

22

THE AIR-CONDITIONER COOLED the interior of the Fiesta to a pleasant temperature and lifted the sweat from her body. She sat up but did not let go of Zack's hand. The car smelled like sex. Outside, two cars drove past the convenience store parking lot. One had a bad muffler. It roared. Then the street was quiet again.

"It's okay," Zack said. He smiled reassuringly. "You can tell me another time."

A tear slipped down her face, surprising her. Zack touched it with his finger and wiped it away. The A/C chilled the wet streak. Another tear followed. "I don't know why I'm crying," she said. She was surprised again—this time by the sound of her voice. All choked-up.

"Ashley."

"I got into porn when I was twenty," she said. She did not know how else to start. "Tara was eighteen. We left home together, after she graduated high school."

"Whose idea was it?"

"Mine. I thought ... I don't know what I thought."

He nodded. "What happened?"

"I liked it. I mean, not the sex itself. That always felt like work, all the anal stuff and weird positions and multiple partners. But I liked the celebrity. The fans and the photo shoots and the box covers and the events. You know? Tara and I came from a ... not a great home. My grades in school weren't spectacular either. And then, all of a sudden, I was making a lot of money. Random people would recognize me and tell me how sexy I was and ask for my autograph. And I made friends. A lot of them. In high school, I never really fit in. But in the industry, it was like everyone was an outcast. I don't know if you can understand that, but to me, it was like I had finally found a place where I belonged."

She paused for a breath. He said, "I do understand."

"I don't know why the luster faded. Maybe I just grew up, you know? Getting attention became less important to me, and the negatives started to bother me more. The regular STD tests, the drama and bullshit."

"That's why you left?"

Another car sped past the lot, a flash of red. Ashley's hand tightened on Zack's.

"No. I probably would have stayed, but—" She felt a lump gathering in her throat and took a deep breath. "I got pregnant. Gonzo fans don't like seeing condoms in their videos. Of course I was on the pill. But sometimes birth control fails. I still don't know who the father was. There are literally dozens of possible fathers. I didn't know what to do. Who to tell. I kept it a secret. I had an abortion. Tara was the only person I told. She went to the clinic with me. And ... after the abortion, I had a kind of panic attack. I knew I couldn't do it anymore. I wanted a normal life. So I left the industry. I left LA. I broke off contact with all of my old friends—even Tara. It was terrible and selfish and now she's dead—"

Zack leaned across the console and gathered her into his arms. She cried against his chest. Her face rose and fell as he breathed. The rhythm was soothing. She did not want to part from him.

"You have nothing to feel guilty about," he said. "Tara could not have asked for a more devoted sister."

"That's bullshit and you know it." She pressed her cheek against the wet spot her tears had made over his heart. "I didn't even return her calls."

"You needed time away from all of this. Eventually, you would have called her."

"We'll never know." She pushed herself off of his chest, wiped her eyes and sniffed. "Okay. Enough crying. I'm okay."

"You don't look okay."

"We need to find Billboard Ben. Finish this. It's what I need to do. It's the only thing that's going to make this feeling go away."

Right. As if she would ever stop feeling the guilt of turning her back on Tara. As if it would not be with her for the rest of her life.

————

BECAUSE ZACK HAD NEVER MET Billboard Ben, they decided that it would seem less suspicious if he made the phone call from the set of a porn shoot. Zack had established himself in the industry as Kingsley Nast's new editor. If he called under the pretext of needing "refreshments" for the cast and crew of Tyrant's latest masterpiece, then hopefully Ben would not think twice. That was the plan, anyway.

After a quick call to Angela, they learned that Kingsley was shooting at the house in Granada Hills.

"The same one he used on Tuesday," Ashley said.

"Where we met for the very first time," he said in a singsong voice that made her laugh. "How romantic."

When they arrived, the driveway was more crowded than it had been on Tuesday, and there were several cars parked along the curb. Ashley wondered how many more times Kingsley would get away with using this place before one of the neighbors caught a glimpse of something nasty and complained to the police. This time it was the second-floor that had all of its window shades pulled down. Kingsley must have moved the action upstairs in an attempt to make his recycling of the set less obvious.

Beth Baldwin answered Ashley's knock. The makeup artist looked frazzled. Her spiky blue hair drooped and she had ditched her studded choker. A sheen of perspiration glistened on her forehead. When she saw Zack a look of relief flooded her face. "Where have you been, Cutter? Never mind. I'm just glad you're here."

"A little overwhelmed?"

"I think Kingsley's trying to shoot six movies at the same time. I'm not fucking exaggerating. I've already redone Autumn Wood's makeup twice. Glamour for one scene. Goth for the next."

"How many scenes is he shooting?"

Beth shrugged and led them into the house. The foyer smelled like personal lubricant. Moans and grunts filtered down from the upper floor, along with creaking bed springs. Ashley raised her eyebrows at Beth. Back when she had worked with Kingsley, he never would have shot a scene on a bed. He had always insisted that there was nothing visually interesting or exotic about fucking on a bed—it was literally flat. Apparently his standards had changed.

As Beth led them deeper into the house, Zack leaned close to Ashley. Warm breath touched her ear as he whispered, "He shoots all the time now. Quantity over quality. Trying to appease his new business partners."

Beth glanced back at them, caught them with their heads pressed together. Her eyes widened. Then she grinned. "The amazing Ashley Hale. She comes to town for a few days, she steals the most eligible bachelor."

Before Ashley could respond, Beth bounded up the stairs. Her fatigue had apparently faded.

In the master bedroom, they found the usual porn amalgam of intimacy and show-business—a man and woman naked in bed, and a whole bunch of other people standing around them, working or looking bored. Ashley saw a guy stuff what looked like the end of a Baja Fresh taco into his mouth, then wipe grease off of his lips with the back of his hand. Beside him, a brunette in goth makeup—Autumn Wood, presumably—was texting someone with her phone. The smell of lube was stronger in here, a rubbery odor that Ashley remembered well. The performers on the bed moaned and gasped. The headboard knocked against the wall.

Kingsley turned and smiled at Zack. The smile faltered when he saw Ashley. He held up a finger in a *give me a minute* gesture, then focused his attention on his camera's LCD screen.

Ashley had worked with one of the performers, Jake Garrett. His partner in the scene was a young blonde she did not recognize. The blonde's large, natural-looking breasts flopped and swung in a way that could not feel good as she and Jake fucked in the anal-reverse-cowgirl position. The blonde was doing a good job of looking turned on, but Ashley spotted a telling pulse in her right thigh. The muscle that pivoted her body up and down looked ready to give out at any moment.

"Okay, Jake. Stand up and pop on her tits."

Jake was old-school. He could come on command. Ashley watched him do it now. Semen jetted across the blonde's breasts. She grinned and massaged the sticky fluid against her chest as if it were an exotic lotion.

"Good," Kingsley said. "Cut. We're done." He turned and clapped Zack on the shoulder. "I'm glad you're here. I need you to grab the second camera from downstairs. Pick up some alternate angels for me during the next scene."

"No problem." Zack gave Ashley a meaningful stare and she realized that he was planning to use this opportunity to make the phone call downstairs.

Kingsley waited until he was gone, then took a deep breath and met Ashley's gaze. "You're still in town?"

"I told you I'm not going anywhere until I find out what happened to Tara."

"Cheryl told me about the talk you two had at my house the other night. Your unexpected visit. The accusations you made."

"You should have just told me the truth from the beginning. You would have saved me a lot of wasted time and energy."

She saw his cheeks redden at the edges of his goatee. "Some things are personal, Ashley. Even in porn."

"Yeah, well," she lowered her voice, "I'm glad you didn't kill her. I would hate to think of you as a murderer."

She watched his face closely as she spoke the words, but if he had been involved in Brewster's disappearance, his expression did not betray his guilt. He met her stare. He even smiled. "I'm many things, but I'm not that."

"Well, I just came by to apologize. You know, for suspecting you."

"You and I go way back," he said.

"You, me, and Brewster."

Again, no reaction. He said, "You should visit him, now that you live on the east coast. See how the legit film business is treating him."

"I plan to."

Kingsley nodded. A few seconds passed in silence. He fidgeted.

"So we're good?" Ashley said.

"Of course. We'll always be good." He looked up. Smiled. "Hey, as long as you're here, you should stick around. I ordered a platter from Tony's. Your favorite, if memory serves."

She tried to look pleased, even though food was the furthest thing from her mind.

———

DOWNSTAIRS, she found Zack sitting alone at the kitchen table. There was a cordless phone in his hand. When she pulled out a chair and sat next to him, he covered the mouthpiece and whispered, "Singer must have warned him."

"What?"

Zack gave a quick shake of his head, then said into the phone, "I don't know who you're talking about, dude. There's no one named Ashley here." There was a pause while he listened, then he said, "Jenna, Autumn, Brianna, Jake, some other people. No Ashley. Look, man, King said to call you. If you want me to call someone else—" He listened some more. "I don't know what you're talking about—" He placed the phone on the table. "He hung up."

"What do we do now?"

Zack shook his head. "I don't know." He leaned back in his chair.

Above them, she could hear chatter and footsteps. Kingsley had probably moved everyone to a different room and started setting up equipment for the next scene. In a few minutes, Kingsley would start to wonder where Zack was with the second camera.

The phone rang. Its shrill cry made both of them jump.

Zack looked at Ashley, then picked up the phone. "Hello?"

Ashley slid from her seat to his, pushing him half out of the chair so she could press her ear close to the phone. His body was warm and still smelled vaguely of sex. She had to resist the urge to snuggle. Then she heard a gravelly voice from the phone and her body went cold.

"You and the dead bitch's sister want to talk to me, you're gonna have to do it on my terms. And it's gonna cost you."

In a voice that was remarkably laid-back, Zack said, "I told you, man, I don't know what you're talking about."

"What I'm talking about is you and Ashley Hale think I killed the bitch on account of the fact I hate her."

"I don't—"

"Shut up, now. Maybe I know who killed her, okay? Maybe I'll even tell you. For a price. But I'm not walking into no trap. I'm not stupid. You want to talk to me, you'll meet me where I tell you to. There's a warehouse on Sherman Way in Reseda. Used to be owned by Cat Scratch Video, before they went bust. Meet me there. You and Ashley. Alone. I see anyone else, I'm gone and you'll never find me. There's dangerous people involved in this and danger is definitely *not* my middle name, understand?"

"No, I don't understand," Zack said. "You come here. Sell some coke or crank or whatever. No one's setting any kind of trap, dude."

"Bring five-thousand dollars in cash."

Zack dropped the pretense of confusion. "That's too much money."

"It's a seller's market. Bye, now."

"Wait, Ben—" He leaned forward, almost knocking Ashley off the chair. "Hello?"

The line was dead.

23

"Shit." Zack stared at the cordless phone. His face was taut.

Ashley was already on her feet. Her heart was racing. A sour, unpleasant taste filled her mouth. She recognized it as fear. But at the same time, she felt relieved. She had begun to doubt that she would ever find Tara's killer—or even prove that Tara had been killed. Now she was on the trail again.

Whispering, she said, "Do you think the FBI would be willing to front you five-thousand dollars?"

"No time. I'll get it from my checking account."

"You would do that for me?"

He flashed a wry smile. "Well I'm sure as hell not doing it for *him*."

"Let's go."

Zack did not move from his chair. The smile was gone. Lines of concern bracketed his eyes. "I know the warehouse he's talking about, Ashley. It's abandoned. Been in foreclosure for almost a year. There's no one around."

"Didn't you hear what he said? He knows who killed Tara."

"Why would he want to meet us alone in an isolated place? It doesn't sound like he wants to have a friendly conversation."

"What are you saying? He's going to try to kill us?" She felt silly just voicing the words. "It's the middle of the day. It's sunny outside."

Zack passed a hand over his face. He looked tired. "If he murdered Tara, and he knows we're closing in on him, then he might be desperate enough to try to kill us, yes."

"You heard what he said. He wants money."

A door banged open in the hallway and a man stepped out, zipping his fly. He glanced at them before jogging toward the staircase. Any minute and Kingsley was going to start hollering for Zack.

He took a deep breath. "I need to talk to Kingsley, give him some excuse for bailing. We'll go to the bank. Then we'll stop by my house. I'm not doing this unarmed."

She hugged him. "Thank you."

————

ASHLEY HAD THOUGHT that the midday sunshine would burn away the creepiness of the abandoned warehouse, but if anything, the brightness highlighted the building's sinister aspects. Sunlight traced the jagged edges of broken windows, lent rust-spotted gutter pipes a reddish glow, and revealed the fine details of a fat wasps' nest clinging to the side of the building. The lot behind the warehouse might as well be located in the middle of the desert. She could hear the sounds of traffic on the far side of the warehouse, but the structure blocked the street from view completely. Smashed beer bottles glittered in the dirt.

Reflexively, she reached for Zack's hand and squeezed it. Privacy was not high on her list of desires right now. A crowd of people, that would be nice.

"Okay," she whispered. "Now what? Where's Billboard Ben?"

Zack stared at the building. She followed his gaze. A narrow back door looked warped, as if someone had forced it open with a crowbar.

"You think he's inside?" Ashley said.

"Possibly. Were you familiar with this place? I mean, back when

Cat Scratch Video was still in business? Is there any chance you would remember the layout?"

"I've never even heard of Cat Scratch Video."

Zack nodded. "Okay. Then we're staying outside. We came this far. If Ben wants to talk to us, he'll have to come out."

A wasp hovered near one of the building's grimy windows. It's long, narrow body bounced against the building a few times, then disappeared inside the papery nest that clung to the side of the building. Ashley shivered.

"Hello, hello."

They swung around. Ben had not been waiting in the warehouse after all. He had crept up behind them. He looked even worse than his mug shot. His face was doughy and patterned with red splotches. His teeth were brown and there were gaps between some of them. His hair, long and uncombed, fell past his shoulders. She could smell the greasy tangles from where she stood, five feet away from him. Dark aviator sunglasses masked his eyes.

If it was true that this guy had once been a model, he'd definitely let himself go.

He was shaped like a bear—tall and wide and powerful-looking. The gun he gripped looked cheap and small in his bloated hand.

"I know you're carrying," he said to Zack. "Put your piece on the ground. Slow."

Zack's shoes crunched dirt as he squatted to place his gun on the ground. He rose slowly with his hands in the air. "Tell me, how does a male model become a drug dealer?"

"I didn't think we were here to talk about me."

"We brought the money," Ashley said. "Tell us what you know about Tara."

She could not tell if Ben's gaze shifted toward her. The sunglasses were practically opaque. But his gun did not move. It remained trained on Zack.

"Meth," he said. "A little too much meth." He shrugged his wide shoulders. "I'll always have the memories."

"The money is in my pocket," Zack said. Ashley did not like

seeing him with his hands in the air, his chest and face exposed to the gun. She felt an irrational and surprisingly compelling urge to put herself between him and Ben. He gave her a quick, reassuring look, as if sensing her thoughts. "I'll reach for it now, slowly. None of us wants trouble. This is a simple transaction. You want to sell us information. We want to buy it. After that, we'll go our separate ways."

"Is that the plan?" Ben said.

"That's the plan."

"Unless you killed my sister," Ashley said. "In that case—"

"If that were the case," Zack said, "he wouldn't have agreed to meet us. Right, Ben?"

"It's not like I needed Tara dead. You think one prissy porn bitch preaching the evils of drugs put a dent in my earnings? You gotta be kidding. Smack beats K-Y any day. I didn't kill Tara. I threw a party when I heard she was dead, the meddling bitch, but I didn't kill her."

"But you know who did," Zack said. "That's what you said on the phone."

"Really? Were you taking notes? Because I think I said *maybe* I know. Take your hand away from your pocket and kick that gun closer to me."

Zack complied with the demand. His semi-automatic skidded across the ground and stopped about a foot from Ben.

"What about the money?" Zack said.

"All in good time, my friend."

"Please," Ashley said, "if you know something, just tell us. I don't care about you, or drugs, or anything. I just want to know what happened to my sister."

"I'm a fair person," Ben said, "that's why I'm gonna tell you this, Ashley Hale. Your sister didn't hang herself. Someone did it to her. I think you got the right to know that, on account of you two being blood and all."

"Who? Who did it to her?"

"Get on your knees now. Both of you."

Ashley felt a spike of fear in her chest. She looked at Zack. This time, he had no reassuring look to offer her.

"Why?" he said.

"*Because I fucking said to!*"

Ben's voice reverberated off the side of the warehouse. Zack gave her a quick nod, then slowly lowered himself to a kneeling position. Ashley gave the ground a leery glance before touching it with her bare knees. The grit was uncomfortably hot, like sand on a beach, and packed hard.

"Now put your hands on the ground in front of you," Ben said.

Zack caught her eye. "It's okay. He just wants to make sure we don't follow him out of here. After he leaves, we'll be free to go. Right, Ben?" He spread his fingers and placed his hands on the dirt. After a few seconds, Ashley did the same. She had to crane her neck to see Ben now, stepping toward them.

Ben swept Zack's gun off the ground and examined it. "This thing loaded?"

She could not see Zack's expression. She was too terrified to take her eyes off of Ben. Zack's voice was grim when he said, "Yes."

"Nice piece."

"You can keep it."

"No, I don't think that would be a smart idea." He racked the slide.

"What are you doing?" Zack's voice cracked on the last word. Ashley could hear the confidence draining out of it and that terrified her. Ben's shoes crunched grit as he drew closer. His greasy smell filled her nostrils. "You don't want to do this, Ben," Zack said. "Think about the consequences."

"Thinking's never been my strong-suit." He stopped about two feet away from them and aimed the gun at Zack's head. "Violence, on the other hand—that's always come real natural."

Ashley's heart was beating so hard it hurt her chest. A column of vomit raced up her throat, hot and bitter. She choked it down. Winced at the burn in her throat. She forced her gaze away from the gun and looked at the hard-packed dirt between her hands. There were a few pebbles, the aluminum tab from a soda can, a rock. Her gaze fixed on the rock. She gnawed her lip. The rock was big enough, heavy enough. If she threw it at Ben, it would sting. But it wouldn't stop him. Not by a long shot.

Sting.

She looked past Zack at the sun-blanched wall of the warehouse. The wasps' nest was about halfway up the side of the building. She could see it, like a pimple on the otherwise smooth surface. It was large, but that didn't mean it would be an easy target, especially if she threw from a kneeling position.

She slid her right hand along the ground, careful not to draw Ben's attention. She palmed the rock and closed her fingers around the warm, solid weight.

"You said you didn't kill Tara," Zack said. "If that's true, then why kill us? You'll get caught. You know how hard it is to get away with murder these days? Don't you watch TV? You want to spend the rest of your life in prison?"

Ashley took a breath. Ben's attention was focused on Zack. She reared up on her knees, raised the rock, and pitched it at the side of the warehouse. Ben jumped and swung the gun from Zack to her. She could see his startled expression around his sunglasses. She could also see the black tunnel of the gun barrel. It turned her insides to liquid. Her stomach clenched painfully. Then the gun wavered as a buzzing sound rose in pitch.

A funnel-shaped swarm surged from the ruined nest. It was hard to believe that so many wasps could fit in that papery shell, but she didn't have time to ponder the physics. The first sting felt like someone pinched a wad of skin from her forearm and twisted. The second was like a needle stabbed into the back of her hand. Tears flooded her eyes. She rolled to her feet and ran.

Ben was running, too, an ungainly stagger that she might have found comical if not for the insects raging around her head. Zack put on a burst of speed, launched himself at the big man, and drove them both to the ground. Ashley slowed and turned, ignoring the stings, not sure what to do. Ben was screaming. Zack had his teeth gritted and was wrestling the guns from him. When he had them, he lurched to his feet and sprinted, yelling for Ashley to follow.

She did not dare to answer him. She was sure the wasps would pour into her mouth the moment she opened it. One had already stung her nostril and it was getting harder to keep her eyes open because the lids were swelling.

She risked a backward glance at Ben. He had clawed his way up off the ground and was swatting and batting at the wasps as he ran after her.

She rounded the corner of the warehouse seconds after Zack. They had left the Fiesta on the paved loading dock, in front of a padlocked garage on the side of the building. Zack had the key—thank God Zack had the key. He used the fob now to unlock the doors from a distance. The car beeped. Ashley reached it first, wrenched the door open, and threw herself across the backseat. Wasps crawled in her hair, on her legs. She slapped at them. Zack slammed her door and then opened the one in front of it and scrambled into the driver's seat. He pulled the door closed after him. Through the window, she watched Ben stagger toward the car. He had lost his sunglasses. His eyes were wide.

"What, does he think we're going to give him a lift?" Zack reached for the door lock.

"Let him in!"

Zack looked at her. His face was rubbery and discolored, already swollen. "Ashley, he tried to kill us. He was going to take the cash off of my dead body and leave us there to rot."

"He knows who killed Tara!"

Ben's oversized body slammed the side of the car. The impact rocked the Fiesta on its wheels. Ashley could hear his fingers scrabbling at the door handle. She opened the door and he fell on top of her. His odor was overpowering. She pushed him and he rolled off of her. His body wedged in the well between the front and back seats. Ashley pulled the door closed.

The cloud of wasps was gone, but her ears continued to buzz.

Ben's eyes were closed. The lids were red, swollen lumps. His mouth hung open. His tongue looked huge. Air wheezed in and out of his throat. His jowly face had a purple tint.

"Zack, he's not breathing right."

Zack twisted around in his seat. His face looked almost as bad as Ben's, but he didn't seem to be having any trouble breathing. "He must be allergic to wasp stings," he said. "He's gone into anaphylactic shock. His throat is closing up." Zack righted himself in the driver's seat and started the car. "We need to get him to a hospital."

One of Ben's eyes opened to a squint. The fear she had seen earlier was gone. Now he watched her with a serene, almost resigned, calm.

"Ben, tell me who killed my sister," she said. "Who killed Tara?"

The Fiesta dove into traffic. Ben's wheezing grew louder, more strangled. One of his hands clutched her arm and squeezed.

"Listen to me, Ben," Zack said from the front seat. "We're taking you to a hospital. We're saving your life, even though five minutes ago you were going to take ours. Now tell Ashley who killed Tara. You owe her that much."

A car horn blared. Ashley felt the car jerk sideways as Zack swerved through traffic, but she did not take her eyes off of Ben.

Ben's lips moved. A wheeze trickled past his swollen tongue.

"I can't understand you." She elevated his head and cradled it with her hands. Damp, greasy hair oozed between her fingers. A dead wasp fluttered to the floor.

Ben hissed and gasped. His face was dark purple now, and getting darker.

"Was she killed because of drugs?" Ashley said.

Ben shook his head. Then he nodded.

"Which is it? Yes or no? Was Tara killed because of drugs?"

Another breath rattled out of him. His eye closed. His neck went slack and his head drooped in her hands. Ashley shook him. No response. She moved one hand near his mouth and waited to feel his breath touch her skin.

Nothing. He was gone.

24

ASHLEY LEANED BACK in the metal chair, then immediately regretted it when a swollen knob high on her back sent a flair of pain through her body. She sat up straighter in the chair, but that did little to relieve her discomfort. The surface of her skin felt bloated and sore. And things felt even worse underneath—a sensation like barbed wire squeezing every bone and muscle. The doctor at the ER had counted twenty-eight stings.

She supposed she should consider herself lucky. Zack had been stung thirty-one times. And Billboard Ben, who had suffered only eighteen stings, was in the morgue.

But it was hard to feel lucky when she was back in Northridge, sitting in the same Devonshire Community Police Station interrogation room she had visited twice already.

Instead of easing her pain, the cream she had rubbed all over her skin only filled the room with its sweetly medicinal odor. The pills the ER doc had given her were not helping much either. She wished she could just turn off her nerve endings.

In the chair next to her, Zack looked equally miserable. His hands looked like Mickey Mouse gloves. He stared at them as if willing them to shrink to normal proportions.

"Let's go over this one more time," Detective Heather Collins said. They had been doing this for hours. First the police had interviewed her and Zack separately, then together. Collins's pale face still held the look of fascinated revulsion that had appeared on it when they'd arrived. She touched her notebook. The metal spirals clinked against the table's metal surface. "Benjamin Crowder, aka Billboard Ben, tried to kill you, and the only way you could think to escape was to disturb a large nest of paper wasps."

"Hey," Zack said. He managed to hitch his swollen mouth into a half-smile. "It worked. It was a good idea."

"Tell me again why you believe that Crowder had information regarding Tara Latner's death."

"He told us he did," Ashley said. "He told us she was murdered. And he might have told us more, if...."

"If multiple wasp stings to his face and throat had not triggered an allergic reaction," Collins said, referring to her notebook, "resulting in anaphylactic shock and death by asphyxiation."

"Yes!"

Collins leaned back in her chair, crossed one leg over the other, and sighed. "This kind of insanity isn't *too* hard to understand in a grieving sister, but a trained FBI agent?"

Ashley was not sure how much of the redness in Zack's face was from the wasp stings and how much was from indignation, but his glare made Collins look away.

"It's not insanity," Ashley said. "You're a detective. If you learned that a murder victim had been provoking drug dealers, and that one drug dealer in particular had made it clear that he hated her, wouldn't you want to talk to that man?"

"Yes," Collins said, "in a room like this one. Which is why you should have come to me instead of setting up your own meeting in an abandoned lot in Reseda."

There was a knock on the door. Two quick raps. A man in a suit ducked into the room and made a visible effort to keep his gaze on the floor. *Don't stare at the freaks,* Ashley thought. He passed a folder to Collins, then fled.

Collins placed the folder next to her notebook and flipped it open. The room was silent as she read the first document. Finally, she looked up. "Crowder was in a jail cell on the night of Tara's death, an overnight stay at Van Nuys Station for drunk and disorderly behavior. He couldn't have killed her."

"Just because he wasn't there doesn't mean he didn't know what happened," Ashley said.

"We'll never know," Collins said. She let out another sigh. "Jurisdictionally speaking, this bee-sting fiasco should have been West Valley's problem. Do you know why I took it off their hands? Because I'm trying to help you. Now return the favor. Stop antagonizing drug dealers and stinging insects. You go home," she said to Ashley. "And you," she said to Zack, "go back to whatever undercover FBI bullshit you were doing when you decided to shirk your responsibilities and become Ashley Hale's personal hero."

Had Zack been shirking his responsibilities? Ashley wondered what excuse he had given Kingsley for leaving the set. Was Zack jeopardizing his investigation to help her? She looked at the red and puffy skin around his eyes. She had almost gotten him killed.

Outside the police station, after they settled into the Fiesta, she said, "I'm sorry."

"For what? Saving my life?"

"It's my fault we were in that mess. I was too ready to believe that Ben only wanted money. You were right. It was stupid and dangerous. Now look at us."

He flipped down the visor and regarded his reflection in the mirror. "Good thing neither of us works in front of the camera."

"Ha ha," she said dryly.

"The question is, what are our options now? What do we do next?"

The smell of their ointment began to stink up the car. She started the engine and got the air-conditioner running. The cold air dissipated the smell. "Maybe Detective Collins is right. You should go back to doing your job. Kingsley is probably pissed off at you right now. If he fires you, that kind of screws up your undercover thing, doesn't it?"

"I told you, the investigation is basically dead. He's covered his tracks too well."

"If you keep watching him, he's bound to slip up. Especially with all of this pressure on him." Zack was watching her. His loopy grin had somehow fought its way through his swollen face to make an appearance. "What?" she said, smiling herself.

"Are you seriously trying to talk me out of helping you? Because you're not doing a bad job. If you keep it up, I might abandon you."

"I'm trying to do what's right."

"Well, knock it off. You can do what's right after we figure this thing out. And don't think I'm being totally selfless, either. I personally can't wait to deliver the perp to Collins. Her reaction is going to be priceless."

"You're just saying that."

"True, but does it matter?"

"I guess not."

She kissed him. It was a strange kiss. His lips felt cold and puffy, and the only feeling in her own lips was a dull pain. That didn't stop sparks of pleasure from shooting through her body. He pulled back. She expected to see the grin again, but his expression was serious.

"What?" she said.

"There's one thing about this case that's been bothering me for awhile now."

"Only one thing?"

"Selena Drake. Why was Tara so convinced that she was using drugs? Would your sister be wrong about something like that?"

Ashley thought about it. Tara had plenty of experience watching people she cared about struggle with drugs and alcohol. Hell, she had probably learned to read their mother's pupils before she'd been able to read Dr. Seuss.

"If she thought Selena was using, she had a reason," Ashley said. "She saw something, or heard something."

"Right. And here's something else to think about. Who suggested to us that it might be a good idea to meet with Billboard Ben?"

"Selena."

He nodded. "Right again."

The thought made Ashley queasy.

"I don't know about you," he said, "but I think she owes us some explanations."

———

ONLY THREE DAYS had passed since the first time Ashley had visited the townhouse that Selena, her sister Janie, and Rob called home, but it felt like weeks. The last time she'd been here, she had been positive that Rob was a killer. She had accused him to his face, while he cooked a grilled cheese sandwich for a girl with Down syndrome. Since then, she had cycled through a few more suspects, and now she had returned to accuse his girlfriend.

No, not to accuse her. Just to get some answers.

"This is where they live?" Zack gazed up at the powder-blue two-story townhouse. A bush near the front door shook and a chipmunk scurried out of it.

"Cute, isn't it?" she said.

"That's one word." He looked around at the other townhomes. "I wonder what the neighbors think."

"Somehow I doubt they've invited Rob and Selena to join the book club."

"Unless it's a club for adult books."

It hurt to smile. She touched her face, pressed gingerly against the swelling. Zack knocked on the door. She heard the sound of heavy footsteps clomping toward them. Zack shot her a quizzical look. Then the door was flung open. Janie's large body filled the doorway.

Janie's eyes popped almost comically wide. Her lower lip quivered. Ashley sensed that in a matter of seconds the girl was going to let loose a scream that would rock the townhouse.

"It's okay," she said hurriedly. "It's me, Ashley. We met a few days ago, remember? I just ... hurt my face a little. So did my friend. His name is Zack. But we're okay. We look scary but we're okay."

Ashley's words—or maybe just her voice—seemed to soothe the girl. Her lower lip stopped twitching. She moved a large hand across her face to wipe away the spittle that had collected at the corner of her mouth.

A slimmer figure appeared behind Janie. It was Selena. Her expression looked almost as horrified as her sister's. She gently guided Janie out of the doorway and beckoned Ashley and Zack inside.

"Oh my God. What happened?" She led them to the living room. The house smelled like recently baked cookies. Selena gestured for them to sit on the couch. Ashley heard footsteps upstairs. Apparently, they'd stopped by while the whole family was home. Lucky them. "You look like—did something attack you?"

"Something or someone," Zack said. He eased himself onto the couch. Ashley sat next to him and tried to ignore the flare of pain when her back touched the cushion.

Selena remained on her feet. She wore a dark blue sweatsuit. Her black hair was tied up in a ponytail. She looked like a different person than the sultry stripper they had seen the night before. "Did you ... did you talk to Billboard Ben?"

There was no mistaking the note of guilt in Selena's voice. Ashley felt her body tense. "Billboard Ben is dead," she told her.

Selena nodded slowly. "Janie, go upstairs and play cards with Rob."

Janie's eyes lit up. "Can we play Go Fish?"

"Any game you want. Tell him I said so."

"Yay!" Janie barreled up the staircase. The pictures on the walls shook.

Selena watched her go, then returned her gaze to the couch. "What happened?"

"He tried to kill us," Zack said. "But Ashley turned the tables on him."

Selena began to pace in front of the couch. She looked troubled, but not particularly surprised. "What do you mean, he tried to kill you?"

"Is there something you'd like to tell us?" Zack said.

Selena hesitated. "I ... I called him. Right after we talked at the club. I called him and told him you would be looking for him."

"You told us you didn't have his number," Ashley said.

"Technically I didn't. But I knew Max did. Max has everyone's number."

"Max?" Zack said.

"Rob's personal assistant. After you left Gloss, I called Max, got Ben's phone number, and called him."

"Why would you do that?" Ashley said.

"It's complicated."

"So explain it," Ashley said. "We're smarter than we look."

"No, I mean—" Selena chewed her lip. "Did you ... have you talked to the police?"

"Of course," Ashley said.

"Are they going to, you know, come here?"

"I doubt it."

Selena exhaled. "It was a mistake, obviously. I made a mistake. I thought—I don't know—that I could use Billboard Ben to stop you. Stupid, right? I've seen too many movies."

"Selena, what are you talking about?"

"I didn't think he would actually try to hurt you. You must know that, right? I mean, you know me. A little. I'm not—" She shook her head as if to shake her words into a more orderly sequence. "I told Ben I would pay him a thousand dollars. He was supposed to scare you. Make you give up and stop, you know, asking questions."

"Scare us?" Zack sounded dubious. "He held my own gun to my head. My loaded gun."

"Oh God. I'm sorry."

"Why would you want to stop us?" Ashley said.

"*Because she's trying to protect you, you stubborn bitch.*" A shadow fell across the couch. Rob Rourke stepped into the room. Selena glared at him. The room became eerily quiet. Ashley thought she could hear the ticks and creaks of the building settling on its foundations.

"I can handle this without your help," Selena said. "Go upstairs. Janie needs—"

"You obviously *can't* handle this."

"He's right," she said to Ashley. "I was trying to protect you. I'm trying to protect all of us."

"Tara believed you were using drugs," Zack said.

"She was wrong."

"Who are you trying to protect us from?" Ashley said.

Rob's face radiated anger. "My fiancée doesn't have to answer your questions."

"Fiancée?" Ashley said. The image of Sean's face flashed in her mind. She had not thought of him in days. It was amazing to think that last week, she had wanted to spend the rest of her life with him. "You're engaged?"

"Congratulations," Zack said. "Now you can be her husband and her suitcase pimp."

Rob turned his sneer on Zack. "What's your angle here, Cutter? You barely knew Tara."

"I'm just a good Samaritan helping Ashley out."

"Right. Well, you can help her out the door. Now."

"How about if you tell us what's going on so we can protect ourselves?" Ashley said.

Rob shook his head. "As usual, you don't have the slightest idea what you're talking about. You always were the dumb sister. For God's sake, get on a plane and go back to Jersey. And you—" He looked at Zack. "Join a church group or something."

Zack rose from the couch. "At least let me use the bathroom."

Rob shrugged and gestured at the hallway. Zack slipped out of the room. Ashley assumed there was a bathroom on the first floor, but the creak of the staircase was unmistakable. She started talking to cover the noise.

"Insult me all you want, Rob. I'm not leaving here without answers."

"I'm as heartbroken as anyone that Tara is dead," Selena said. "But if you keep digging, more people are going to wind up dead."

Her words did not sound like a threat. There was genuine concern in her voice. To Ashley, that was even more frightening.

"Who killed her?" Ashley said.

"I can't tell you that."

"Then I'll call the police."

"We'll deny that this conversation ever took place," Rob said.

"What about Billboard Ben's phone records?" Ashley said. "Selena called him. Are you going to deny that?"

"Please," Selena said. Now there was desperation in her voice. "You can't bring Tara back. You're only going to hurt more people."

Zack stepped into the room. "Come on," he said. "It's time to go."

Ashley lifted herself from the couch. Her body ached. She faced Selena. "Just so you know, I'm not giving up. And I'm not afraid."

"That's because you're stupid," Rob said. He walked them to the front door and opened it. "Have a great day."

———

IN THE CAR, Ashley said, "Please tell me you found something up there."

"No. But I did have an interesting conversation with Janie."

Ashley pulled her gaze from the road long enough to take in the excitement in his eyes. She said, "I'm guessing it wasn't about Go Fish."

"I asked her if she ever heard her sister talk about Tara."

"And?"

"Well, it was difficult to get a coherent story from her. She's easily distracted. But I managed to get the basics. I guess you could say I have a way with people of limited intelligence."

"I hope you're not including me in that category."

He laughed and shook his head. "Hardly. I realized right away that Janie doesn't know Tara is dead. She speaks about her in the present tense. I guess Selena's trying to shield her from the knowledge, or something. But Janie picks up a lot more than Selena probably realizes."

"Such as?"

"She told me that Selena was mad at Tara. When I asked her why, she said it was because Tara followed Selena."

"Followed her? Funny that Selena never mentioned that to us."

"Isn't it?"

"Where did she follow her? And when? And why?"

"I wasn't able to get the when or the why. Or the where, actually. All Janie said was that Tara followed Selena to someone named Rosie."

"Who's Rosie?"

"That's the question."

"I've heard that name." Ashley's foot lifted from the pedal as she searched her memory. She felt that familiar sensation again, the tingle of a thought that was just out of reach. The car behind them honked and swerved, then blew past on the right. The jolt brought her back to the moment.

"Are you okay?" Zack said.

"Yeah. I just...."

Then it came to her.

She pulled the Fiesta to the side of the road and grabbed her purse from the back seat.

"What are you doing?"

She rummaged through the purse. "A few days ago, when I was looking around Tara's apartment, I found something that I thought might be important. But I didn't know how to interpret it at the time, and then I guess I just forgot about it." She pulled the slip of paper from her purse and handed it to Zack.

"A receipt?"

"Tara always kept all of her credit card receipts."

She watched him squint at the blurry print. "Rosie's. It's not a person. It's a place. A bar in West Hollywood."

"Look at the date and time," Ashley said.

His gaze returned to the receipt. "Last Tuesday. 8:52 PM. That's the night before Tara was killed."

Ashley shifted the car back to drive. "I guess we know where to go next."

25

THE WEHO ADDRESS led Ashley to anticipate a trendy hotspot, but the only remarkable feature of the squat, faded gray building—and the only reason she didn't drive right past it on La Cienega Boulevard —was the large crowd of smokers loitering in front. Only then did she see the sign in the window. *Rosie's.*

"We're not exactly going to fit in at this place," Zack said after they parked the car and they returned to the building. They could hear the chatter of the crowd.

"Why do you say that?"

He smiled and tilted his chin. The smokers were all men. Mostly young, in their twenties and early thirties. As Ashley and Zack passed through them and entered the building, Zack said, "I need to start hitting the gym more often. No one is checking me out."

"You're a very attractive man, but right now your face looks like a Macy's Day balloon. Come on, I see an empty stool at the bar. I'll sit. You stand. Maybe your butt will get a better reception than your face."

"Story of my life."

The bar was a long strip of dark mahogany. He pulled out a stool for her. She put a hand on his shoulder and leveraged herself up onto the padded seat. He helped her with a hand on her back. His hand felt good there, a warm pressure. She wished he would leave it there, but he took it away as soon as she settled onto the seat. He leaned over the bar, rested his elbows on its glossy surface, and played with a cardboard coaster.

"Tara followed Selena here?" Ashley said, thinking out loud. "Not what I expected."

"Me neither."

The guy on the stool next to him turned with a smile, but the smile faltered when he saw Zack's swollen, red face. He offered a polite, "Hello," before turning away.

"I think I'm making people uncomfortable," Zack said. He turned the coaster in his hands. The St. Pauli Girl did cartwheels.

"Now there's a waste of advertising dollars," Ashley said, looking at the busty blonde.

He smiled. "But if you think about it, this place makes sense if Selena wanted to go somewhere she wouldn't be recognized. She's not likely to run into many fans of her work here."

Ashley turned on her stool to look around. The mahogany bar ran across one side of the room. Tall, round cocktail tables were arranged in the middle. Booths lined the far wall. The place was dark, but she could see smiling faces in the dim light. Conversations babbled around her, loud but not rowdy. People must have carried the odor of cigarette smoke inside on their clothing. It tickled her nostrils.

"But what was she doing?" Ashley said. "Buying drugs doesn't make sense. Why would she come here to buy something she could get for free? And even if she did want to buy drugs herself, why would she care so much about not being recognized?"

"Tara was probably asking herself the same questions when she followed her here. Do you have any pictures of Tara on your phone?"

"Yeah, but they're not recent." Ashley dug out her phone. "There are two photos of Tara. Even when I stopped returning her calls, I never had the heart to delete them. One is from when we were kids and the other is from an AVN Adult Entertainment Expo years ago."

She handed the phone to Zack and looked away when he flicked to the childhood photo, but she saw it in her mind's eye anyway. She and Tara clung to the monkey bars at a local playground in Tarzana. She still remembered the place vividly, everything from the pleasurable burn of the metal slide on her legs to the sound of sneakers crunching gravel, but she had no memory of who had taken the picture. She doubted the photographer had been their mother. Gail had spent most of that time period snorting cocaine—and sometimes mainlining it. Maybe a mother of a friend. It didn't matter. Ashley had kept the photo for years. It had migrated from the corner of her bedroom mirror to the inside of her high school locker to a plastic picture holder in her wallet and eventually into a digital file on her phone. The color was faded and the brittle corners of the original photograph, where she'd trimmed it with scissors, were visible in the digital version.

Thinking about it made her eyes tear. She blinked.

Zack had moved on to the second photo. Ashley could look at this one—although it still hurt to do so. She and Tara stood on the floor of the Sands Expo Center in Vegas, smiling, arms around each other's waists.

"Jeez, I've gotten old," she said.

"I think you're more beautiful now. I mean, when your face isn't all swelled up."

"Thanks."

Zack waved for the bartender, a good-looking guy dressed in black designer jeans and an expensive-looking shirt. Young, like most of the patrons. Probably an aspiring actor or model. He pushed a lock of black hair from his forehead and smiled at them. He had friendly blue eyes that did not reveal any reaction to the swollen, wasp-stung faces in front of him.

"Happy hour special, two-dollar martinis."

"Just a gin and tonic for me," Zack said. "Tanqueray."

"You got it. And for the lady?"

"Diet Coke," Ashley said.

The bartender dropped ice cubes into a tumbler, added Diet Coke and a slice of lemon, and put it down on the St. Pauli Girl's face. After he mixed Zack's drink and put in on the bar in front of him, Zack turned her phone to face him and showed him the adult expo pic.

"The woman on the left," Zack said. "We'd like to know if you've seen her here."

The bartender leaned forward for a better view. "I don't think so."

"Are you sure?" Zack pushed the phone closer to the man's eyes. "Take a closer look. Please."

The bartender shook his head slowly. "Sorry."

"What about last Tuesday," Ashley said, "around 9:00 PM?"

"I was working, but I don't remember her."

"Are you sure?" Zack said.

The bartender's friendly smile faltered. "Look, I don't make a mental note of every woman who comes in here, okay? I spend most of my time pouring drinks and counting change." He glanced down the bar at his waiting customers.

"There can't be too many women who come in here," Zack said.

"You'd be surprised. Some have gay friends, others want a place where they can have a drink and not get hit on." He gave the photo another look, then turned to Ashley. "Your sister?"

"Yeah."

"Good gene pool."

She felt herself blush, but she doubted he could see it through the red lumps on her face. "Thanks."

"Is she missing or something?"

"Something like that."

"That sucks. I'm sorry." He frowned. "You want to settle up now or run a tab?"

"We'll run a tab," Zack said.

"You got it." He moved down the bar to tend to his other customers. Zack sighed and handed the phone back to Ashley.

"She was here," she said. "There's no other explanation for the receipt."

"I agree. But she did a good job staying inconspicuous. She probably wore something dark, maybe stood close to a large group so she would appear to be part of it. Ordered her drink and paid her bill quickly and without making any small talk. She obviously didn't want Selena to notice her."

The smell of alcohol saturated the air. It stirred a craving in her that she had managed to suppress for a long time. The photos had weakened her. She looked at the rows of bottles behind the bar. Grey Goose, Bombay Sapphire, Johnny Walker, Cuervo. Even with the sweet fizz of Diet Coke on her tongue, her mouth felt dry.

Suddenly, a thought struck her. "We should have shown him a picture of Selena. That was stupid." She accessed the Internet with her phone, ran a Google search for *Selena Drake*, and was rewarded with hundreds of pictures. She settled on a professional-looking headshot.

Zack waved the bartender over again. Again, he showed him the screen of Ashley's phone. "How about this woman? Have you seen her?"

The bartender took the phone from Zack and peered at the screen. "Yeah. She drinks gin, like you, but without the tonic. I didn't know she was a model." He looked impressed.

Ashley and Zack exchanged a glance. "She comes here a lot?" Zack said.

"I wouldn't say a lot. She's been here three, maybe four times."

"Hanging out with gay friends, or drinking without being hit on?"

The bartender smiled and returned the phone to Zack. "Gay friend. What's his name? Derek something. He comes in here a lot. Although I haven't seen him this week."

"What does he look like?" Zack said.

"Tall. Really skinny. Good hair, though. I'd say he's in his mid-twenties. He's kind of a showoff. Always telling stories. Real loud voice."

"What are his stories about?"

"I'm usually too busy to pay attention. I've heard him spout some celebrity names. Gossip. Like if someone famous picks up hemorrhoid cream, that sort of thing."

"He's a photographer or something?" Zack said. "Paparazzi?"

That made the bartender laugh. "No, man. He works at a pharmacy. I forgot the name of the place, but it's on Robertson Boulevard. He's always telling me I should stop by, and he'll take care of me."

"Thanks," Zack said.

The bartender looked at Ashley, then at Zack. "Was that helpful?"

"I hope so," Ashley said.

———

ASHLEY SLID INTO THE FIESTA. The sun was low in the sky. Its rays speared through the windshield. She squinted against the glare and wished she had thought to bring a pair of sunglasses.

"So it's back to drugs," she said.

"Derek works at a pharmacy. He met with Selena. Tara suspected Selena of using drugs. It might be a coincidence."

"But you don't think so?"

"I'm FBI. We don't believe in coincidences."

"You think this guy Derek is selling drugs on the street?"

"Or at Rosie's. It wouldn't be that unusual. There's a huge demand for black market prescription drugs. Vicodin, OxyContin, even Ritalin."

"It still doesn't make sense."

"But it's a lead. Leads are good."

"So now we visit every pharmacy on Robertson Boulevard?"

"Derek supposedly saw a lot of celebrities, so we know to focus on the northern part of the street. That narrows it down."

She nodded. The tree-lined boulevard was home to plenty of trendy boutiques, designer clothing stores, and chic restaurants, but she doubted they would find many pharmacies.

"Remember," Zack said. "Investigations are ninety-percent legwork."

"Good thing I'm wearing heels." She looked at her feet, which were already aching, and sighed.

———

TWO YEARS HAD PASSED since Ashley had last walked Robertson Boulevard. She had not realized how much she missed shopping in LA. Beautiful women strolled past them, their slim arms laden with bags from Lisa Kline, Tory Burch, Maxfield Bleu. A gorgeous pair of boots caught her eye and she stopped in front of a window to stare.

Zack waited while she ogled the footwear. His patience was admirable.

They had already visited two pharmacies. Zack had questioned employees at both, with no success. Ashley was debating taking a five minute break to try on the boots when Zack pointed down the street. "There's another one."

He was right. Sandwiched between two clothing stores was a narrow brick building. *Whole Care Pharmacy*. Ashley lost interest in the boots and quickened her step. She and Zack cut through the ambling shoppers. A bell chimed when Zack opened the pharmacy's door.

Ashley's first thought was that the place seemed more like a Los Angeles souvenir shop than a drug store, but as they walked past overpriced T-shirts and mugs, they eventually reached shelves of painkillers and other over-the-counter medications. Finally she spotted the counter labeled Pharmacy in the back of the store.

As soon as she saw the man behind the counter, she knew they had found Derek's workplace.

The pharmacist, a petite, middle-aged Indian man in a white coat, had a bandage on his forehead and some kind of splint on his nose. The faded remains of bruises were visible around his dark eyes.

She and Zack approached the counter. The pharmacist observed them for a moment, then said, "Wasps?"

"Yes," Zack said. "But that's not why we're here."

"My son disturbed a yellow-jacket nest when he was five," the man said. "It was awful. I assume you've been to a doctor?"

The splint on his nose distorted his voice, but Ashley detected a hint of a British accent. "Listen," she said, "Mr...."

"Dama." He smiled at her.

"You're one of the pharmacists here?" Zack said.

"*The* pharmacist. And owner."

"We're looking for somebody." Zack leaned his elbows on the counter. "A tall, skinny man in his mid-twenties. We think his first name is Derek."

The pharmacist's olive-complexion blanched beneath the bandages and bruises. "Are you a policeman? May I please see some identification?"

"We're not with the police. My name is Zack Cutter. This is Ashley Latner."

"I don't believe I can help you." His dark eyes gazed past them at two young women browsing the aisles. "I have customers."

"Please," Ashley said. "We think this person may have hurt someone we care about. We just want to talk to him."

"As I said, I really don't think I can help you."

"Because you don't know the man we're talking about?" Zack said. "Or because you do know him and you're afraid of him?"

"I'm sorry. I have a shop to run—" He looked around, as if for help. None of his employees were in sight.

"What happened to your face?" Zack said.

"I had an accident." The pharmacist straightened up, rolled his shoulders back. "Not that it's any of your business."

"It looks like someone hit you," Zack said, "several times."

"I know how it looks. The truth is that I bumped into a wall. Clumsy."

"Just because we're not with the police doesn't mean we can't get the police involved," Zack said. "Is that what you want?"

Dama's eyes widened. "No."

"Really? Because there is a homicide detective who might be interested in talking to you. I can call her now, if you'd like."

"Homicide?"

"That's what I said."

"There's a reason I didn't go to the police," Dama said. "I don't need the bad publicity. Nor do I want ... further episodes with this person. If I answer your questions, you have to promise not to take what I tell you to the police."

"I can't make that promise," Zack said. "But I can promise you that if we go to the police, it means your friend is guilty of a lot more than assault and battery. Revenge against you will be the furthest thing from his mind, and trust me—the evening news will have a lot juicier details to obsess about than his employment here."

Dama looked intrigued. "I suppose I can accept that."

"Tell us what happened."

"Not here," Dama said. "In the back."

Dama opened a gate built into the counter. Zack and Ashley followed him into a backroom that smelled of pills and powders. The walls were lined with shelves, cabinets, and refrigeration units. Two of the larger cabinets had locking mechanisms built into their doors. Ashley guessed that these held the narcotics. There was a desk and two plastic chairs. Dama gestured for them to sit down, then leaned his hip against the desk.

Zack took a seat in one of the plastic chairs. She sat next to him. The chair was hard plastic, uncomfortable, and the legs wobbled.

Dama looked at his shoes. "Derek started working for me about a year ago. He told me he was a college student. I had no reason not to believe him. I hired him part-time, as a pharm-tech. He seemed honest and capable. I had no idea he was doing anything untoward."

"Until last week," Zack said.

"Yes. A young woman came to see me last Wednesday. She told me that she suspected that Derek was selling drugs on the street. I didn't believe her at first. I showed her my controlled drugs cabinets. Nothing was missing. But after she left, I checked the rest of my inventory, just to be sure. It seems Derek had been supplementing his paychecks by selling Estinyl and Premarin."

Zack's brow furrowed. "I'm not familiar with those drugs."

"Estrogen hormone treatments," Dama said.

"You can use estrogen to get high?" Ashley said.

The pharmacist's laugh was a little shrill. "No. But it turns out there is a thriving black market for the stuff among transvestites and transsexuals."

Ashley looked at Zack. Their "lead" was a dead end. It had to be.

Tara had been following Selena, and Selena had no reason to buy black market estrogen.

Unless it wasn't for her.

"Is there any reason that a woman with Down syndrome would use estrogen treatments?" Ashley said.

Dama looked surprised by the question, but after a moment, his eyes lit up. "Actually, there have been studies observing pathological similarities between Down syndrome and Alzheimer's disease. But estrogen replacement therapy in women with Down syndrome is hardly common. I believe researchers are still experimenting on lab animals."

"Where is Derek now?" Zack said.

"I don't know. After I discovered that he had been stealing from me, I fired him and I told him I would have to go to the authorities. He, ah, disagreed with that point. Quite violently. Then he left. That was Wednesday of last week. I haven't seen him since."

"What about the woman?" Ashley said. "The one who told you she suspected that he was selling drugs? Have you seen her?"

Dama shook his head. "No, I haven't seen her, either."

"Was this her?" Ashley showed him the photo of Tara on her phone.

Dama nodded. "That's the woman who visited me. Is she ... the person who may have been harmed?"

"She's dead," Ashley said. "She was murdered that night. Wednesday night."

Dama's face grew paler. "You shouldn't have come here. I have a wife and a son. What if ... what if Derek is watching me? What if he finds out that I talked to you?"

"What's his full name?" Zack said.

"Derek Randall."

"Do you have any photographs of him?"

"I photocopied his passport for tax purposes." Dama walked across the room and opened a small file-cabinet. He flipped through some folders, then returned with a sheet of paper.

Ashley gasped. Even in the stark black-and-white tones of the photocopy, she recognized the face. "That's Max. Rob's obnoxious personal assistant."

Zack shook his head. "Actually, his name is Dimitri Sidorov."

"No," the pharmacist said. "His name is Derek Randall. I held his passport in my hand. He showed me a social security card."

"Forged documents," Zack said. "Derek Randall is an alias." He turned to look at Ashley. "So is Max, apparently."

The small backroom of Whole Care Pharmacy suddenly seemed smaller. Ashley stood from the wobbly plastic chair and paced, running her fingers along the smooth doors of the refrigeration units. Dama looked equally agitated. His hand touched the bandaged splint that covered his nose.

"Dimitri Sidorov is the nephew of Konstantin Kazakov," Zack said. "I had no idea he was in Los Angeles. This changes everything."

26

A STUNNED SILENCE fell over the pharmacy's backroom. Ashley could hear the ticking of a small clock on Dama's desk.

"You mean he's part of the Kazakov crime family?" she said.

"No." Zack rubbed his face. "That's what doesn't make sense. Dimitri was expelled from the family the day he came out of the closet. Hell, he would have been killed if his mother hadn't pleaded with Konstantin to spare him."

Dama's gaze ticked from Ashley to Zack. "You said you weren't the police."

Zack said, "Listen, it might be a smart idea for you to close the store for a few days. Take your wife and son on a vacation."

Dama looked ill.

"Come on," Zack said to Ashley. "We'll talk in the car."

The slow crawl of traffic made Ashley vibrate with frustration. She squeezed the hard plastic steering wheel. She wanted to cruise, wanted to feel the steady thrum of wheels on pavement. She knew it would set her mind free to arrange everything she had just learned into a logical pattern. But it was 9:00 PM on a Friday night. The only pattern was the mosaic of red brake lights in front of her. Her foot moved from the pedal to the brake and back again.

"It's got to be the estrogen," she said. "The estrogen's the key."

"Why do you say that?"

"Think about it. Selena's been taking care of her sister for a long time. It makes sense that she would stay current on Down syndrome research. She read or heard about the potential of estrogen replacement therapy and thought it would help Janie. But because the treatment's effectiveness hasn't been proved, Janie's doctor wouldn't go along with it. So she found another source. Dimitri."

She turned to Zack and expected to see her excitement reflected in his face. But he looked skeptical. "I told you, I don't believe in coincidences."

"You said the Kazakov family has been expanding its influence in the porn industry. Maybe someone connected to the family knew that Dimitri was selling estrogen to transvestites. Isn't it possible that that person also heard about Selena's problem and decided to help out two friends at the same time? It's not that big of a coincidence. The porn business is very insular."

"Your theory is possible," Zack said. "But it's just a guess."

"It's not just a guess. It explains everything. Tara was on a mission to keep the Pinnacle girls clean, right? And Selena was Pinnacle's biggest star. Somehow, Tara found out that Selena was buying drugs. She didn't realize the drug was estrogen. She would not have even considered that possibility. Not in this industry, and not with her —*our*—background. She followed Selena. To help her. And then she followed Selena's dealer back to the pharmacy. She probably figured she could rid the industry of one more sleazebag. So the next day, she talked to Dama. Dimitri lost his pharmacy job and almost got in trouble with the police. He flipped out and got revenge by killing Tara."

Zack's expression remained guarded. "Tara's death was not a 'flipped-out' kind of scenario. Her killer was careful and smart. He made her death look like a suicide and left no evidence behind."

"Maybe Dimitri was afraid of pissing off his uncle. If a member of the Kazakov family—even an estranged member—got arrested for killing a porn star, it would kind of screw up the family's plans in the industry, right? So he would have been careful."

Zack sighed. "Okay. But explain the Max alias. Why would Dimitri adopt a new name and start working as Rob Rourke's personal assistant?"

"That's easy. For one thing, he's out of work. His access to estrogen has been cut off. He needs a steady paycheck. He probably used Selena to coerce Rob into hiring him. By getting a job at Pinnacle, Dimitri put himself in a position to observe the police investigation and make sure no one suspected that Tara was murdered. Rachel, the receptionist at Pinnacle, told me that Max was new. Rob must have hired him right after Tara's death. It all fits, Zack! It explains why Max was so hostile to me when I met him, why he didn't want me around. And it explains why Selena and Rob have been trying to get me to stop asking questions about Tara's death."

Zack nodded. "It's a theory."

"Selena told us that she called Max last night to get Billboard Ben's phone number. Remember? When Dimitri got that call, he knew we were closing in. So he set us up to be killed."

She cut into a gap in traffic to their right and spurted past an Infiniti. She did not gain much ground, but at least she had a new license plate to stare at.

Zack said, "Are you driving to the police station?"

"We need to talk to Detective Collins."

"Ashley, I need to get in touch with my superiors. If we go straight to the police, we risk compromising a major federal investigation."

Ashley leaned back against the seat. Frustration burned through her.

"Head for my house," he said. "I'll make some calls and find out what the Bureau thinks of your theory."

———

"YOU'LL SPEND THE NIGHT?" It was the first thing Zack said after unlocking the door and ushering her into the duplex. She suspected that part of his motivation was to keep an eye on her, but she didn't care. She leaned into him as they stepped into the shadowy entryway.

Upstairs, she kicked off her heels and took off her skirt and top. She changed into one of his T-shirts, a gray Pirates of the Caribbean souvenir from Disneyland. It was comfortably big on her, hanging almost to her knees. Then she padded downstairs, where she found him in the kitchen spooning decaf into his coffee maker. She was about to crack a joke about how domestic they'd become when she noticed the phone clamped between his ear and his shoulder.

She sat on his kitchen counter and watched him. At first, he did most of the talking. After that, he was mostly silent, his lips pressed together in a thin line. He muttered responses like "yes" and "that's correct" and "that is my understanding" as he poured water into the coffee maker. He turned on the coffee maker and ended the call at the same time.

"Well?" she said.

"They're going to call me back."

She hugged herself, not because she was cold but because she liked the feel of his T-shirt against her skin. The material was soft. His smell lingered in the cotton.

"You look good," he said.

She scooted her butt over the edge of the counter, reached her leg out to hook her ankle behind one of his thighs, and drew him closer to her. "The ER doc didn't say anything about refraining from sex while our stings heal, did he?"

Zack made a face. "I think it's kind of assumed."

"Rain check?"

"Definitely."

He propped himself onto the counter beside her and put an arm around her waist. They listened to the coffee maker gurgle. A rich and nutty smell filled the kitchen.

"Will the FBI arrest Dimitri?" she said.

"They don't have jurisdiction. They would have to turn it over to the LAPD. But they won't."

"Why?"

"First they'll try to figure out a way to use Dimitri against the Kazakov family. They'll threaten him, then bring in the state district attorney with an offer. A reduced state sentence in exchange for information and testimony against the Kazakovs in a federal RICO case."

She jerked out of his embrace. "And you're okay with that?"

"It's the best solution." He touched her hand. "I know you're excited about your theory, but that's all it is. A theory. From an evidence standpoint, the case against Dimitri is too weak to take to trial. We can connect Dimitri to Selena with an eyewitness, and we can maybe prove the theft and drug dealing—assuming Dama cooperates—but we have no evidence connecting Dimitri to Tara's death. Even a very confident prosecutor would think twice about filing a first-degree murder charge in this case. But if Dimitri accepts a deal, that means he'll plead guilty. No trial. The gaps in the evidence chain won't matter."

"I'm not stupid, Zack. I know what a deal would mean. The FBI nails the Kazakovs and Tara's killer gets a slap on the wrist."

"Trust me, any amount of time spent in a maximum security prison will not be a slap on the wrist for a guy like Dimitri Sidorov."

Ashley shook her head. "You're not even giving the police a chance. If we tell them what we've learned, maybe they can find the evidence you say is missing, the link between Dimitri and Tara."

"I'm sure that's an option that the Bureau will consider. But it's their call to make, not ours."

"Bullshit. Tara's my sister. It's my call." She hopped down from the counter. The kitchen tiles felt cool under her bare feet. She tried to remember where she had put her purse. It was in the bedroom. She had left it on the bed when she changed out of her clothes.

"At least wait until the morning," Zack said. "Sleep on it. Think about everything I said. If you still disagree with me when you wake up, you can call the LAPD. I won't try to stop you. But I'm asking you not to do that. I'm asking you to trust me."

The decaf finished brewing. She looked at the full pot, then turned away. Her stomach felt too agitated for coffee.

"Fine. I'll sleep on it."

———

SHE WOKE IN HIS ARMS. Sunlight pressed against the mini-blinds covering the bedroom window, lending them a soft glow. The rest of the room was still comfortably dark. She closed her eyes. She had hoped that she would pop out of bed knowing exactly what to do, but she felt just as conflicted as she had the night before.

She wanted justice for her sister. She wanted Dimitri Sidorov to pay. But she could not ignore the man who had helped her puzzle out Tara's murder in the first place. The man whose warm, strong arms were holding her now. The man whose deep, even breaths made her feel peaceful, secure, happy. The night before, he had asked her to trust him.

Zack shifted in the bed, tugging the sheet with him. It slid off of her legs. She felt goose bumps rise on her thigh. She leaned forward to grab the sheet and saw a man. He stood in the shadow of the doorway, watching them.

She sat up and gripped the sheet against her chest. Her heart jack-hammered. Zack muttered in his sleep, then came awake suddenly, popping up beside her. His hand swung to the nightstand but came back empty. After the incident with Billboard Ben, the police had confiscated his gun.

The man who stood in the doorway of Zack's bedroom held a revolver.

"Kingsley," Zack said. There was no trace of grogginess in his voice. She could feel the tension in his muscles. "What are you doing here?"

Kingsley stepped closer to the bed. The lines in his face looked deeper. More gray hairs than she remembered streaked his head and goatee. The smell of sweat and body odor clung to him and almost made her gag.

"What's your real name?" he said. His arm trembled under the revolver's weight. He sucked in a breath and steadied the gun. She heard a click as he pulled back the hammer. The barrel was aimed at Zack's bare chest.

"I don't know what you're talking about," Zack said. "Put the gun down and we'll talk, okay?"

"And Ashley," Kingsley said. "I don't know what to say to you. I thought we were friends."

"We're all friends," Zack said. "Put down the gun, King. You shoot videos, not people."

Kingsley's mouth hitched up in a grimace. "That's cute, Zack. Did you make it up yourself, or did someone at the FBI just feed it to you through an earpiece?"

"What are you talking about?"

"Cut the shit." Kingsley looked enraged, but only for a second. Then fatigue seemed to drag him down. The gun wavered. "I've got a Devonshire uniform on my payroll. Can't be too careful these days. He told me he's been seeing the two of you in the station a lot lately. I told him to look into it. What do you think he learned?"

"I don't know," Zack said.

"The fuck you don't." He jerked the revolver upward and aimed it at Zack's face. "You've been lying to me since the day we met. Spying on me. Trying to take me down. You're with the fucking feds."

Zack's hand found hers under the sheet. "Get out of the bed, Ashley."

"She moves, I'll kill her."

"Like you killed Brewster?" Ashley said. Zack squeezed her hand, crushing her fingers. She registered the silent warning but could not hold back her anger. "He thought he was your friend, didn't he? Look how that turned out."

She saw muscles twitch under Kingsley's skin, below the tangles of his goatee. "I didn't kill Brewster. I told them they could trust him. I begged. But they don't trust anyone. They used one of their own people. One day Brewster was here, the next he was gone. *Gone.* That's how they do shit, Ashley."

"The Kazakovs," she said.

He flinched at the name. "I took their money. Keeping Tyrant alive seemed so important at the time." He laughed. His eyes were shiny. "A fucking joke, right?"

"I can help you," Zack said. "Put down the gun."

"I'm fucked."

"You're not fucked. You're in an excellent bargaining position. Put down the gun and I'll get on the phone and set up a meeting. Work with the good guys."

"Right. And risk—" His face bunched. He looked away. "Do you know what they would do to Cheryl and the girls?"

He raised the revolver, then turned it around and pressed the barrel to the underside of his chin.

"Kingsley, don't!" Zack launched himself across the bed. His ankles tangled in the blanket and sheet. His naked body tumbled onto the floor. Kingsley sidestepped away from him.

"I didn't tell them about you," Kingsley said. "Maybe you can still take the fuckers down."

"Kingsley, no!"

The gunshot sounded like a bomb detonating in the small bedroom. Ashley had been to firing ranges as a kid, but she'd never heard the report of a revolver without the protection of ear plugs. She felt a burst of pain in her ears and then heard a whine. Tears filled her eyes. She blinked until she could see.

The wall was splashed with blood where Kingsley's body had crumpled. His head lulled forward, revealing a snarl of wet, lumpy hair. She smelled gun-smoke and blood and urine.

Zack lunged across the room. He lifted Kingsley's head and revealed a hole under his chin. It had ragged, crispy edges where the blast of heat from the revolver's barrel had burned him. Ashley's stomach lurched and her mouth filled with warm saliva and she rolled over the other side of the bed and threw up on Zack's floor.

"Kingsley?" Zack's voice sounded distant. Her ears were still ringing. "Can you hear me?"

She crawled around the bed and joined him at Kingsley side.

Kingsley was still alive. She could see his chest rising and falling and she could hear shallow breaths. His eyes were glassy.

"Russell," Zack said, using his real name, "don't slip away on me. Think of Cheryl and Valerie and Kate."

Kingsley's eyes remained unfocused.

Ashley said, "I'll call 911."

27

THE ER WAS out of view around the corner, but isolated sounds still reached her where she sat in a small waiting area. The clatter of a clipboard, the rattle of a privacy curtain tugged around an examination table, the scrape of a metal implement. She heard a woman ask someone named José about his medical history, first in English, then Spanish. The staff must have sprayed air-freshener to cover the odor of antiseptics and blood. The air had a flowery, artificial smell. An out-of-date issue of *Us* magazine rested on a table to her left. Its corners were bent. Fingerprint smudges blurred the cover photo of Reese Witherspoon. She wondered how many people had touched it.

The staff was prepping Kingsley for surgery. Cheryl had arrived and was with him. So was Zack—just in case he came around, had some last words, some vital information to whisper on his dying breath. Ashley thought of the exit wound on the top of his head and forced herself to think about something else.

She had not felt this alone since arriving in Los Angeles. The adrenaline that had coursed through her body when she and Zack had seen Dimitri's photo at Whole Care Pharmacy was now barely a memory. Sadness had replaced it, an emptiness that made her want to lie face-down on the checkered linoleum tiles and close her eyes and block out everything.

The worst part was the impulse to call Tara. She remembered what Cheryl had said. *Sometimes, I think of something, you know, that I want to tell her. And I pull out my phone and I actually start calling her before I remember.*

She needed air.

She wandered out of the hospital. An ambulance braked in front of the building. She watched its back doors fly open. A sweetly medicinal odor spilled from the back. Paramedics maneuvered a stretcher to the ground. An old man was strapped to it. He looked dead until his head turned and his eyes found hers. They were watery and unfocused. The stretcher rolled past her. Its wheels clattered on the pavement.

"You and Grayson were friends."

She had not heard Heather Collins come through the doors behind her. She turned and looked at the detective's pale, weary face and shrugged. "We used to be. During the years I was gone, he changed a lot."

The detective's eyes narrowed and she took a step closer. "I don't suppose you have a better explanation for Russell Grayson's actions tonight than your partner provided."

Her partner. Collins probably intended her tone to annoy Ashley, but it only made her sad. She had thought of Zack as her partner, in more ways than one, until he had decided to offer Dimitri to the FBI as a bargaining chip instead of turning him in to the police.

She could turn him in now. She could tell Collins everything.

But Zack had asked her to trust him. And even though the idea of the FBI making a deal with Dimitri sickened her, she did trust him.

"I guess he was depressed," Ashley said. "His company has been losing money, and I think he's having marital problems." It was the same story Zack had told. It was the truth, minus the Kazakovs. A lie of omission. They had agreed upon it while following the ambulance to the hospital. "I don't know the details. We're not that close anymore."

Collins looked skeptical. "This has nothing to do with your sister, does it?"

Ashley looked at the cement edifice of the hospital. "How's Kingsley?"

"Grayson? He's probably going to die. And even if he doesn't, the brain damage...." She trailed off. Her voice softened. "I wouldn't hope for too much."

"This has nothing to do with my sister."

"Then it has to do with Special Agent Foster's federal investigation?"

"I don't know."

Collins drew closer and lowered her voice. Her eyes flashed. "I've been a detective for a few years, Ashley. I'm pretty good at sensing when someone is hiding the truth from me. Considering how eager you've been in the past to share all of your theories, your reticence now is suspect. My guess is that Foster convinced you that whatever is going on here would be better handled by the FBI than the LAPD."

"Your guess is wrong."

"I see." Collins touched one of the swollen marks on Ashley's face. She felt a burst of pain. "You've stirred up a lot of hornets' nests since you came back to LA. Maybe it's time you went home."

Collins turned away without waiting for a response. Ashley watched her step through the automatic doors and enter the hospital. Cool air drifted out before the doors slid shut.

"Bitch."

She considered following Collins back inside the hospital, but what would she do in there but sit and wait? She was tired of waiting. Waiting for Kingsley to die. Waiting for the FBI to make a decision about Dimitri. She was restless and frustrated.

She wanted to *do something.*

Zack had told her that the case against Dimitri was full of holes, that the chain of evidence—as he called it—was missing the link that connected Dimitri to Tara's death. That missing link was his justification for turning Dimitri over to the FBI as a bargaining chip instead of turning him over to the LAPD as a murderer.

If Ashley could find that missing link, maybe she could make sure Dimitri received the punishment he deserved.

She pulled out her phone and called Selena Drake. The line went straight to voice mail, but it only took one call to Pinnacle to track her down. Rachel was happy to tell her that Selena was shooting a scene for Dingo Digital at their warehouse in Van Nuys. Ashley thanked her and disconnected.

She had found something to do.

———

DINGO'S WAREHOUSE was boxy and nondescript. When she entered, a man rose from a desk and approached her. "Can I help you?" He wore a tailored suit, and when he extended a hand to shake hers, she saw the glint of a bulky class ring. "Do you have an appointment?"

"Actually, I'm looking for a friend. Selena Drake. She's shooting a scene here."

"Uh, I know Ivan is shooting some content today." He led her back to his desk and picked up the phone. "I'll ask who he's working with. I'm Kevin, by the way."

"Nice to meet you."

He held her gaze, apparently waiting for her to offer her name. She didn't. Why give Selena advance notice that she was here? Kevin leaned his butt against the edge of the desk. She waited while he waited. After a moment, his gaze wandered to her legs.

"You work in the industry?" he said. He still held the phone to his ear, but apparently no one was picking up on the other end of the line.

"Used to."

He nodded. Then he jerked forward. "Hey, Josh. Is Ivan shooting Selena Drake today? I've got a woman here looking for her." Ashley could hear the buzz of the other person's voice, but could not make out the words. She waited while Kevin listened. "Cool. Thanks." He hung up the phone.

"Yeah, she's here. Ivan's shooting new content for the *Nympho*

Babysitters Web site. If you'd like to wait for her here, that would be fine." He gave her what she assumed he considered a charming smile.

"Would it be alright if I waited on the set?"

Kevin checked out her legs again. He acted as if her request required a lot of thought. What did he think? That if he kept her here for an hour, she would be helpless to resist his animal magnetism? Maybe he had watched too many of his employer's nympho-themed videos.

"You know what?" she said. "This place can't be that big. I'll find her myself."

She walked past him toward the tinted-glass doors that led deeper into the warehouse. Two seconds passed before she heard the slap of his leather-soled shoes on the floor.

"No, it's no big deal," he said. He drew even with her, matched her pace, and resurrected the charming smile. "I'll take you."

———

THE SET of *Nympho Babysitters* was familiar. Ashley thought of it as *the little girl's bedroom* set, a porn cliché that never seemed to go out of style, no matter how much unwanted interest the government showed in the industry. It always sported the same accoutrements: a bed with a big, puffy, pastel-colored comforter, lots of pillows, and at least two stuffed animals. This time, the stuffed animals were a teddy bear and a penguin. The penguin had plush yellow feet, one of which was currently crushed between Selena Drake's teeth. Tony Bragg—a male performer Ashley had worked with back in her performing days—looked uncomfortable in a business suit. Ashley supposed he was playing the role of the babysitter's employer, but he seemed more focused on his costume than on the babysitter he was screwing. He kept fidgeting with the knot of his tie and seemed almost unaware of the sex going on below his waist. Selena's grunts and squeals were muffled by the stuffed penguin foot.

The room smelled like lube and overheated stage lights. The director—a guy Ashley did not recognize but assumed must be Ivan

—crouched as close to his performers as possible without climbing onto the bed with them. The camera was aimed at Selena's ass, shooting a close-up. He pulled out to a wider shot, getting Selena's pigtails, white socks, and plaid schoolgirl skirt into the frame. For some viewers, the costume would be as important as the sex.

Tony must have glimpsed Ashley in his peripheral vision. After a quick glance at the camera to make sure his head was not in frame, he flashed her a smile and mouthed a silent *what's up?* A few of the other people in the room followed his gaze, but seemed to lose interest when they did not recognize her. One woman was squinting at her phone's display. Ashley remembered her own phone and pulled it from her purse to put it in silent mode. It was still in her hand when it started to vibrate.

She looked at the display. Zack.

Her first instinct was to not answer the call. But what if he had news about Kingsley or Dimitri?

She stepped into the hallway and lifted the phone to her ear. "Hello?"

"You disappeared."

"I took a drive. I needed to get out of that hospital."

"I understand. I know how— Why are you whispering?"

Selena and Tony were both making noise now. Ashley cupped her hand around the phone to try to block out their moans. "I'm not," she said.

"Kingsley's dead. The doctors did all they could. Cheryl is pretty upset, as you can imagine. She doesn't know what to tell the girls. Looks like the industry is going to have another big funeral."

Ashley leaned against the wall. She closed her eyes. "Any word from the FBI? About, you know...."

"Not yet. You should go back to your motel. I'll stop by later."

She glanced down the hallway at the set and considered telling him where she was. She decided against it.

"Listen, I'm, uh, it's hard to talk while I drive. I'll see you later, okay? Bye."

She ended the call and dropped the phone into her purse. As she walked back to the set, Selena was yelling, "Come on my face! Come on my slutty babysitting face!"

The scene was finished.

———

SELENA SAT on the side of the bed and mopped her chin with a washcloth. When she noticed Ashley, a look of weariness filled her eyes. Ashley sat next to her on the bed, careful not to sit on anything sticky.

"You just don't give up," Selena said.

"I know about Dimitri Sidorov. AKA Max. AKA Derek."

"You're making a huge mistake. If he finds out that you know his name...."

"He'll hang me? Let him try."

Selena's expression changed to one of disbelief. "Ashley, you really don't know what you're talking about. What this guy is capable of."

"But you do. That's why I'm here. I want to know everything you know. Now."

"There's nothing I can say. Don't you get that?"

"What if someone murdered Janie?"

Selena did not answer, but Ashley watched her fingers close around the edge of the sheet and twist it.

"Sisters share a bond," Ashley said. "You know that better than anyone. A responsibility."

"Don't use Janie like that. To try to win an argument."

"How did you meet Dimitri?"

The anger faded from Selena's eyes. She glanced at the people milling around the room. "Let me get cleaned up."

In a dressing room down the hall, Ashley waited while Selena scrubbed her face and throat with a wet towel, then dressed in a pink Victoria's Secret sweatsuit. She pulled her hair free of the little-girl pigtails and shook it loose. It fell in a jet-black cascade behind her shoulders.

"I was trying to get a drug—"

"Estrogen for Janie," Ashley said. "I already know that. How did you meet Dimitri?"

At the mention of estrogen, Selena's eyes widened. "How did you find out—"

"The same way Tara did. I went to Rosie's. Then I went to a pharmacy on Robertson Boulevard called Whole Care. I talked to the pharmacist."

Selena licked her lips. "Tara shouldn't have done that—invaded my privacy like that. And you—"

She asked the question for the third time. "How did you meet Dimitri?"

"Through Simone Santiago, a friend of mine. She's a pretty big name in the chicks-with-dicks genre. She mentioned that she gets her estrogen on the black market. She hooked me up." Selena shrugged. "I wasn't hurting anyone. If Tara hadn't followed me and then messed with Dimitri's business.... And what if I *had* been using Oxy or something? So fucking what? Why did she have to care?"

"Our mom was a drug addict. And I ... well, I had some problems with alcohol. I guess Tara grew up feeling like it was up to her to save the world from addiction."

Selena looked down at her hands. "I didn't know that."

"Dimitri killed her. I need proof. Can you help me?"

Selena shook her head. "I don't know."

"You don't know if you can, or you don't know if you will?"

"Last Thursday—the same day Tara's body was found—I found a note pinned to the back of Janie's shirt. A threat. Janie had no idea it was there. She was walking around with a big smile on her face, talking about a chipmunk she saw in the yard. I went cold when I saw the piece of paper. I knew what it meant. It meant the gossip I was hearing was wrong and Tara's death wasn't really a suicide."

"The note was from Dimitri," Ashley said.

"A few hours later, he showed up. At my house. While Janie and Rob and I were watching TV and eating dinner. He introduced himself as Max and he asked for a job. Rob resisted, but after the note, what could we do? He started as Rob's personal assistant that Friday. Now he's always around. Watching everything we do."

"What did the note say?"

Selena shook her head.

"It's okay," Ashley said. "You can tell me."

"It said retards die young."

Selena held her gaze for a moment, then started to cry.

28

THE DOOR OPENED and a petite brunette stepped into the dressing room. She had a phone pressed to her ear. Her voice stopped mid-chatter when she saw Selena with her hands pressed to her face and her shoulders quaking. She retreated quickly, leaving them alone again.

"Where is Janie now?" Ashley said.

"Rob took her shopping. At the Beverly Center. Janie likes it there."

"I think you should call him. Tell him it might not be safe to go home right now."

Selena did not probe for more information. She went straight to a black leather handbag on the makeup counter, opened it, and withdrew her phone. She called Rob. Minutes passed. Her expression grew more concerned. When she spoke, there was an edge of panic in her voice. "It's me. Where are you guys? Call me back as soon as you get this message. It's important. It's about ... you know. And don't go home until you call me. Bye." She took the phone away from her ear, then brought it to her face again and added, "I love you. Tell Janie I love her, too. Bye."

Ashley had not realized she was holding her breath until her lungs began to burn. She forced herself to breathe.

"Now tell me what's going on," Selena said. "Why isn't it safe for them to go home?"

"I told you I went to the pharmacy." Ashley took a deep breath and tried to think of a way to warn Selena about the danger she was in without blowing Zack's cover. "Zack was with me. After we found out about Dimitri, Zack made a phone call. To the, uh, the authorities."

"Zack Cutter?"

Ashley nodded. "He's just trying to help. He's trying to do the right thing."

Her impulse to defend him surprised her, but no defense was necessary. Selena did not look angry.

She looked terrified.

"We need to call him," Selena said.

"I don't know if we'll be able to reach—"

"Not Zack. Dimitri. We need to call him and explain. I'm going to put you on the phone with him. Tell him that Janie and Rob and me had nothing to do with this. We didn't tell you anything. You found everything out yourself. We had nothing to do with it."

"Do you think he'll listen? Or care?" Ashley backed away from Selena as if the phone in her hand were radioactive. She had been hunting the man for a week, but suddenly, the thought of hearing the voice of her sister's killer petrified her. "Maybe this is a bad idea. Maybe we should let the police handle it."

Selena was already thumbing through her phone's contact list. It made Ashley queasy to think that all of this time, the killer's contact information had been sitting in the memory chip of Selena's phone.

Selena tapped her screen. Watching with her lower lip in her teeth, Ashley expected a repeat of the previous phone call—a slow, agonizing wait followed by a voice mail message. Her expectation was wrong. Selena started talking almost immediately. Dimitri must have picked up on the first ring.

"It's Selena. No, I understand. I'm not calling for that. Listen,

Ashley Hale knows about you. And, um, it's possible that her friend went to the pol— No, wait! Just listen to me. Please! It's not my fault. I — No, I'm not going to do that. Please, just listen to Ashley, she'll tell you I didn't tell—" She thrust the phone into Ashley's hands.

The phone was warm and seemed to exude menace. Ashley almost dropped it. She fumbled it to her ear. Channeling every movie heroine she'd ever seen, she said, "It's over, Dimitri. You hurt anyone else, you'll just make the prosecutor's job easier."

She held her breath waiting for his response. None came.

"What is he saying?" Selena said. Her voice was tight.

Ashley shook her head and handed the phone back. "He must have hung up. What did he say to you?"

Selena's face was pale. "He hung up?"

"Selena, please. What did he say to you?"

"He said ... he wants to meet in person. Me, you, and him. No one else."

Flashbacks of a desolate warehouse, of Billboard Ben racking the slide of Zack's loaded gun. She touched her swollen face.

"I need to call Zack."

"No." Selena grabbed her wrist. Her grip was surprisingly firm for such a delicate hand. "Let's just do what he says. Please."

"I've made that mistake before."

"What if he finds Rob and Janie? If we disobey him, he'll take out his anger on them!"

Ashley could not summon much concern for Tara's ex-boyfriend, but she flinched at the thought of Janie being harmed.

"Rob has a gun," Selena said. "He bought it illegally, from some guy who works in shipping at Dynamo. He keeps the thing at Pinnacle. We can go get it, bring it with us. If Dimitri tries to hurt us, we'll shoot him."

Looking at this skinny, terrified eighteen-year-old made Ashley feel suddenly sad. "Do you even know how to fire a gun?"

"How complicated could it be?"

"Does Rob keep it loaded? Does he have ammunition?"

"It's loaded. Rob showed me the, you know, the stick-thing that goes up into the handle."

"The magazine," Ashley said. Selena looked confused, so she added, "That's what it's called. My mom had a lot of boyfriends. One of them liked to take his gun apart and clean it in the living room. He let me help him. Took me to the range, sometimes, too."

"Your mom was okay with that?"

"She was probably unconscious."

"This is good," Selena said, looking more confident now. "You can handle Rob's gun. All we need to do is go to Pinnacle, pick it up, and then meet Dimitri. We have a plan."

"That's not a plan, Selena. I still think we should call Zack."

"Why? It's not like he's a cop or anything. He's a video editor."

Ashley had no answer to that. She looked around the dressing room and sighed. "Where does Dimitri want to meet us?"

THEY TOOK SEPARATE CARS, Selena leading in her Audi TT, Ashley following in the Fiesta. About halfway to Pinnacle, traffic slowed to a bumper-to-bumper crawl. Ashley smelled the reason for the slowdown before she saw it. A smoky, metallic odor seeped into her car. The accident came into view a minute later. A car and a minivan had collided head-on. Ashley tried not to look, but the scene pulled her gaze toward it. She recalled the impact of the Volvo that had hit Zack's Corvette. The memory was so vivid that she had to unclench her jaw and shake her head to clear it. The Volvo and the Corvette faded from her mind, but Zack's face remained.

Fuck it.

She called him before she could change her mind.

"Hey," he said. "I was about to call you."

She could see the back of Selena's head through the Audi's rear windshield. "Did the FBI get back to you?"

"Yes."

She sensed reluctance in his voice. Anger swelled in her chest.

"What are they going to offer him, Zack? Ten years in prison for murdering Tara? Five? Just tell me."

"Dimitri is dead."

Traffic had thinned since she passed the accident. Selena's Audi cut between two SUVs in the left lane. With her arms and feet on autopilot, Ashley followed. She pushed the pedal to the floor and the Fiesta's little engine roared.

"Ashley? Are you there?"

"What do you mean, dead?"

"Police recovered his body four days ago in San Bernardino. He overdosed on Oxycodone. That's what it looked like, anyway. The LAPD is going to take a closer look now."

"Four days ago," she repeated. Her hands felt numb on the steering wheel. She glanced at her knuckles. They were white. "That means he couldn't have called Billboard Ben."

"There's another thing," Zack said. "I did a little research on Selena Drake. Tyrant's records include her driver's license number, her social security number, everything. Her real name is Jennifer Hundley. She was born in Blue Bell, Pennsylvania. I had a colleague pull some public records, and here's the strange thing. Jennifer Hundley doesn't have a sister."

The Audi darted through traffic. Was it picking up speed? Ashley accelerated. She slipped the Fiesta through a gap between a Jeep and a Mustang and emerged two cars behind Selena.

"Ashley? Are you there?"

"Maybe the records are incomplete," she said.

"My colleague made a few quick phone calls. Jennifer had a brother named Jeremy. Jeremy and Jennifer disappeared a few years ago after their house was destroyed in a fire. Their parents were killed."

"It's the wrong family, obviously. We're looking for sisters, not a brother and a sister."

"According to a woman who used to live next door to the Hundleys, Jennifer has Down syndrome." He paused. "Ashley, *Janie* is Jennifer Hundley."

Ashley remembered her first meeting with the girl. *They call me Janie.*

"Then who is Selena?"

The Audi pulled ahead again. Was Selena trying to lose her, or was she just an aggressive driver? On open road, the Fiesta would never be able to keep pace, but LA traffic stripped the Audi of its advantage.

"Suppose Selena lived in the neighborhood and knew the Hundleys," Zack said. "Maybe she was even a girlfriend of the brother, Jeremy. One day, she gets into some trouble with the law, wants to start fresh. So she starts the fire, kills the parents and maybe the brother, too, abducts Jennifer, and assumes her identity. She moves to LA with a clean slate. She's Jennifer Hundley now. No criminal record, no history at all."

"Then why continue to take care of Janie? Why bother to try to get her estrogen?"

"It's just a theory," Zack said.

"In other words, we have no idea who Selena Drake really is." She pulled closer to the Audi and saw the dark head through the rear windshield. A chill passed through her. "Zack, there's something I need to tell you."

"What?"

"I didn't drive back to my motel room. I went and talked to Selena. I felt like, if I could get a little more information.... Selena called—or I guess she pretended to call—Dimitri. She was very convincing."

"Where are you now?"

"In my car. I'm following her. We're driving to Pinnacle. At least, that's where she said we were going. From there, we're supposed to meet Dimitri."

"Listen to me. Do you think you can interact with her without letting on that we had this conversation?"

"I think so."

"Stall her at Pinnacle. Do whatever you need to do. Give me five, ten minutes. I'll bring the cavalry. Ashley, don't go anywhere else with her. *Keep her at Pinnacle.*"

She had not been afraid before, but hearing the barely controlled panic in Zack's voice twisted her stomach.

"Ashley?"

"I can do it."

———

WHEN THEY ARRIVED at the former optometrist's office, there were no vehicles in the parking lot. None parked at the neighboring businesses, either. It was a quiet Saturday afternoon. Selena parked in the spot closest to the building's entrance. Ashley parked next to her.

"Who were you talking to?" Selena said as they headed for the door. The heels of her sandals clicked on the pavement. "I saw you using your phone in the car."

"My mother. I wanted to say a few things. You know, in case something happens to us."

The answer seemed to satisfy her. She unlocked the door and held it open for Ashley. The lobby was dark. Ashley felt the wall with her hand, ran her fingers along the textured wallpaper until she found a series of switches. She flicked them on. The room brightened.

Selena stepped past her. "Come on."

They walked through the waiting area to the long hallway of offices. To Ashley's surprise, Selena stopped at the open door to Tara's office. She didn't need to turn on the light in this room. Plenty of sunlight streamed through the window.

"Rob keeps his gun in my sister's office?"

"He owns it illegally. I guess the idea is that if it's ever found by the wrong person, he can deny that it's his."

Nothing in the office had changed since the last time Selena had brought her here. No one had removed the computer docking station or monitor from the desk, even though they were useless without Tara's laptop. The tall file cabinet in the corner looked untouched as well. She thought she caught a trace of Tara's perfume in the air, but knew she was probably imagining it. As before, she felt a pang of sadness, as if she were glimpsing Tara's stolen future. This time, though, the sadness hardened quickly to anger.

Zack's voice sounded in her head. *Keep her at Pinnacle.*

Selena closed the door behind them. Then she walked behind Tara's desk and rolled the swivel chair a few feet toward the corner of the room. "The gun is up there," she said, indicating the top of the file cabinet.

Ashley felt a surge of alarm as Selena put one foot on the seat of the chair. She hurried forward and took Selena's arm. "Wait."

Selena turned, looked down at her.

"I'm more comfortable with guns than you are. You don't want to, you know—"

"Shoot my hand off?"

"Right."

"That would make it harder to accept my AVN awards."

Selena stepped down from the chair and made room for Ashley. A water pipe ran along the ceiling, secured by metal brackets. There was an empty space of about five inches between the pipe and the top of the file cabinet. Ashley hoisted herself onto the office chair and reached a hand into the pocket of shadow.

Her fingers touched wisps of dust, nothing else.

Before she could move, she felt the chair rock as Selena climbed on behind her. Selena's chest pressed against her back. Her arm reached over their heads. Ashley tried to turn. A length of rope dropped from the water pipe. It had been coiled there, out of sight. Ashley tried to duck, but Selena guided the loop over her head. She knew the moment the coarse rope touched her throat what it was. A noose.

She twisted around. Reached for Selena. But Selena had already hopped off the chair. Now she grabbed the backrest and pulled. Ashley felt a sickening unsteadiness as the seat of the chair slid out from under her heels. Gravity yanked her downward. The noose cinched tight around her neck.

"No bees to save your ass this time, bitch."

Ashley clawed at the rope. She couldn't work her fingers into the knot. She kicked at the file cabinet behind her. It clanged, but offered no foothold. She kicked at the desk. Her left toe nudged a mug full of pens off the edge. Pens scattered on the floor. She kicked off her left shoe and stretched her leg as far as it would go. Her toe brushed the side of Tara's monitor but could not reach the desk's surface. The noose tightened. Black spots bloomed across her vision.

Selena watched her. Her expression was unnervingly calm. "You wanted the truth of what happened to Tara? Enjoy it."

More black spots popped in front of Ashley's eyes. Her range of vision seemed to shrink, the borders darkening. She tried again with her toe to reach the surface of the desk, but it was useless. She clutched the rope above her head, pulled, tried to take the pressure off of her throat. The muscles in her arms throbbed.

"It will make a good story in AVN," Selena said. "'Grief-stricken Ashley Hale commits suicide in Tara Rose's office, doubling tragedy.'"

Ashley hauled on the rope. Her body rose half an inch. She sucked in a lungful of air. "Zack knows I'm here with you!" It was all she was able to say before her muscles shuddered and she dropped again. The rope cinched tight under her chin.

"Knowing and proving are two different things. A lot of people in Pennsylvania knew I set my family's house on fire, but no one could prove it."

Her family? So much for Zack's theory.

"Please," Ashley said. Her voice was a croak.

"I gave you a thousand chances to walk away. You refused. Just like your sister, you couldn't mind your own business. You had to ask questions. You had to follow me. You had to snoop."

Selena turned away, and there was something about the way she moved that triggered a memory. Suddenly, Ashley was sitting with Kingsley in the coffee shop down the street from the funeral home, and Kingsley was filling her in on the hot date that Rob Rourke had brought to his ex-girlfriend's funeral.

I think it's her hips. They're kind of straight, like a dude's.

The rest fell into place, a cascade of mental flashes as the noose choked the oxygen from her brain. The almost masculine aggressiveness in her sex scenes. The traces of surgery Ashley had noticed when she'd seen her naked body up-close. The black-market estrogen.

Selena had her hand on the doorknob when Ashley said, "What's the rush, Jeremy?"

Her green eyes flashed with rage. All the confirmation Ashley needed.

"Who else knows?" Selena took two steps closer to Ashley's thrashing legs. "Tell me now, you washed-up whore. Who else—"

Ashley kicked out. Her bare foot almost hit Selena's chest, came within inches, but flailed harmlessly in the air.

"Who else knows—"

A low groan cut her off. The noise came from the pipe above Ashley, the pipe supporting the rope. The metal groaned again, then bent. Ashley dropped an inch. Her throat bounced painfully in the noose. There was a louder, wrenching noise, and the pipe segment holding the rope separated at a joint and dropped again. Water surged from the broken pipe and arced to the floor, pooling on the carpet. The loop of rope slid forward, then jerked to a stop when it hit the metal bracket still clinging to the ceiling. Ashley swung. Her toes were still too far from the floor, too far from the desktop, too far from Selena.

Water cascaded around Selena's sandals. The carpet was soaked. She seemed oblivious to it. Her eyes, glaring, were locked on Ashley.

"Tell me who else knows!"

Black spots crowded Ashley's vision. Her lungs burned. She kicked, thrashed. Her toe touched the glass screen of Tara's monitor. The monitor rocked on the desk.

"I've earned this life," Selena said. "I've earned it."

The muscles in Ashley's thigh and calf ached. Her toe brushed the face of the monitor again. A plan formed in her mind.

"This ... is gonna make it harder ... to accept ... your AVN awards."

With all of the strength she had left, she drove her foot into the monitor. It rocked on its stand, then toppled off of the desk. Its power cord snaked after it. The monitor hit the carpet with a thump and an electric crackle. A blue streak flashed from the monitor to Selena's toes, searing the soaked carpet.

The air filled first with an ozone smell. Ashley felt her hair rise on her scalp. An uncomfortable pressure vibrated in her teeth.

Selena's legs twitched. Her left arm jerked. Ashley heard a bone crack. The stink of burning meat filled the room. One of Selena's eyes bulged.

The electrical current popped once more, then quieted. Selena's body thudded to the floor. Smoke drifted from her skin and hair. The bulging eye had burst. Whitish gel leaked down the side of her face.

Ashley gripped the rope above her head, but the strength had left her arms. She could not lift herself. Could not give her throat even a centimeter of breathing space. She was going to die here, with only the corpse of her sister's killer for company.

Then she heard her name, and the sound of running footsteps.

Zack was calling her name.

29

A WHITE CEILING shifted into focus. She was horizontal. Lying on an unfamiliar bed. She jerked a hand to her neck. Her throat was wrapped in a bandage. She fingered the soft gauze.

"Ashley? Are you awake?" Her mother's face appeared above her. "Oh, thank God."

"Gail?" Pain lanced up her throat. She winced.

Gail leaned closer. The loose flesh around her mouth puckered into a smile. "You did it, Ashley. Tara didn't kill herself. The insurance company is going to pay."

She tried to push the woman away from her. The weakness in her arm surprised her. Gail did not budge.

"Don't look at me like that. You know it's not the money I care about."

"You—" She winced again, but fought past the pain. "You lied ... to me. The will. The stalker. Lies. You and Tara never reconciled."

Gail smiled condescendingly. "I had to tell you something."

She was using again. Ashley could see it in her pupils, could smell it on her skin. She tried again to push her away. There was still no strength in her arm, but this time Gail moved backward. Zack came into view behind her. He had a hand on Gail's shoulder and he was pulling her back from the bed. Gail started to protest, but his look silenced her. She shrunk away from him, then slipped out of the room.

Zack sat down. He inched the chair closer to the bed. Its metal legs squeaked against the floor. "Hey."

She opened her mouth to answer, but he put a finger to her lips.

"Don't talk. Your throat is bruised pretty bad. You're lucky you didn't fracture your larynx." His hand moved down the side of her face. His fingers felt warm against her cheek. "You're going to be okay. The doctor wants to run some tests and lab work, but he thinks you're going to be fine." He smiled. "Turns out you're tough as nails. Who'd have thought?"

"Selena?" Her voice was a croak.

"You fried her. And listen to this. It looks like Selena—*you're not going to believe this*—it looks like Selena—"

"Was a dude."

His eyes widened. "Damn. You're a better investigator than I am."

She smiled. He had not removed his hand from her cheek, and she was glad.

"Anyway," he said, "here's what we've learned. Jeremy Hundley grew up in suburban Pennsylvania. His father was a middle-management type. His mother was a housewife who worked part time at a department store. Most of the money they made—not to mention their attention—went to Jeremy's sister Jennifer, who was born with Down syndrome. Maybe Jeremy felt lonely or neglected. We don't know. But people familiar with the family remember Jeremy watching a lot of TV and reading a lot of Web sites and entertainment magazines and tabloids. Apparently, he was obsessed with celebrities. He idolized them."

There was a soft knock. Zack looked up, but he did not move from the bed. Detective Heather Collins stepped into view. She looked at Ashley with a concern she had never shown before. "The nurse told me you were awake." She approached the bed. "So, let's hear it."

"Hear what?" Ashley said.

"'I told you so.' Come on, get it over with."

"I told you so."

Collins nodded. "I shouldn't have been so quick to dismiss your suspicions."

"I told you so."

"Okay." She smiled. "Once was enough. How do you feel?"

What she felt was physical pain and the lingering ache of loss. "Been better."

"You need anything, call me."

Zack waited for the detective to leave. "Where was I?"

"Jeremy. Lonely and neglected."

"Right. Well, things got worse when he hit puberty. He realized he was gay. There was an incident in high school. Apparently, some jerk led Jeremy on, got him to do his school work for him, that kind of thing. Then he tried to convince Jeremy to let him have sex with Jennifer. That was going too far. Jeremy beat the guy to a bloody pulp. He was given probation.

"A few years later, he started college at Penn State. Joined a gay and lesbian student group. Apparently that's when he started thinking seriously about sex reassignment surgery. I guess he looked at his skinny body and decided that with some surgery, he'd make a pretty damn good-looking female. When the semester ended, he went home and confronted his parents and told them he needed money for the operation. According to neighbors, they could hear the yelling up and down the street. Are you okay? Do you need me to call the nurse or anything?"

Ashley shook her head. She gestured for him to continue.

"Sex changes aren't cheap. His parents barely had enough money to care for his sister and themselves. He begged, then railed at them. They refused. That night, he offered to take his sister to a movie. They left the house. What happened next is debatable. Officially, a tragic fire took the lives of their parents. But the local cops still don't believe that. They were never able to prove it, but they think that before leaving the house, Jeremy turned on the gas range. Jeremy knew his parents would use the fireplace later. The house filled with gas and exploded when his father lit the fireplace. Jeremy and

Jennifer returned from the movie to find their house in flames and their parents dead. Jeremy waited for the life insurance check to clear, then took Jennifer and left town. The payout was more than enough money for the treatments and operations he wanted.

"We don't know what happened next. Not the details, anyway. Obviously, Jeremy's procedure was a success. He got his female body. He adopted his sister's name and social security number and her age —eighteen. He surfaced in Los Angeles. Tax records show that Jennifer Hundley worked as a waitress in a Hollywood diner. According to her boss, she was very popular with the customers. She got a lot of male attention. One of those men was our buddy Rob Rourke. He must have pitched porn as a career, and she must have recognized it as a chance at being a celebrity. I doubt Rob ever suspected the truth about her past."

"Tara...."

"Tara probably had no idea either. My guess is that she liked Selena. She admired the way Selena cared for Janie. But something tipped her off that Selena was using drugs. She didn't realize the drugs were estrogen treatments. She confronted Selena about it, and Selena denied that she was using anything. So Tara followed her. She learned about Dimitri. She would have learned about the estrogen, too, and figured out the rest eventually. Selena realized that and got scared. She had murdered once. She figured she could get away with it again. The first time, she had made it look like an accident. This time, she made it look like suicide."

"*Knockouts*," Ashley said, remembering the behind-the-scenes feature on the DVD. "Kingsley showed her how to make a noose."

"After Tara's murder, it was like a domino effect. She had to kill Dimitri, too. You were last on her list."

"No," Ashley said. Selena's cries of *Who else knows?* echoed in her head. "You were."

———

SOME NEGATIVE EFFECTS of strangulation can manifest days after the event. That was what the doctor said, anyway, and it was all the excuse Ashley needed to stick around the Valley for another week. She gave up her room at the motel, though, and moved her suitcase to Zack's place. Temporarily, of course.

"My SAC has made a decision," Zack told her one night, after making love. His forehead gleamed in the lamplight. She gripped his bare shoulders, pulled herself up to a sitting position beside him, and kissed the sweat from his brow. "He thinks it's too dangerous for me to continue here undercover."

"So what does this mean?" She already knew what it meant, of course. They had talked about the possibility—the *probability*—of the termination of Zack's assignment. It meant that "Zack Cutter" would cease to exist, and James Foster would be recalled to Washington, D.C.

"It's a relief, in some ways," Zack said. "But I sure would have liked to nail the Kazakovs."

"Hey." She kissed the dimple in his cheek. "You helped catch a murderer. Isn't that enough?"

"Maybe." Zack swung his legs over the edge of the bed, then stood up. She watched him pad naked across the carpet to the dresser, all rangy muscle and smooth skin. He came back holding a folder. "But there might be another option. Another way to get at the Kazakov organization. They own a string of strip clubs on the east coast. Fronts for money-laundering, we think, but also part of their effort to muscle into the porn industry." He had not opened the folder yet. It remained closed on his lap. His gaze fixed on her. "The Bureau thinks I might be able to investigate the Kazakov family by working under-cover in their strip club businesses." He opened the folder. It was a dossier on a man named Zack Tipper, complete with a passport-sized photo.

"You're going back undercover? Already?"

"I'd like you to come with me." He paused and studied her for a few seconds. "If you don't want to, I understand. You have your own life to get back to—"

"I'll have to pretend you're a different person?"

"I know that part sucks. But we would be together."

"You think doing this will help prove that the Kazakovs murdered Brewster?"

"Among other crimes, yes."

Ashley nodded. She wished she could believe that the voice screaming *Yes!* in her head was motivated by a pure desire to see justice served and avenge her old friend's death, but she could not deceive herself.

She leaned into Zack and pressed her lips against his. The folder fell to the floor. Papers scattered.

Zack pulled back and smiled his loopy grin. "Does this mean you'll come?"

She pushed him back on the mattress and climbed on top of him. "Count on it."

THE END

Thank you for reading Hardcore!

If you enjoyed the book, please post a review on Amazon and let everyone know. Your opinion will directly influence the success of the book. It doesn't need to be an in-depth report—just a few sentences helps a lot. If you could take a few minutes to help spread the word, I would greatly appreciate it.

—Larry A. Winters

WANT TO SEE MORE OF ASHLEY?

If you enjoyed Hardcore, and would like me to write more books about Ashley, let me know!

All you need to do is sign up to my email list (which is free), and in addition to expressing your interest in more Ashley Hale books, you'll also receive notices of new book releases, sales and discounts, and other fun stuff.

I promise not to spam you, and you can unsubscribe at any time.

Sign up here:

http://larryawinters.com/more-Ashley

Thank you for being a fan. I appreciate it.

—Larry A. Winters

BOOKS BY LARRY A. WINTERS

The Jessie Black Legal Thriller Series
Grave Testimony (prequel)
Burnout
Informant
Deadly Evidence
Fatal Defense

Also Featuring Jessie Black
Web of Lies

Other Books
Hardcore

Visit my website for an up-to-date list of books:

http://www.larryawinters.com/books/

ABOUT THE AUTHOR

Larry A. Winters's stories feature a rogue's gallery of brilliant lawyers, avenging porn stars, determined cops, undercover FBI agents, and vicious bad guys of all sorts. When not writing, he can be found living a life of excitement. Not really, but he does know a good time when he sees one: reading a book by the fireplace on a cold evening, catching a rare movie night with his wife (when a friend or family member can be coerced into babysitting duty), smart TV dramas (and dumb TV comedies), vacations (those that involve reading on the beach, a lot of eating, and not a lot else), cardio on an elliptical trainer (generally beginning upon his return from said vacations, and quickly tapering off), video games (even though he stinks at them), and stockpiling gadgets (with a particular weakness for tablets and ereaders). He also has a healthy obsession with Star Wars.

Email: larry@larryawinters.com

Website and Blog: www.larryawinters.com

Facebook: www.facebook.com/AuthorLarryAWinters/

Twitter: @larryawinters

Made in the USA
Monee, IL
29 June 2020